I0611285

THE NEWSTEAD PROJECT

THE NEWSTEAD PROJECT

MELANIE SCHULZ

BLACK AND WHITE PUBLISHING CO.

This is a work of fiction. Names, characters, places, and incidents are products of the author's imagination or are used fictitiously. Any resemblance to actual events, locales, organizations, or persons, living or dead, is entirely coincidental.

No part of this publication may be reproduced, stored in a retrieval system, or transmitted in any form or by any means, electronic, mechanical, photocopying, recording, or otherwise, without written permission of the publisher. For information regarding permission, write to Black and White Publishing Co. Attention: Permissions Department,
1395 Quaker Road, Barker, NY 14012

Copyright 2013 by Melanie Schulz
All rights reserved. Published by
Black and White Publishing Co.
ebook
Paperback printing
Printed in the U.S.A.

ISBN-13:978-0615669021

FOR MY MOM

warrior 勇士 joel

beautiful 美人 rachel

The art of war is of vital importance to the state. It is a matter of life and death, a road either to safety or to ruin. Hence it is a subject of inquiry which can on no account be neglected.

-Sun Tzu, *the Art of War*

chapter one/ the invitation

Do not swallow bait offered by the enemy.
    –Sun Tzu, *the Art of War*

It was one of those moments in my life I wish I could have a do-over on; like that instead of going to my coach's office between third and fourth period, I would've done something else; anything else. Even that wasn't my last chance to escape what seemed to be a fixed course. If I'd just pulled my head back into the hall once I saw my coach's blank stare, then maybe I wouldn't be writing this now. But I didn't do either of those things. I went to my coach's office and I turned on the light and when I did, I didn't walk away.

"You must be Joel," the man standing behind my coach's desk said confidently, like he already knew it was me. He held out his hand and I stepped into the room to shake it. "My name is Mike Arberdean. I'm here to represent Newstead, a private high school in Vermont, that—"

"Newstead—never heard of it," came Coach's cocky voice from somewhere behind Mike.

Mike's smile stayed fixed on his face, at least the outline of it. There's something freaky about a mouth that's smiling and eyes that aren't. After a second or so of that, I decided there needed to be some more space between us, so I took a step back and took my hand with me.

Surprise flashed across his fiery eyes before they dropped to my freed hand. I took another step back and angled myself toward the door. My breathing was the only sound in the room until Mike looked back up and cleared his throat, smiling brightly again, like nothing had happened.

"Like I was saying," he continued, sitting back down. "We are a school that helps to develop the gifts of our students, and from what I saw of you playing last Friday night, you certainly are gifted."

He's a recruiter? I wondered, before following his lead, sitting in the chair that was always in front of Coach's wooden desk.

"So, tell me about yourself, Joel. Your coach says this is the fourth season you've been playing on his team, and that they've done very well, mainly because of you." He leaned back, like he was expecting me to talk for a while.

"There's not really much to tell," I answered, feeling my face flushing.

Mike looked at me quizzically. "But didn't you guys win state last year?"

I nodded.

"And didn't you score five touchdowns that game?"

I nodded again, my face getting hotter.

"And that's not much to tell?" he asked, incredulously.

I shrugged. His eyes never left mine as he started to shake his head. My chair scraped back; his face was getting that look again, but he burst out laughing instead.

"Joel, you *need* to come to Newstead." He continued to laugh to himself, but I didn't know what was so funny about that; I still don't.

I looked over at my coach. I couldn't believe he wasn't busy spouting off all the reasons I needed to finish my high school career in St. Louis. But I guess whatever made him shut-up while Mike was glaring agnostically at me was still fresh in his mind, because self-preservation won out over professional achievement. He never said another word, at least not while Mike was there.

"What is it you're offering?" I asked. There was no point dancing around it. If it was anything short of a free ride, we were just wasting each other's time. There was no way my mom could afford some private school in Vermont, no matter how good it was.

"The world," he answered.

I looked at him to see if he was mocking me, but he wasn't laughing anymore. He looked like he was serious. I leaned towards him as he continued.

"I have been authorized to offer you a full scholarship to Newstead for the remainder of your education. The ones I represent would be very pleased to have you be a part of our program."

I'd been expecting an offer like the one he'd made; only I expected it later, and from a college. Both my mom and my coach talked about it almost every day. They said it was my chance, but even back then I knew that wasn't entirely true. If it was anyone's chance maybe it was my coach's chance for a letter from the governor or something. My mom wasn't looking for a letter, but she had reasons of her own.

Each of them, and truth be told, me too, had been waiting for that day, but when the words were said for real, they felt off. I wasn't excited about it like I'd always thought I would be. It probably would've helped if it was from Ole Miss, or some other school I'd at least heard of.

It also would've helped if they'd sent someone else.

"I'll think about it," I said. It was the best I could give him.

"You do that." Mike stood and handed me a stack of

information and forms to fill out.

My hand was on the door when he called out after me, "Make sure you go home and talk this over with your mother and see if it's a good fit for her." He paused briefly before continuing, "I mean the two of you. If it is, give us a call."

I froze. I turned back around and looked at Mike who had a knowing smile on his face. I left without answering him.

I didn't need to ask my mom, I already knew what she'd say. Hadn't she said it often enough? She'd want me to go for it, not waste the chance. But I knew the real reason she said it, and it didn't have anything to do with me. She was thinking about her own life, her own mistakes, and I'd better not make the same ones.

chapter two/ the voice

The difficulty of tactical maneuvering consists in turning the devious into the direct, and misfortune into gain.
-Sun Tzu, *the Art of War*

While Coach hadn't said much during the offer, he said plenty during practice. I guess he figured it was safe with Mike gone. At first he was subtle, mainly going on about how you don't ditch your team and some stuff about loyalty. But by the end of practice he must've felt more desperate because he even mentioned his pancreatic cancer. He swore the doctor told him once that stressful events would make it come out of remission. He knew I wouldn't want that, would I?

I was used to him by then, so I just ignored him. I knew he wanted my mind made up before my mom got involved. He knew what she would say, too.

I'd been playing for him since I was thirteen, when he saw my freakishly large frame at one of my J.V. games. He'd planted himself next to my mom and filled her head with more B.S. than a fertilizer factory. She was waiting for me outside the locker room after the game. I didn't stand a chance.

What followed was my first shunning; the sixteen to eighteen year olds already on the team didn't take it too well when I showed up and creamed them all. My second happened a couple years later, when my own grade caught up with me. They made sure I knew I was only good for one thing: winning.

They were the ones who started calling me Goliath. One of my teammates forgot my name once and called me that instead. Then all of them started. I'd always answer them, but I never really got it, not until that day when I was standing next to Mike and had to look way up to be able to see his face. I guess it was something you had to see for yourself to understand.

I wasn't mad at my coach for using me, but I didn't trust him either. So I didn't tell him anything as I left practice, but I didn't go straight home, either. My mom's voice could get just as loud as Coach's, only her manipulations hit better marks.

Instead, I went across the street to my place.

I gripped the ledge and pulled myself up and in the first floor window. I'd taken the boards off that particular window years ago. The smell didn't bother me anymore; the rats didn't bother me either. They needed a place to go to, too.

The floor boards creaked under my weight as I made my way up to the fifth floor. My floor. There were no boards on the windows that high up. I guess they figured you'd have to have quite an arm to break one of those. I sat down in one of the chairs I'd dragged up there.

What are you going to do? the voice inside my head asked. I ignored it, like I usually did. Instead, I grabbed my journal from under the loose floorboard next to my chair. My eyes did a quick scan of the apartment; I bet I had a few dozen of them hidden in various places up there.

I pulled out my pencil and started writing. *What am I going to do?* The question sounded familiar. Too familiar.

I ripped the page out and crumpled it into a ball and threw it towards the toilet at the end of the hall. It landed in the empty bowl with a soft thunk.

Definitely a three pointer, I thought proudly. I started writing again, only that time I was careful to write something different.

Where do I belong? I sat back and thought about that question; thought hard.

You don't belong there, the voice interjected.

I pressed my hands to my temples, trying to force the voice to shut up. I wanted to decide this one on my own.

Think about it all you want. In the end you'll admit I'm right.

"Just shut up."

The words echoed through the apartment. Speaking out loud to the voice was worse than writing down what it said. It made it too real. I pressed my temples harder and started humming, trying to drown it out. It worked; the voice faded to the background.

I turned back to my journal and wrote down one last line. *What do I want?*

The world, I thought, thinking back to the pamphlet I'd read a few hundred times that day. It was full of promises and warm fuzziness. I knew I wanted to go, really wanted to go. All I needed was an excuse to ignore my gut that was telling me every one of those promises was a lie.

A picture of Mike's face filled my mind, not his too bright smile or even his smugness. The picture was when my coach interrupted him and he looked like killing him would've been the most natural thing in the world. It was the not killing him part that was hard.

My gut twisted uncomfortably and for the first time in my life I decided to trust it. There was something seriously wrong there, something I'd be better off staying away from.

I stood up and stretched. I was ready to go home.

You are forbidden to go there.

I froze mid-extension. *Forbidden?*

The future that I'm living in solidified as the voice's words swirled around my brain.

"I can do what I want," I called out into the empty apartment. The only response I got was the scurrying sound of a few surprised rats.

"I can do what I want," I repeated and turned to go out the way I'd come in.

chapter three/ hitting the mark

Rouse him, and learn the principle of his activity or in activity. Force him to reveal himself, so as to find out his vulnerable spots.
   -Sun Tzu, *the Art of War*

I paused as I stood outside our third floor apartment. It was my last chance to change my mind—my course—but I didn't. I took the crumpled pamphlet out of my back pocket and tried to smooth it out. It was the least I could do after ruining her life.

"I'm home," I yelled as I dropped my dirty sweats from practice into the hamper in the tiny bathroom we shared. The smell of Hamburger Helper wafted down the short hall that led to the kitchen. Mom wasn't much of a cook, but at least she tried.

"Here goes nothing," I muttered under my breath as I went into the small kitchen to help set the table for dinner. Mom noticed my hesitancy right away. She could read me like a book.

"What's going on?" she asked, looking up from the stove as I placed the last fork down.

I handed her the pamphlet from Newstead and sat down so I could get a better look at her face as she read.

"I don't understand; what's this about?" She looked at me cautiously before turning back to the smoking pan.

"There was a guy from there in Coach's office this morning. I guess he caught my game last Friday and he's interested in me going there."

My mother's shoulders slumped. She kept stirring the Cheeseburger Mac. It smelled burned, but that didn't matter; she stirred it anyhow; anything to keep from looking at me.

"I wish you could go..."

I could see the spot in the pamphlet where she'd stopped reading, the part about the tuition.

"Yeah, about that, I guess they have a scholarship fund set up that I qualify for—you know—based on our income." I said them, the magic words.

Mom turned at them and her face was just what I'd expected. She wrapped her arms around me, tears of joy streaming down her cheeks.

"I haven't decided if I'm going yet," I answered quickly, although I knew I'd decided the minute I gave her the pamphlet. But it felt like I needed to say it so she wouldn't go and think she'd made up my mind for me.

The shocked anger on her face gave me a minute to prepare for the coming assault.

"Of course you're going...why wouldn't you go?" I'm sure her voice was louder than she'd meant it to be.

"Mom...," I sighed and couldn't go on. Mike was right. She was their trump card.

"You're going to go and show them what you're made of and get the hell out of this slum." She said it with such finality; I knew it was useless to argue with her.

I guess it's decided. I'm going to Newstead.

chapter four/ preparations

When the enemy is close at hand, and remains quiet, he is
relying on the natural strength of his position.
   -Sun Tzu, *the Art of War*

It wasn't until the middle of November that I sent Newstead all
their forms. I couldn't put it off any longer. Besides, I was
getting tired of my mom's daily reminders.

Four days later I got a response. The letter felt like it weighed
twenty pounds as I carried it up the flight of stairs to our
apartment. I put it under the socks in my dresser drawer and
didn't open it for two days. When I finally did, it was just a single
sheet of paper welcoming me to Newstead, telling me about the
school. I looked down at it. How could one piece of paper
change so much? But it did; it changed everything.

There were a lot of things Mike didn't tell me. He didn't tell me
that it was a guy's only school. He didn't tell me that it went year
round, with only a two week break after every fifteen weeks of
classes.

Talk about sucking. I took the paper and wadded it up into a
ball and tossed it behind my bed. I already wasn't looking
forward to going, and that was before I'd found out I was giving
up my summer vacation, too. But at least the letter said it was

right in the middle of one of their trimesters, so I wouldn't have to start until January. That would make my coach happy; I'd get to finish his season.

Every couple weeks I had to lug something else out of our mailbox and up the three flights of stairs. Each time felt as heavy as the first. Sometimes it was a letter, telling me how much they were looking forward to me going there, sometimes it was more. It was like they were afraid I was going to change my mind.

They didn't have to worry about that; they had their best helper in my mother. If it wasn't her bragging to anyone and everyone, it was her beaming face every time she came home from another twelve hour shift at the diner. It was the first time in my life I'd seen her actually happy.

Each passing game put me that much closer to leaving. I was the only one on my team who wasn't excited when we went to sectionals, then state. It meant my time was almost up.

The only good thing that happened was that I hadn't heard the voice since it forbid me to go to Newstead. I guess it didn't take it too well when I defied it. If

If knew it was that easy, I would've done it a long time ago.

chapter five/ the dean

Carefully compare the opposing army with your own, so that you may know where strength is super-abundant and where it is deficient.
    -Sun Tzu, *the Art of War*

My mom wanted to drive me, even though I tried to talk her out of it. It was over eleven hundred miles, and in January there was no saying what the roads would be like, especially up north. But she insisted, even after Newstead sent the bus ticket.

I don't know if it was because the mountains made radio reception impossible, or the eerie silence coming from the driver's seat, but that was the longest twenty hours of my life. Eventually we got there, though. She pulled off the interstate into the small town of Weston, Vermont.

I looked out my passenger window as we drove through the town. It was like one of those Norman Rockwell prints my mom tacked up all over our apartment. There were yards there, and porches; our neighborhood in St. Louis had neither.

A small wooden sign on the edge of the road was all that told us we'd arrived, but I couldn't see any school. There was just an open gate followed by a narrow drive that curved around a cluster of trees. It seemed to go on forever. The last bend brought us abruptly to a large clearing with the campus centered in front of the Green Mountains. They were a lot closer there than in town.

The school looked nice from that distance. Old Norman would've had a field day there. It was perfect; too perfect. The brick buildings were all evenly spaced, forming a semicircle that faced the parking lot. There was an occasional tree, just where it needed to be.

Of course there is.

My mom turned off the car, but neither of us made a move to leave. There wasn't even the sound of us breathing to break up the silence, but we must've been, because the windows fogged over, which was good because it kept me from seeing anything. That made it easier to forget I was freakishly large, going to a school for rich kids.

She opened her door. I followed, not bothering to lock mine. Looking at the other cars in the lot, our '87 Buick LaSabre would be the last one anyone would be breaking into.

Our meeting with the dean wasn't until one o'clock; we'd purposely gotten there an hour early to check things out for ourselves. I pulled out the map he'd sent in one of his many care packages, but I didn't need it. The campus was pretty small; even I could figure it out.

There were only twelve buildings in all and my mom and I slowly walked past each one. They all looked the same to me, old brick covered in dead ivy. Only one thing didn't go with the rest of it: the angel-lady fountain that was right in front of the dining hall, in the exact center of the semi-circle. We'd walked by it twice, but on our third pass I decided to stop looking at old buildings and look at an old fountain instead. It's not like my mom was talking to me yet.

I walked up to the only girl I was going to get to see for the next year and a half. She was pretty, but I personally would've preferred one with a pulse. She was small for a fountain, probably not any bigger than me and she was dry, just like all the ivy on the buildings.

I turned back to look at the campus. It looked different close up. I couldn't see the fountain from the car, but it was more than that.

Maybe it'll look better in the spring, when people are outside, and there's water in that fountain.

Maybe.

But not then, right then everything looked barren and dead. A dry, frigid breeze blew as if to prove my point.

Nearby a bell rang. The doors to the building closest to us opened and twelve guys pushed past each other to get out.

Two things struck me immediately. First; they were all in uniforms.

I groaned. *I hadn't thought of that.*

Second; they were all about my size; a couple of them were even taller than me. That was definitely something I hadn't expected. I was used to being the biggest. The freak.

Instead of walking past us, the largest of them came over to where we were standing, watching them.

"Are you Joel?"

It was strange hearing someone call me by my real name. It took me a minute to answer him.

"Yeah, that's me." I hoped he hadn't noticed the pause.

He didn't seem to. "I'm Marcus. I'm going to be bunking with you."

All the air left my lungs. *Guess that's something* else *they forgot to tell me.* No one, not once, had mentioned I'd be sharing a room. I'd never shared a room in my life. *What else did they conveniently leave out?*

My mother's interrupting cough saved me from having to

answer him. We both looked down at her as she motioned toward her watch. I nodded; it was time to go to the meeting with the Dean.

Marcus went back to the other guys who'd come out of the building with him. I was sure we'd have plenty of time to get to know each other later, probably more than either of us wanted.

I looked towards the last building of the semi-circle that went to the right of the fountain: the Administration building. I only hoped the Dean wasn't anything like Mike.

There was more snow crunching and silence as we made our way toward it. It took longer to get there than it did when we were just walking to waste time.

I opened the heavy, wooden door with the bronze handle. The inside of the building didn't match the outside. On the outside everything was old and cold. On the inside it looked like any other modern waiting room.

Maybe a waiting room for giants. I smiled to myself. It was true; everything about the place was scaled extra, extra large. I went to the counter to tell them we were there as my mom tried to sit in one of the oversized chairs. I heard her struggling, but by the time I turned around she was already sitting on one, with her legs dangling feet from the floor.

She was beautiful, even I could see it. Her looks were probably the reason she could support our small family on a couple of waitressing jobs. She always got very nice tips.

It was funny; I didn't look anything like her, not even the slightest resemblance. Her hair was black, mine was brown. My eyes did have some green in them, like hers, but even my driver's license didn't call them green. Instead, they were classified hazel, a name you gave something when you couldn't think of anything else to call it. Even our skin didn't match. Mine was ruddy, making it look like I was always blushing, which was something I hated. Hers was porcelain white.

I often wondered if I looked like my father, but I'd never met the guy and my mom didn't like to talk about him, so I never brought it up. But sometimes I'd catch her looking at me and something in her eyes told me it wasn't me she was seeing. Something told me I looked just like him.

Dean Erikson came to the door to welcome us. He filled the entire opening. He had at least that much in common with Mike, but he was younger than I'd expected, probably not over thirty. He ushered us into his office and asked if we wanted anything to drink. After we both said no, we sat in more oversized chairs as he oriented us to the campus.

"Welcome, Joel. I'm so glad you're going to be joining us here at Newstead." His smile was bright and full as he repeated verbatim the opening line of each of the letters he'd sent me.

I don't know why I didn't believe him, but I didn't. No one was that happy, unless they were faking it. My mother seemed to buy it, though. I could see that at least *her* smile was genuine.

"I've got your schedule right here. We've only got you taking six courses this trimester. No need to overwhelm you all at once." There was more of that fake smiling as he handed me my list of classes. I looked down at it. Math, Literature, Science, History, Gym, and Leadership/tactics.

"What are Leadership and Tactics?" I asked, leaning in.

"Oh, that." He laughed lightly. "That's required coursework for all of our students."

I didn't miss that he hadn't answered me.

He quickly moved onto other topics, like he was purposefully avoiding that one. "The trimester has just begun today, so you'll be starting classes first thing in the morning."

Guess that's his way of saying I'll just have to wait and see for myself.

I nodded and looked out the window as he continued his conversation with my mother. I tried not to listen as she recounted my football/basketball/baseball career of the last eleven years.

I stood up and walked to that same window when the pictures came out. *I can't believe she brought those.*

But at least she was smiling again.

After about an hour or so there was a light tugging on my sleeve. I turned around and saw my mom looking up at me. "I better get going; I need to make it to Cleveland by nightfall."

I nodded and followed her to the door. I turned to say good-bye to the dean, expecting him to be behind his desk, but he wasn't. He was standing right by the door, holding it open for us.

I flinched back, seeing him so close, especially when I wasn't expecting him there. He just smiled again, showing off more of his bright, white teeth. I don't know why, but that made me flinch, too.

He stopped smiling and looked down at me seriously. "Again, if there's anything I can do to make you comfortable here, just let me know. My door is always open."

He looked me over, starting at my head, then slowly going to my feet then back up again. "Mike was right. I think you're going to be our best yet." He looked me square in the eyes when he said it. It felt like the first time that day he'd told me the truth.

"Thank you. I hope I won't let you down," I said, looking him in the eye.

"Me, too." He laughed. My mom joined him, but I didn't.

"I am very involved with the training of our students, so I'm sure I'll see you around, soon. But remember, if you ever need anything–"

"I'll come and see you."

"That's right. I can see you're a quick learner, Joel. Yes, Mike was definitely right about you."

I turned and left with my mother and tried to block out how

much Dean Erikson reminded me of Mike Arberdean.

My mother didn't look happy anymore as I walked her to her car. *I guess talking about me leaving is more fun than me actually doing it.*

When we got there, she hugged me tightly, her face pressed against my chest. That was the only way I knew she was crying, otherwise she would've let me see her face. I humored her and pretended I didn't notice.

I pulled back and went to the trunk to get my one small suitcase. The car rocked as I closed it a little harder than I'd meant to.

So much for keeping it light.

She looked up at me and I could see that her tears had been wiped away. *Of course they were. We wouldn't want to be honest with each other, would we?*

I followed her lead and turned to go toward Chapman Hall, my home for the next eighteen months. If she wanted to ignore the elephant in the room, then so could I.

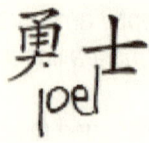

chapter six/ chapman hall

Concealing courage under a show of timidity presupposes a
fund of latent energy; masking strength with weakness.
    -Sun Tzu, *the Art of War*

I walked straight toward Chapman. I didn't have to go far; it
was right next to the dining hall. There were three more housing
buildings beyond it, making up the majority of the semi-circle
that went to the left of the fountain. The only other buildings on
that end were the library and the gym. But I didn't bother going
to either of those. I'd seen enough of Newstead for one day. I
just wanted to crawl into my bed and pretend I didn't have a
roommate.

Chapman was quiet when I walked in. But I figured I couldn't
always count on that, most of the people who lived there were
probably still in class. I climbed the stairs that ran through the
middle of the building until I got to the last one. I was on the
third floor, just like at home.

The hall that ran down the center of the building reminded me
of home, too. It was just a row of closed doors with numbers on

them. I found mine and opened it.

I saw then that there wasn't just one thing Mike and the dean had forgotten to tell me, there were two. In my new room there were three beds. The bunk bed was already claimed, leaving a single bed that I guessed was for me pushed against the far wall, like an afterthought. It was stripped bare, with a sheet set neatly folded on top.

My eyes went to the one window in the room and I breathed slowly in and out a few times. That helped a little. I grabbed my new pillow and put it on the other end of the bed and laid down and looked out the window some more. It didn't take long for me to fall asleep. And it didn't take long for me to wake up, either. All it took was school letting out for the day.

I heard them coming in downstairs and progressively make their way up, building volume the closer they came, like a tidal wave. It peaked and crested with my door being pushed open and two guys falling inside. I recognized one of them right away. Marcus was hard to forget. His hair took the word towhead to a whole new level. His white hair only made his ice blue eyes more freaky looking. He almost didn't look real, especially right next to the other guy's dark skin.

They were too busy wrestling to notice I was in there.

Marcus and the other guy, who I assumed was my other roommate, circled each other in the small room. Marcus grinned at him as he swatted at his leg, tauntingly. The other guy dove into his chest and they both toppled to the floor. They only stayed down for a few seconds before it all started again.

I watched, smiling.

The other guy stood, looking like he was going to do another one of his diving maneuvers, but at the last second his whole body stiffened. He turned slowly until he was looking right at me. My breath held as his eyes narrowed, taking me in. Marcus didn't realize that his opponent wasn't in the game anymore as he tried to grab him by the knees to reengage him, but he was immovable as stone as his eyes stayed fixed on me.

Eventually Marcus gave up and tried to see what was commanding his attention.

"Oh, Joel, you're here," Marcus said. Hearing my name didn't make the guy back down any. If anything, his eyes got more intense.

But I'm no coward, so I stood and faced the man who had spent the better part of two minutes staring me down. He didn't flinch as I stood up to my full height. He still had me by at least four inches.

He swallowed hard, his jaw tight. I pushed my sleeves back. My heart began to pound in my chest as I forced myself to focus on his weak points. He didn't seem to have any.

He nodded once briefly and then turned and swung himself onto the upper bunk. The silence in the room was palpable. Marcus was the first to break it as he turned to me and started talking, but I wasn't paying any attention to him. I was too busy staring at the broad back on the upper bunk. *What the hell is his problem?*

"Joel, did you hear what I said to you?" Marcus asked, as I continued to stare at my other roommate. I forced myself to give Marcus my full attention. It wasn't easy.

"What? I'm sorry, what were you saying?"

"I said I think Erikson gave us the same schedule so I could show you around."

I pulled out the piece of paper that I'd shoved in my front pocket and handed it to him.

"Yeah, they're the same. That's cool. I'll make sure you feel at home." His eyes lifted briefly to the upper bunk and the guy lying on it.

"Thanks," I answered as I tried to forget I even had a second roommate.

Marcus was pretty good at distracting me. He rambled on about nothing for almost an hour when, for no particular reason, he decided to introduce us to each other.

"That's Steven," he said as his eyes rose again to the upper bunk.

Steven.

Steven didn't seem any happier than I was about our meeting each other. Ever since he'd planted himself on his upper bunk, he'd been furiously reading a book.

With Marcus's introduction, Steven looked up briefly and then nodded before returning to his book. At least it was better than the last time Steven had noticed me.

Marcus didn't say anything, so I had to assume that was normal behavior for Steven. I didn't know what to make of him.

Guess I'll be sleeping with one eye open. It was a good thing I'd gotten a nap that afternoon.

I think Marcus would've talked all night, but a loud bell stopped him mid-sentence. He looked toward the clock on his dresser. The bell and the time meant more to him than it did to me.

"You hungry?" asked Marcus.

Dinner; it was a good thing. I was starting to wish I'd taken my mom up on her offer of hitting one more drive-thru before pulling off the interstate. I was starving.

Steven, in one graceful bound, leaped off the upper bunk and was standing beside me. Everything about him was intense, poised, almost like he was a caged animal. He didn't say one word to either of us as he pushed past me and walked out of the room.

I followed Marcus when he left a minute later. *Guess he wants to put some distance between Steven and me. That's probably a good idea.*

Good idea or not, it made us one of the last ones to leave

Chapman, even though I seemed to be the only one anxious to get there. After I saw the food I realized why.

I'd thought my mother's cooking was bad, but she had nothing on that place. I had no idea what bad was until I heard the plop as various piles of unknowns were dumped on my plate.

Steven sat as far from me as the cafeteria would let him. I don't know if that was intentional or not. For all I knew, that was where he always sat. But it felt off. Before Steven had noticed I was in the room with him, he and Marcus had been acting like they were best friends. I'm sure they would have been eating together, too.

I tried not to think about it as I forced the food down.

Marcus was as good as his word. He introduced me to everyone. By the end of the night I knew more people than I could possibly keep track of. *I'll be lucky if I remember half their names tomorrow. But there's one name I know I won't forget. Steven.*

He was in bed when Marcus and I came in, right before lights out. That was the first time in over two and a half months that the voice in my head made an appearance.

I'm not going to tell you I told you so, it said. I ignored it as I smiled to myself before rolling over on my side. Crazy as it seems, I was actually glad to hear it. The voice was the only thing about my old life I had with me. It was comfortable. It was safe.

chapter seven/ the other roommate

Therefore, just as water retains no constant shape, so in warfare there are no constant conditions.
-Sun Tzu, *the Art of War*

Marcus was in my face first thing the next morning.
Guess he wanted to get to me before Steven does. I looked up at the upper bunk. It was already empty, so my eyes closed again.

"Hey, Joel. Rise and shine." I felt a strong hand grip my shoulder and shake it until I forced my eyes to stay open. Marcus laughed at me as I tried to orient myself. I looked at the clock. Six-forty. Somehow I'd managed to sleep through the whole night.

"Sorry to wake you up, but they really don't like it when you're late."

"No, that's fine. I needed to get up anyhow."

"Here's your uniform; Erikson dropped it off about an hour ago."

I looked at the blue pants and shirt that were just like the ones Marcus had on. *It's just like a jersey,* I lied to myself as I stood and walked to the bathroom to take my shower and get dressed. At least it fit.

Marcus was waiting for me outside the bathroom. From the lack of noise in the house, I guessed we were the last ones to head to breakfast. But Marcus didn't seem to mind. He talked my ear off all the way to the dining hall.

Some of the guys from the previous night had saved us a couple seats at one of the tables. It was a good thing; the place was packed. There was double the number that had been there for dinner.

So Marcus made himself busy, introducing me to the rest of them. Everyone seemed very eager to be my friend, almost too eager. It made me feel a little uncomfortable. I just like to be alone. But Marcus wasn't having any of that. He never left my side all day. He was in every one of my classes, just like he'd said.

I didn't see Steven again until the end of the day for Leadership and Tactics class. But that was only because all of us were there, all forty-two of Newstead's Juniors.

Class was held in the gym. It was the only place that could hold all of us at once. I followed Marcus in and sat on the floor next to him. It got pretty loud until the teacher came in. And then, just like a switch, you could hear a pin drop.

He wasn't as big as Mike or even Erikson. But that didn't seem to matter to the guys around me.

"Good afternoon, gentlemen. Welcome back to another fun-filled day of drills. I know how much you love them." There were a few groans that quickly cut off.

"On your feet, soldiers."

I looked to my right, then to my left. *Is he talking to us? Who is this guy?* I wondered, but decided I didn't want to find out. I followed the lead of the rest of the class and quickly stood up.

I soon found out what drills were, and they weren't fun. They made my coach's practices feel like a cakewalk. But I didn't mind. I liked pushing myself.

Steven stayed as far from me as he could in there, too. It was almost like the teacher was in on it too because I was paired up at different times with just about everybody. Everybody but Steven.

We ended class with a jog around the perimeter of the building. I could've passed Marcus, but I didn't. He'd gone out of his way for me that day, and the night before. So I slowed my pace to keep in time with his.

After chow I followed Marcus back to Chapman. I knew where he was going before he turned to go down the flight of stairs: the rec room. We'd gone there my first night. It looked the same; same guys playing pool, same guys fighting over the remote.

And just like the night before, Marcus and I sat on the sectional in the corner. It didn't take long for the rest of them to join us there. Marcus had a group of six guys who followed him around almost as much as I did. But mine wasn't out of choice.

The stories soon started. I couldn't believe it when the first guy began. It was exactly the one he'd told the night before. And just like the night before, all of them reacted at just the right spots, like they'd never heard it before.

I sat back and silently watched them. *Are they for real?*

They didn't seem to notice I wasn't talking. I stopped listening after the fifth guy started.

I need to get out of here.

But I didn't get to, because we stayed right until twenty-three hundred—lights out.

I followed Marcus up to our room. Steven was already asleep in his bed. I laid down in mine and heard the familiar voice ringing in my ears.

You need to get some balls.

I nodded to myself. It was right. I needed to come up with a way to separate myself from Marcus. The guy was alright, but I just wasn't wired that way. There was no way I could survive if I had to be around all those people all the time.

The next day started exactly the same. I followed Marcus around, but instead of automatically going down the stairs to the rec room, I stopped and called after him.

"Listen, I think I'm going to do something else tonight."

Marcus stopped mid-step. The muscles in his neck tensed up. "Do whatever you want," he answered, without turning to face me.

He started walking down the stairs again, but I turned and went back to my room. I didn't have any place else to go.

I was already halfway into the room before I realized it wasn't empty. I almost turned back around, and I think if it hadn't been for the voice in my head, I would've done just that.

Are you telling me you're afraid of a guy reading a book?

I decided I wasn't. So I finished walking into the room and sat down on my bed.

Steven didn't look up. The silence was almost worse than the noise in the basement. But at least the silence was familiar to me. I don't mind silence.

I rummaged through my things and grabbed my Algebra book. I settled down on my bed with my back against the wall and did the problems for the next three weeks. Every couple minutes, I heard Steven turn a page in his book. Fifty-four pages later, I decided to call it a night. Marcus's bottom bunk was still empty when I pulled the covers up over my head.

That time I was the first one to wake up. I jumped in the shower before anyone else and put on the uniform that had been placed on my dresser sometime during the night. Another blue one; I was starting to hate blue. I missed my t-shirts.

The room was empty when I went back to grab my stuff. I

knew I'd blown off his night of story-telling, but I couldn't believe Marcus would've left without me. I waited in the room for a while just in case he was in one of the other shower rooms and I'd missed him, but as the voices in Chapman grew fainter, I knew he wasn't coming back. *Guess I really pissed him off.*

The mess hall was full again, only that time there was no seat saved for me. I scanned the room looking for someplace to sit. I noticed a gap between two backs and made my way for it.

I sat down and found myself directly across from Steven. He looked as surprised as me.

We both quickly looked down at our plates and gave the piles of eggs our undivided attention. Time went by very slowly as I tried to decide how long was long enough before I could make my exit. But I got that wrong too, because we both stood at the same time. It was too late to sit back down, so I followed him to the trash.

Out of the corner of my eye I saw Marcus sitting at his usual table with his usual group of followers. He was staring right at Steven and me. A couple of the other guys he was with turned around to look at us, too.

Steven paused briefly before shelving his tray. His whole body seemed to stiffen. Then it relaxed and he continued on his way. I left too, but my class was in the opposite direction of his.

I turned to watch him as he walked toward the gym, alone.

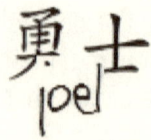

chapter eight/ the waitress

If you know the enemy and know yourself, your victory will not stand in doubt; if you know Heaven and know earth, you may make your victory complete.
    -Sun Tzu, *the Art of War*

For the second night, Steven and I occupied a silent room. Even the voice in my head wasn't saying anything. I finally gave up all pretenses and went to sleep.

I don't know if Marcus slept there or not. He wasn't in his bed when I fell asleep and he wasn't there when I woke up. It was a Saturday, so I got dressed in clothes, real clothes, and they were anything but blue, except for maybe the jeans.

I went to the mess hall by myself. It was fairly empty; there were any number of seats to choose from. I ate as quickly as I could and then went back outside. I almost didn't go back to Chapman. There was no reason to go there. There was no reason to go anywhere.

I looked towards the parking lot and the long winding drive in front of it. And then I turned and went back to my room. Steven was in the room and the clock was in the room.

Zero nine hundred....eleven hundred and four...eleven hundred and twelve.

The sudden thud of a closing book made me look up from staring at the clock. Steven wasn't lying on his bed anymore; he was sitting up with his legs dangling over the edge, looking at me. He didn't even look angry.

"Hey, you want to head into town, get something to eat?"

I turned to look behind me to see who he was talking to, but there wasn't anyone there.

"Sure," I answered. By that point I would've said yes to just about anyone.

We met another couple guys on our way out of Chapman who Steven asked to come with us; Seth and Tom. Together we turned and walked down toward the parking lot, then the drive that led out of Newstead.

The air was brisk. I breathed it in, long and deep.

Steven seemed to know where he was going, so we just followed him. We walked by a couple other restaurants before we finally stopped.

I think the neon sign that was centered on the front window was supposed to say Fred's Pizza, but the e and two z's were only a dull pink, while the rest of it was glowing bright red.

Steven stood by the door, waiting for me. I followed him inside.

It was packed. *Guess that answers why Newstead looked so empty; everyone is here.* We stood by the counter and waited for someone to seat us.

It turned out I was wrong about not seeing any girls.

She was behind the counter, the pretty waitress, trying to ignore all the overgrown guys gawking at her. Her dark brown hair with soft curls was pulled back into a loose ponytail that was stuck through a stained, well-worn baseball cap. Pizza sauce and cheese splattered the front of her apron as the pizza she was carrying almost slid to the floor. From the looks of her, that wasn't her first near miss. She raced past us to a waiting table that thankfully hadn't noticed that their food had almost tested the five second rule.

My eyes followed her as she darted around the small dining room. She was always in motion: delivering pizzas, waiting on the counter, working the register. It didn't occur to me at the time that she was ignoring us, but now I know that she was. Finally, she turned to wait on us.

"Table or booth?" she asked, not looking at any of us in particular.

"Right this way," she replied as I took the lead and spoke up, saying we'd like a booth.

The other guys didn't move, not at first. They were too busy staring at me. I turned even redder; wishing I'd just let one of the other guys answer her.

The girl led us to a booth in the corner and I took the lead again and followed her. The rest of them followed silently behind.

I pretended to look at my menu, describing the thirty-six varieties of pizza Fred's was supposedly famous for: Home of the original meat lover's pizza. *Funny, I could've sworn we had meat lover's pizzas in St. Louis.* I chuckled to myself and then looked up again.

She was at a different table, taking their order. I don't know what they were saying to her, but she didn't like it. She went back into the kitchen for a while and then came out with a pizza that she dropped off to some guys two booths down. Then she came over to us.

She looked taller than she had before, but maybe that was just because I was sitting. If I had to guess, I'd say she was five six or seven. She tucked a curl behind her ear and pulled out a pad of paper.

"What can I get for you?"

That time Seth spoke up and told her we wanted four cokes

and two large pizzas, extra everything. For some reason she smirked before turning to go back into the kitchen.

I watched as she carried pizza after pizza. They all were exactly the same. All of them were larges, loaded with toppings.

She paused briefly to drop off our drinks, throwing a pile of straws in the middle of the table. I picked one up and took off the paper wrapping and put it in my pocket. She was back a few minutes later with our pizzas. They looked like all the rest of them.

The first pizza was gone in five minutes. The second didn't last that much longer.

My cup was empty halfway through the first one. It stayed empty for a while. I pushed it towards the edge of the table, hoping to get her attention. She ignored it.

I was too busy watching her to realize that Seth was watching me. I know he thought he was being helpful when he reached out and grabbed her arm just as she was walking by. I know that, but it didn't change the way I wanted to rip his arm off when he did it. She looked like she felt the same way.

"Can you get my friend a refill?" he asked, still holding onto her arm. Her face was beet red. I don't think she was scared, I think she was angry. She reached over and grabbed my cup. She never looked at Seth; no, her scowl was only for me.

My breath held until he let her go.

"Hey Joel, why don't you get a job here?"

We all turned to look at Steven who was only looking at me. Everyone laughed, even me; everyone but Steven, who looked like he'd been serious.

I cleared my throat. He was still looking at me expectantly.

"I've never had a job before," I said, avoiding all eyes but his.

"Now's as good a time as any," he answered. His eyes looked intense again, like the night I'd first met him.

I just chuckled as the waitress brought me my full coke along with our check.

Maybe I will.

I pushed the drink to the side and pulled out my wallet. I put my last five on the table and waited for Seth to stand up so I could slide out of the booth. I left them standing there as I went up to the counter and the girl who stood behind it.

"Excuse me, can I have an application?" I asked, trying to ignore the snickers coming from behind me. I was hoping they'd wait by the table, but I guess that was too much to expect.

She looked stunned. She blinked twice before answering me. "What would a Newsteader need a job for?"

"What makes you think I go to Newstead?"

She looked at me incredulously.

Guess I can see her point.

I almost walked away, and if Steven hadn't suddenly appeared at my side, I probably would have. As I looked at him he nodded slightly. So I told her the truth, "I just wanted to make some extra money to send back to my mom."

She looked dumbfounded. After all, what could she say to that? I could tell she was trying to come up with something, though. Failing, she reluctantly reached under the counter and pulled out a white sheet of paper with the words "APPLICATION FOR EMPLOYMENT" typed across the top.

"Thank you," I said as I took it, folded it in half, and tucked it into my jacket pocket.

Steven smiled. Tom and Seth stared at me in astonishment. I think they'd thought the whole job thing had just been a big joke. I did, too.

As soon as we left Fred's, the bantering began.

"Looks like Joel has a girlfriend," they teased, laughing heartily at my expense. My flushed face was answer enough to continue the jokes all the way back to the dorm.

I ignored them. I was glad I'd asked for the application. It gave me something to look forward to.

All I could think about was the idea of working there. It was what helped me get through that Sunday, when the nothingness was too much. I don't know why I was so excited; the place was a dump and she was a bitch.

Late Sunday night I sat down on my bed and tried to fill out the application. I'd never had a job before. My mom would never let me. She was afraid it would get in the way of that scholarship she kept harping about. But my mom wasn't there.

When I was done I looked down at it. Even I could see it looked pretty sparse. But I reassured myself with the thought that you probably didn't need to be a rocket scientist to work at Fred's Pizza.

I walked down the long drive towards town right after chow on Monday. That time I went alone. I got there quicker than on Saturday; in a little over fifteen minutes I was standing in front of Fred's with the application clenched tightly in my hand.

I walked to the door and pushed it open. It was a different Fred's than the one I'd been at on Saturday. It was mainly empty, with only a few old guys sitting on the swivel stools at the counter. One of them turned to look at me when I walked in.

"Can I help you?" he asked as I approached the counter. I paused a minute before answering him. My eyes scanned the restaurant. She wasn't there.

I turned my attention back to the one who had spoken to me as he stood up and reached over the counter to grab himself another donut. He shoved it in his mouth, whole. I didn't know it then, but I was looking at the infamous Fred.

"Yeah, I was here on Saturday and noticed the help wanted sign. The waitress that was on gave me an application." I handed him the piece of paper.

"Rachel?" he asked; his mouth overflowing.

"I guess so. She didn't tell me her name."

Rachel.

He scanned my application as he half-sat, half-leaned on the counter. I guessed he needed it to support his enormous stomach that was protruding out from beneath his stained t-shirt.

"No experience?" he asked. That was the one question I was hoping he wouldn't get to.

I looked him in the eyes and tried to ignore the chocolate frosting smear that was across the bottom half of his face as I answered him, "No, but I work hard and am available every weekend."

He turned to look at me, like it was the first time he was really seeing me. Something made him smile.

"Can you start on Friday?" he asked, trying with some difficulty to meet my gaze.

"Sure," I responded, with more confidence than I felt. I turned to walk away before either of us could change our minds.

"Be here at five p.m. sharp. Don't be late, and don't wear that goofy uniform," he called out as I opened the door.

I turned around to show that I'd heard him and then sprinted back to campus.

chapter nine/ rachel's frustration

Never take life too seriously. Nobody gets out alive anyway.
    -Author unknown

Fred met me at the door with a huge grin on his face; that alone should've warned me that my day was about to get very bad. Fred never met me at the door. Never.

"So, Rachel, how are you doing?" His eyes were brimming over with some secret.

I walked past him to drop off my backpack in the back room. When I turned around he was still there, with the same stupid smile on his face.

"Okay Fred, I give. What is it that you want to tell me?"

I really didn't have time for Fred and his stupid antics. I only had forty-five minutes before the hordes of Newstead kids started showing up. If I fell behind in my prep work, I'd be playing catch-up for the rest of the night. Not that that mattered much to Fred.

"Nothing. Can't I just be glad to see you?"

I shrugged. Fred was always trying to get a rise out of me. It was like he got off on it. Most of the time I ignored him; I was the last one to want to see Fred enjoying himself.

He got out of my way and let me get to work making the

dough. Every few minutes he'd peek his head through the kitchen window to see if I was done yet. By four o'clock, I'd had enough. I went out to the dining room to get whatever it was over with.

The swinging door to the kitchen was still going back and forth when Fred walked very slowly over to the help wanted sign that had lived on the wall above the cash register for at least the last four months. It may have been there longer, but four months was as far back as Fred's Pizza and I went.

His eyes never left mine as he peeled it off the wall. The paint under the sign was a different color. *I guess it's been up there for a while.*

"Are you trying to tell me you hired someone?" I asked, still not connecting the dots at that point.

"Yup, he's going to start on Friday." Fred's smile couldn't have gotten any bigger.

"He?" I asked.

"Yes, he stopped out here yesterday after school. I think he's going to work out great."

"Does *he* have a name?" Weston High was pretty small. I tried to think of who it could be—who'd be desperate enough to work at Fred's? I only hoped it wasn't that goofy kid from my Biology class. He gave me the creeps, the way he kept watching me.

"Joel something or other. I don't know; here's his application." Fred handed it to me and stood back to watch my reaction. It didn't take long. It only took seeing the address.

"He's from Newstead?" I might have yelled it; I don't know. I wasn't exactly in total control of myself at that particular moment.

My heart was pounding in my chest. All the dots connected. I knew exactly who Joel was. He certainly worked fast. It didn't even occur to me that he'd turn it in on Monday, my only day off. If I'd known that I never would've given him the stupid application in the first place. My plan all along was to just throw it out. Fred rarely left his office, especially when *they* started showing up. He never would've known the difference.

"Are you alright, Rachel?"

If his voice had been even the slightest bit sympathetic, I probably would've burst out in the tears that were threatening to overflow from my eyes. But it wasn't. It was all passive aggression, but I was glad when I heard it. It helped me get myself under control. Fred would be the last person to see me break down. I took two deep breaths and squeezed my eyes shut, forcing the tears to stay where they were.

I didn't look at Fred as I went back into the kitchen. I needed to think, to plan.

I knew after the display I'd just given, there was no way Fred was going to fire him. He needed to quit.

After scanning the kid's application for something I could use, I filed it in the trash. There was nothing for me there, just his name and age: Joel Cranston, age sixteen. From what I remembered, he didn't look sixteen. But then again, none of them looked their age.

It didn't matter anyway. I already knew enough about them to know what to do. I just needed to figure out what job there was in that place that would make him want to leave. I laughed to myself as I surveyed the options. It would probably be easier to come up with a list of jobs that would make him want to stay.

My eyes rested on the greasy stack of dishes that overflowed from the washtubs in the far corner of the kitchen. It was perfect.

Being stuck in the back, doing real work for once, not being able to get paid for hanging out with his friends all night and making my life miserable—he wouldn't last a week.

I smiled to myself as I started grating the cheese. It was time for Fred to eat some humble pie.

The bell above the door rang and I went out to wait on my first table of the night. Three huge guys were waiting for me by the counter and, of course, Fred was nowhere in sight. I led them to a table just as the bell rang again.

chapter ten/ the secret

You're only given a little spark of madness. You mustn't lose it.
　-Robin Williams

I left Fred's at a little after nine. I could've left earlier, but I purposely worked slowly at the end. I wanted some time between the last Newsteader and me. I don't know why I bothered—Newstead was in the opposite direction of my trailer—but every night I made sure there were at least thirty minutes between their departure and mine.

It wasn't so bad in town, when the soft lights illuminated my way. It was worse when I turned onto the farmer's lane at the end of Markham Lane. There were no lights there, just a dark path through the woods.

I normally would've walked faster when I got to that particular leg of the journey, but that night I didn't. I wasn't looking forward to telling Nathan about my new co-worker.

Maybe I don't have to tell him. Maybe I can talk about the rest of the stuff that happened and he'll just leave it at that.

The trailer came into view right as the forest turned into a sheep pasture. I stopped and looked at it, our tin box on wheels. The moonlight didn't do it any favors.

Yeah, right. When have I ever been able to keep anything from Nathan?

He was sitting at his normal spot at the booth-style table when I walked in. I almost walked past him to my room, but I knew that would only make him more suspicious, so I sat down on my usual folding chair and waited for him to begin.

"How was work?"

I looked up at him. Did he suspect it already? His eyes didn't reveal anything.

"The usual. Maybe a little busy for a Tuesday, but not too bad."

"Did Sam call in again?" Sam was the cook, who was well known for not showing up for his shifts.

"No, Fred didn't even have him on the schedule."

"Fred needs to hire some more people. It's not right that he keeps leaving you alone." I didn't look up. He paused briefly as my breath held, but he just continued on with his next question.

"Did they bother you again tonight?"

"No worse than usual."

We both knew what the usual was. The usual was most girls' worst nightmare, but for me, it was 'the usual'.

"So, who did Fred hire?"

That time my eyes raised to meet his. He'd figured it out in two minutes; that was a new record for him.

"I don't know what you're talking about," I answered, trying to play dumb. But Nathan knew me too well. He didn't even have to say another word. He just had to look at me with those intense eyes and I spilled it all.

"Okay, so Fred hired someone—what's it to you? It's not like *you* have to work with him."

He raised his left eyebrow.

"I know it's not ideal, but like you said, it's not fair that I keep being put on the schedule alone."

Both eyebrows went up.

"All right," I sighed. "He's from Newstead."

The questions ended. He knew as well as I did what that meant. He knew there was another word I could've used to describe him, but we had an unspoken agreement between the two of us never to say that word out loud again.

He looked over at my Aunt Beth who was lying listless on the couch and I knew my interview was over for the night. He wouldn't want to talk about that in front of his mother.

I stood up and went to my room and tried to focus on Geometry. After about an hour, I went to the kitchen to get myself a drink. Aunt Beth was still on the couch, but that was nothing new. She rarely left it. Nathan had already broken down the booth-style table into his bed.

Guess he's calling it a night; that makes two of us.

I filled my cup with water and turned to walk back to my room when his voice called out to me.

"Rachel?"

I almost kept walking

"Yes?" I answered without turning around. He knew that part of the night was for me.

"Do you ever wish you didn't come to live with us?"

Like I had a choice. "What are you getting at, Nathan?" I asked.

"I don't know. Sometimes I just think it would've been better for you if you'd moved in with someone else."

"What, and miss all this?" I laughed lightly as I looked around our trailer. Our eyes met, but Nathan wasn't laughing.

"You know what I'm talking about."

I sighed. He was right, I did.

We both knew the word I refused to say and we both knew that he was the reason I was forced to work with one of them.

chapter eleven/ nephilim

If you are going through hell, keep going.
  -Winston Churchill

Just a month after we'd moved there I was sitting in my metal chair, giving my usual report. Nathan's questions started out typical, and so did my answers.

"It was busy."

"How busy?"

"I don't know, just busy."

"What type of people does Fred get in his pizza shop?" Nathan continued with whatever mental list he was working off of. He barely looked interested.

"A lot of guys, actually. They all go to that school by the Green Mountains."

"What school is that?"

"Newstead. It's a private school for guys. I think it's a sports school, most of them are pretty big."

His eyes narrowed. "How big?"

I shrugged. "Real big."

That was the point Nathan started getting animated. Nathan never got animated, but he was then. He was leaning towards me, hands planted flat on the table. I think that table was the only thing keeping him in his seat.

"And what do those guys act like?"

"I don't know," I answered, but my flushed face must've given me away. I don't know why I blushed; they really weren't that bad, at least not back then. It was more a feeling, a knowing that they *could* be.

"I see."

I knew better than to elaborate. If Nathan wasn't asking, I wasn't offering. Besides, it looked like I had the rest of the night off; he was too preoccupied with the answers I'd already given him to bother asking more.

As soon as I became distracted by my homework, he slipped outside.

He didn't come back for two days.

Nathan, who usually spent all day, every day, in the trailer, Nathan, who didn't deviate from any of his daily routines, that Nathan was suddenly gone with no excuse or explanation.

Aunt Beth had the same vacant look on her face the entire time. I'd always wondered if she was really as void as she appeared. A small part of me assumed it had more to do with the stagnation of her life. But after those two days of Nathan being gone, I knew it was much more than that.

When he opened the door that second night I almost knocked him over. Physical contact was never a part of my relationship with Nathan, so he looked as shocked as I was as I clung to him. He briefly allowed it before pulling back.

I stood there waiting for something, some kind of excuse or explanation, but Nathan just walked over and sat at the booth that was our kitchen table. It was the same thing he did every other night at that time.

For the first time, I joined him there.

"Nathan, are you all right?"

He wasn't used to me initiating anything with him, so he

looked up, surprised. From that one look I knew he had no intention of telling me anything.

"Are you hungry?" I asked. I knew he was. He looked like wherever he'd been didn't have a shower, let alone food and water.

His eyes measured me. He knew the cost of what I was offering. He licked his dry lips, trying to decide. Eventually, basic human needs won over.

"What have you got?" It was the day before I went shopping, so he knew any food in the trailer would've been in my own personal stash.

"Oh, just some cookies and a bag or two of potato chips."

I watched him salivate. I'd just named his two favorite food groups.

He swallowed hard. "Would you mind getting them for me?"

"I wouldn't mind at all. But first…"

"First?" he asked warily.

"First you have to promise to tell me why you left, where you went, and what you did."

He wasn't used to being on the receiving end of the demands. He looked like he was about to refuse me, but his eyes looked past me to my room. He wanted those cookies.

"Fine. But bring me some milk, too."

I jumped up before he could change his mind. In two minutes he had a stack of cookies in one hand and a cup of milk tightly clenched in the other. I gave him a minute to gorge himself. Nathan was many things, but I knew he wouldn't back down on his word.

Without my prompting, he began:

"I left because of the things you were saying, about those Newstead kids. I knew there was something more, something both of us were missing, so I went to spend some time alone to think about it."

I nodded as my first question was answered. I tried not to look too eager as I waited for the rest.

"I went to the woods that are right behind Newstead. I thought maybe I would see one of them for myself and figure it out. Last night, I did. There were several of them, not too far from me. You were right, Rachel."

His eyes closed briefly, like he was seeing them, even then.

"Right about what?"

"About everything. Their size, their strength. Everything. They didn't stay where I was for too long. They looked like they were hiking, or something like it. I can't be sure, but it felt like they knew I was there."

"What did you do?" I asked.

He opened his mouth and then closed it, like he was about to say something but had changed his mind. He knew me well enough to know I wouldn't miss the gesture, but that didn't seem to matter. Something had happened to him that he wasn't willing to share with me.

He nodded slightly to himself, like he was responding to some internal question. Finally he continued, "After I left the woods, I came to a clearing at the base of the mountains. It was there that I figured out what had been eluding me."

"What was that?" I asked, leaning towards him.

"The boys from Newstead…" He stopped and looked around the trailer, like there might've been someone watching us. I looked too. There was just Aunt Beth sprawled out on the couch, nothing new there. But that pause was enough for me to get another look at Nathan. His face was white and his pupils were dilated. Nathan was afraid.

He ducked his head towards me and whispered, like we weren't in our trailer in the middle of nowhere. Even with him right across the table, I had to strain to hear him.

"Have you ever heard of a Nephilim?"

I shook my head.

"They haven't been here in a long time, not since they were exterminated. But that was only their descendants, a diluted strain. The real ones haven't been on the earth since before the flood."

"I don't understand." I tried to look at the eyes that still wouldn't meet mine.

"Those boys—they're not boys. They're more—and less. They're Nephilim."

"Didn't I already say I didn't know what a Nephilim was?" I asked angrily, but I shouldn't have. It gave Nathan all the excuse he needed to stop giving me answers. Nathan stood, like our conversation was over.

"Where are you going?" I asked as he made his way back to the bathroom. He ignored me. He was done; I'd have to figure the rest out on my own. But at least I had a word to begin my search with: Nephilim.

chapter twelve/ found out

I have learned over the years that when one's mind is made up, this diminishes fear, knowing what must be done does away with fear.

  -Rosa Parks

We didn't have a land line to the trailer while we were in Weston. We were lucky to have running water and electricity; some of the places we'd stayed at didn't. So my search couldn't begin until the next day. It was the first time I actually looked forward to going to school. The library there had computers, and the Internet.

I didn't have any study halls. Most of the schools I went to were determined to transform me into the model student, and Weston was no different. They wanted me to mingle in with as many of the locals as possible.

No study halls.

I didn't even bother explaining to them that it didn't matter how many locals they forced me on. Nothing mattered when you just moved in three months anyway.

So if I was going to have access to the library and their computers, I needed to be creative. Creativity usually isn't a problem for me, and that day was no different. It didn't take me long to formulate my strategy.

My gym teacher, Mr. Clark, had always looked very uncomfortable around me. It was probably because I was the only one of his students he hadn't known since birth. Or maybe it was more than that, because his face always enflamed whenever I walked into class. It didn't matter; both could be used for what I needed.

"Excuse me, Mr. Clark?" I asked at the beginning of class, before we got too involved in whatever bogus thing he'd come up with for the day.

His face became bright red.

"Yes, Rachel?"

It was time to put my plan into action. My timing was perfect; everyone had turned to see what I'd say to him. I rarely spoke in school.

I didn't disappoint any of them.

"May I go to the nurse? I'm having cramps." I wrapped my arms around my waist to leave no room for doubt as to what I was implying.

If possible, his face got even redder as a few of the others snickered. He mumbled something and waved me away before I could say anything else that would mortify him. He even forgot to issue me a pass.

Just like I'd planned.

I walked past the nurse's office on the way to the library. No one stopped me, even though I walked by several teachers. I'd learned a long time ago that if you looked like you knew what you were doing, other people would usually leave you alone.

Even the librarian didn't stop me as I sat down at one of the vacant computers and typed in the word that had run through my mind over and over since Nathan first whispered it the night before.

Nephilim.

Several results appeared, and I clicked on the first one. I wish I hadn't. The second was worse. It wasn't until I got to the fifth that I had to acknowledge they were all talking about the same thing: Nathan's Nephilim.

I went back to the first site. That time, I read every word. According to them, Nephilim was another word for giant. That part didn't frighten me. I already knew they were huge; it was more the reason *why* they were giants that freaked me out.

They were giants because the genetic material that invaded their DNA was too big for their cells to contain it. They were giants because they weren't people at all, at least not the technical definition of a person. A person was human, and a Nephilim was only half.

It was the other half that made them both less and more, like Nathan had said.

I didn't consider myself religious, not since my parents had died. But there were a few words listed on that site that I easily recognized. Like Fallen Angel, and Demon. Nephilim were that half, too.

Nephilim were only human on their mothers' side.

I tried to process it all in my mind: what Nathan had said, what I saw every day at work, and what the computer displayed right in front of me. And then I knew it was true, all of it.

I knew the what, but I couldn't even begin to comprehend the why. Why was such a thing allowed, and why of all places was it happening in Weston? In all our moves, we'd never been to someplace so rural.

Maybe that was the point. It was the perfect place to hide a few hundred giants. No one would ever suspect it, not even me.

But why?

I didn't know, but I had a feeling Nathan did. That was why he'd stopped answering me. He wouldn't have a choice when I got home that night. He was going to tell me everything.

"Rachel Newell? Are you supposed to be in here?"

Her voice came from somewhere behind me, and I knew my cover was blown. Whatever confidence had been on my face had disappeared somewhere around page two of my search. I turned to face the librarian as I shut off my computer.

I doubted she could handle what I'd just seen, especially since she was a permanent resident of Weston. I was just passing through. And from what I'd discovered that day, Weston would be our shortest stop ever.

"I was just leaving," I said as I walked away. I'd never meant anything more.

I felt her incredulous eyes on my back. Her loud sigh was the only response I got.

It was too early to go to my next class, so instead I went to where I'd told Mr. Clark I was going. I went to the nurse's office. It looked like something out of the Twilight Zone, straight from the fifties. Everything was decked out in white, including the nurse who was sitting behind the desk. She looked up briefly from the book she was reading and pointed to one of the two cots that were pushed against the far wall.

I walked over to the one on the left and laid down and stared at the ceiling. There was a clock on the wall right above my head with a very loud second hand. Each time it ticked I saw a different picture in my head. None of them were good.

The last one was of Nathan's face. It was a refreshing change. Not that his face looked good—it looked terrible—but it gave me hope. He was as afraid of them as I was.

I took a deep breath in and stood up. I had five more classes to get through.

The nurse didn't look up as I walked out.

chapter thirteen/ marcus

To him who is in fear everything rustles
  -Sophocles

The final bell rang at a little after three-thirty. Everyone stood up to leave, and I did, too. In a line we streamed out of the room, toward wherever it was all of us were going to for the rest of the day. Some were going to clubs, some to basketball practice, some were just going home. I was supposed to go to Fred's.

That was the real problem, the one I'd spent the majority of the day racking my brain over. I really, really didn't want to go. I didn't see the point, especially if we were just leaving that night anyhow.

Fred's was dark when I walked by. I didn't look back at it, any more than I did at the school. But for some reason, I did look up as I rounded the corner towards my road. The town's only gas station was on that corner. It was a one pump type of place, and that's where my eyes went to, that one pump and the price that was posted above it.

Four freaking dollars a gallon. My feet stopped moving as my mind started doing the math. I had a little over eighty dollars; with gas at four dollars a gallon, our gas guzzling truck wouldn't even make it out of Vermont.

That wasn't nearly far enough, I was thinking more like Canada. That time, I did turn and look back at Fred's. Only five hours. I could do five hours. I had to.

I closed my eyes and put one foot in front of the other as I made my way back into the town. It felt like my feet were made of lead. It didn't take long enough to get there; too soon, I was standing in front of Fred's. I took a deep breath in and pushed the door open.

Fred's was empty, like it usually was that time of day. Newstead didn't let out until a little after four. I could set my watch to them. At four-fifteen Fred's was empty. Four-thirty, packed beyond capacity.

Fred was back in his office. He didn't come out to see who it was; he knew it was me. I started doing what I normally did that time of day: making the dough, shredding the cheese. It kept my hands busy, and my mind, too. I could easily forget what was right outside my door. Until four-thirty.

You wouldn't think it would make a difference knowing what they were. Something deep inside me had already been afraid of them. But it did. Seeing their huge frames so close to mine, having them talk to me, made it very difficult to pretend they were just boys.

Just like with the librarian, they could see my confidence slipping, they saw and capitalized on it. That was the first night one of them asked me out.

He walked over to where I was standing by the register, ringing up a group of them. I didn't notice him at first; there were just too many of them for the individual Newsteader to stand out, but he made me notice him.

"You're Rachel, right?" he asked.

I turned at the sound of his voice. I wasn't used to having them talk directly to me. They would place their orders, they would pay. Until that night, that was the extent of it.

I felt my face flushing. He smiled when he saw it.

He took a step closer and then another one. He stopped when various parts of his body grazed mine: His toes against my toes, my knees against his calves, my chest against his stomach.

I took a step back, and when I did, I felt his light laughter. There were no steps back. I was already pressed right up against the wall.

"Going somewhere?"

My knees started to shake. I knew he felt it too, because he started laughing again.

He stepped back and I had to catch myself from toppling over. I didn't realize how much I was leaning on him to keep myself upright. He laughed again as I yanked my hands off his chest.

His finger went towards my shirt and traced along my name tag, "It says it right here; Rachel."

For the first time, I looked up to see his face. He was smiling broadly, but it was cold, as cold as his ice blue eyes.

"Did you need something?" I asked.

"Not really," he said, still smiling. "I just wanted to give you a good look, since you seemed so interested and all."

I didn't know if there were double meanings to what he was saying or if I was just reading too much into it. But either way, being that close to him taught me one thing I didn't know before. Nephilim fed on fear, meaning the opposite was also true. They starved without it.

"Trust me, I'm not interested," I said with just the right amount of acid in my voice.

He took another step back to look at me, to see if I was serious.

I'm good at masks. I'd worn one for years after my parents died. It kept people from knowing how I really felt. Changing schools three times a year didn't hurt, either. I'd reinvented myself so many times that I had a vast supply to choose from. I picked my bitchiest one and planted it firmly on my face.

He wasn't laughing anymore. He wasn't smiling either. He just shook his head as he watched me glare at him. "You have no idea what you've just started."

I shrugged. He had no idea about me, either.

He shook his head one last time before turning to leave. I didn't look in that direction until I heard the front door slam.

But he was right, something did start that night. The switch had flipped; all pretenses were gone. They were as unrestrained as they wanted to be, all of them. They didn't go to the point of pressing me against the wall like blondie boy had done, but they were pretty close. Pretty close.

At first they looked at me quizzically when I responded with a voice that matched my mask. Then they backed down, just like their leader had done. They didn't know what to make of me. I knew they'd figure it out eventually, but it did buy me the couple of hours I needed.

I flipped the sign to read "closed" and felt myself completely relax. It was over. I threw my name badge in the garbage on my way out of Fred's.

chapter fourteen/ staying

I'm sorry, if you were right, I'd agree with you.
  -Robin Williams

Nathan was sitting in the booth again when I got home. He was watching the news on the tiny TV he had balanced on the ten inch length of counter space the kitchen had. I sat down in the seat across from him. My fingers started tapping on the table as I waited for him to look at me.

When the first broadcast was over, he stood up and twisted the dial until he could find another one. It took him a while; Weston is near a pretty big mountain range. He sat down and pretended to be watching coverage of the local high school's basketball tournament. I wasn't fooled. Nathan hates sports almost as much as I do.

I got up and sat in my chair, only then did he turn to look at me. He opened his mouth to start his usual questions, but something in my face made him stop. I guess I still had my mask on. He looked like he didn't even recognize me.

So I began instead, "I know it's my turn to disconnect the sewer, but I was thinking of a trade. How about I pack the pictures *and* do the laundry as soon as we get to the next place?" I looked expectantly at Nathan, who still looked confused.

"Why would you disconnect the sewer—it's not broken again, is it?"

That time it was my turn to look confused. "We always disconnect the sewer when we move."

Understanding flooded Nathan's face, and then something else, something I recognized immediately: Stubbornness.

"We're not moving," he said quietly, but it felt loud, loud enough to remove the air from my lungs. In all my thoughts that day, I never once thought Nathan and I weren't on the same page. I decided I needed to clue him in on what I'd discovered.

"I know what a Nephilim is."

"So do I," he said, his eyes never leaving mine.

My mask fell and with it my panic was as plain to him as it was to me.

"Then why would you want to stay?" I asked, trying very hard to hold in the tears that were threatening to spill over.

"It's not time for us to leave yet."

I thought he was talking about the fact that we'd only been there a month. I was about to use that against him until his next words stopped me.

"We have a purpose here and we're not leaving until we complete it." His face looked like he meant it.

"Are you serious?" I asked.

"Very."

My mind raced, trying to come up with something, anything. Then I remembered. Nathan was afraid, too. No matter how much he tried to hide it, I knew he was. I could read faces just as well as he could. But he was doing a good job forgetting. That was easy when you spent all day locked in a trailer. It was time Nathan remembered a few things.

My mind reviewed the conversation we'd had when he first

came home. I knew I only had one shot at it before Nathan closed up all together; I needed to make it count. He'd looked the most terrified when he was talking about them at their school. So that's what I brought up.

I waited until he was eyeing me and then I let it fly: "Do you know what they're doing there at that school?"

Bull's-eye.

He paused as he stared at me. He slowly licked his lips that must've gone dry again. His distrusting eyes measured me, trying to decide how much I actually knew and how much of it was a bluff. But enough of the bitch mask must've still been on my face because I think he decided I knew way more than I actually did.

"They can go ahead and build their army. It still doesn't mean we're moving." He looked defiantly at me, his arms crossing his chest. And then he must've looked closer, because his face flashed some of the horror that'd bubbled up inside of me. He knew he'd said way, way too much.

"Army?" I choked over the word, surprised I could get it out.

"Never mind. It has nothing to do with you," Nathan stammered, trying to backtrack. But it was too late, he'd already said it. I knew I was very close to what he'd refused to tell me the other night.

"It has everything to do with me if you expect me to stay." I tried to keep my voice from sounding as desperate as I felt, but it was inevitable. I *was* desperate.

Once I got going, I couldn't stop myself. But in my anguish, I forgot who I was talking to. Nathan was as bad as Fred. My grief would only make him more determined. My only chance was his own fear. I never should have made it about me.

"I'm the one who has to go out there every day, not you. You'll just be here, sitting safely in the trailer while I have to go out there with those…those mutants. No, I won't do it. I refuse."

"You *what?*" He looked at me incredulously. I think the only word he'd heard at that point was refuse. No one refused Nathan, especially not me.

So I said it again, just to let it sink in. "I refuse."

He didn't say another word. He just stared at me. At first I met him square in the eyes, but as the seconds turned into minutes, my eyes dropped to my lap. And still he stared at me. I could feel it.

I closed my eyes and stood up and walked to my room, shutting the door softly behind me. I was out of masks. I was out of reasons. I threw myself on my bed and buried my face in my pillow. Only then did the tears that threatened to come all day finally make their way out.

The next day I woke up with a new mask on my face. It wasn't quite the bitch; that had too much feeling. It was too exhausting to wear that one for long. Instead, it was a nothing mask. I thought about nothing, I cared about nothing. I was nothing.

It was the only way I could stand to live and work around people I knew were monsters.

chapter fifteen/ horrible surprises

There are many things in life that will catch your eye, but only a few that will catch your heart...pursue these.
    -Author unknown

I knew Friday was coming. Fred reminded me every day. But for some reason that week, Friday came extra fast; like it knew I was dreading it.

Fred met me at the door again, with another big smile on his face. I pushed past him and went into the kitchen. It was easier to breathe in there. But I couldn't stay in the kitchen all night, especially because for once Sam, our cook, was actually working.

Fred sat himself at the counter, staring at the clock. I ignored him and started waiting on the tables that were beginning to fill up. I wasn't as busy as I needed to be, though. My eyes went to the clock, too.

Right at five, he showed up. Fred didn't waste any time running over and dragging him to where I was standing, right behind the counter.

"Joel, this is Rachel. If you have any questions at all, she's the one you ask. Got it?" Fred smiled broadly. He smugly walked away, knowing he'd just won. Fred one, Rachel zero.

The kid didn't say anything, but I felt him looking at me, so I looked up, way up. It wasn't very often that I let myself look at any of their faces and it didn't take me long to wish I'd stuck to that line of thinking.

He was gorgeous. Of course he was. Weren't they all? But it was all wasted on me. I knew the why behind the perfect faces and bodies.

But there was something about *his* face that made me want to touch it. I was too preoccupied with the horror of that thought to notice my hand already halfway extended. I didn't see it until it came into my peripheral vision, slowly creeping upward towards his flawless face. I quickly yanked that traitor hand towards the kitchen door to push it open. He wasn't standing as close to me as they usually did, so I think I pulled it off without him noticing. At least I don't think he noticed. He didn't say anything.

I realized I was still looking at him, and he was still looking at me, probably wondering what the heck was wrong with me. I turned towards the kitchen door that was still swinging back and forth from my abrupt shove.

I didn't turn to see if he was following me; I knew he was. I could feel him. I stopped right in front of the washtubs that were overflowing with greasy dishes. It had taken me three days to amass that pile. I was rather proud of it. If that didn't deter him, nothing would.

I turned to face him, carefully focusing my eyes on his chest. It wasn't much better; that was perfect, too.

"This is where everyone starts out," I said, gesturing to the pile. I didn't realize I was holding my breath until I felt myself exhaling deeply as a large shadow moved past me to the wash tub.

I stood there for another minute, waiting. He started stacking the dishes on the floor in order to fill the tub with water. I finally left when the faucet turned on. I'd been defeated twice in five minutes, only that time it wasn't by Fred.

I went back into the dining room. At least the Nephilim there made sense. I'm sure if I'd shown one of them that washtub I would have heard a boatload of hysterics. Fred would've run out of his office and I would've gotten the huge laugh that I'd been counting on since I'd first come up with my stupid plan.

Instead of enjoying my victory, I went back to filling the drinks that I'd been working on before the kid came and ruined everything.

"Hey, you," one of them called from the other side of the restaurant.

That meant me. One of the best things I ever did was throw out my name badge. I hated it when they used to call me by my name. I walked over to the table with four guys sitting at it.

"Yes?"

"Do you know what would look good on you?" one of them asked, while the rest of his friends snickered.

"Not you." I smiled at him as his friends looked as baffled as he did. *Amateurs.*

From the looks of them, they were only freshmen. In the four months I'd been there, I'd heard much, much worse. I almost told them they needed to take some lessons from their upperclassmen if they wanted to shock me. But I didn't. Freshmen were a nice break.

I laid their bill on the table and went to another group that called out to me. Normally I just ignored them, but that night I spent more time in the dining room than I usually did.

But I couldn't avoid him forever, so I lifted the large tub that I'd filled with dirty dishes and pushed open the kitchen door with my back. His pile was almost gone. I walked over to him and heaved the tub onto the metal ledge by the wash basin.

I don't know why I expected him to be mad that time. The new pile wasn't even half the size of the first one. I guess I just didn't want to admit my brilliant plan had failed, mainly because I was having trouble coming up with another one. There weren't many jobs worse than washing the dishes.

He wasn't mad. He just reached over and slid the new dishes into his wash basin. I didn't stand and watch him that time; there was no point.

No point at all, unless–unless I watch him for Nathan, I thought, smiling to myself. It *was* true. I was sure to be grilled especially hard by him that night. It was the closest either of us had come to one of them.

Maybe it's a good thing he was hired there. It's my "in." I'll be like a spy, getting secret information. Maybe then Nathan and I can trade; we'll each tell each other what we know.

So I put Plan B into action. I barricaded myself behind the rows of plastic cups that were the only border between the washtubs and the storeroom. I took one tube out of the stacks and watched him.

I don't know what I expected to see. He was just a guy washing dishes. Nathan would never exchange information for that. *It figures; I have to get the one boring Nephilim in the whole group. The rest of them would've put on a show for sure.*

He started humming.

Really? Is this kid for real? I looked closer.

He bent over to pick up a pan from the floor and for one brief second his face was right at my level, only a few feet away from me. My heart stopped. And then he was standing again. The faucet turned on and the humming resumed.

No freakin' way. My hand went to my chest and I slowly backed up. I swallowed hard and put the tube of cups back in place. *Nathan can keep his information.*

My eyes focused on the kitchen door as I walked past him to go to the dining room. I stayed out there for the rest of the night.

I just put my dishes in the tub under the counter again. I didn't care. There was no way I was going back there again, with him.

He stayed in the back until the end of the night when he quietly stuck his head out the kitchen window, saw me sweeping the dining room floor, and then proceeded to walk over. The front of his shirt was drenched, his hair disheveled.

"I'm all done. Do you need any help out here?" he asked quietly.

I jumped at the sound of his voice. I tried to tell myself it was because I was afraid of him, but even I knew that wasn't the real reason.

"No, I'm just finishing up," I said more forcefully than I'd meant to.

Fred poked his head out the kitchen opening.

"Good job, kid. Come back tomorrow, five p.m. sharp." Fred tried to appear authoritative. It almost made me laugh. He shot me a glare before pulling his head back.

"See ya," Joel said quietly as he turned to go.

I didn't answer. I didn't trust myself with a response.

After he left, I dropped onto a stool. That time my reaction *was* based on fear. I knew it was irrational, but it was there. *How can I possibly be attracted to him?*

Hormones, that has to be it. There's no other explanation for it. I'm just a helpless victim to bizarre female hormones coursing through my veins. My hormones don't know he's a monster, like the rest of me does.

I closed even more slowly that night. That was another sucky thing about the kid working there. Usually they were all gone by eight and I could leave at eight-thirty. But he didn't leave until nine. I sat on a stool and waited for nine-thirty.

The next night was worse. Sam called in, so I was stuck in the back for most of the night. I didn't even notice it was already five until I turned and saw his broad back facing me, already starting to wash the dishes that once again overflowed the washtubs.

I didn't say anything to him before turning to go back out into the dining room. Besides, he wasn't going out of his way to talk to me, either.

I walked up to the table making the most noise.

"Have you decided what you want?"

One of them piped up. "Yeah, we want you." There was always one. He laughed like he was being original. I wanted to tell him he was the fourth guy that night to say that to me, but I didn't. Instead I turned and walked away. Normally when I ignored them for a while, they'd actually order when I went back. That alone told me they were teachable. But the fact that the same ones did it over and over again made me have my doubts.

I went to the next loudest table and asked the same question. I got the same answer. I shook my head as I went to the third.

I knew that group would at least be different. The last two had been freshman, but the third table was all juniors. They didn't disappoint me.

"It's good to see you, Rachel. Why don't you sit down and join us?"

I shuddered. Some of their memories were just too damn good. I hadn't worn my name tag in over three months.

"No thanks. Do you know what you want?"

"The real question is, what do you want?"

"Not you." I smiled when I said it.

He smiled, too, like he was sure I was lying. I was about to leave that table, too, when his hand reached up and gripped my waist, forcing me into the seat next to him. I knew it wouldn't take long for them to figure out they could try new things to scare me. I was human, after all; half more than them.

"Now that's better." He smirked. His hand was still firmly on my waist, like a restraint holding me in place.

"Get your hand off me." I tried to sound bold, but it came out as a whisper.

He smiled as his fingers pressed even harder into my side. Then the smile left his face, which had gone quite white. His hand dropped.

I quickly stood and ran to the kitchen. I told myself I was running to check on my pizzas, but I knew better.

In my hurry to get away from them, I ran smack into the person I'd been avoiding all night. He must've been dropping dishes off in the kitchen, because he wasn't back in his usual hole. His hands caught my shoulders and steadied me.

"Are you all right?" he asked. His voice sounded angry.

I jerked back and he dropped his hands.

"I'm fine," I lied. He didn't look like he believed me, but I didn't care what he thought. I pushed past him and went to the bathroom. I locked myself in.

He was back washing the dishes when I finally came out. I paused when I saw him, and then walked quickly past, but it didn't matter. He didn't turn around.

I grabbed my two pizzas and headed back into the dining room. For the rest of the night I only went in the back when I absolutely had to. Most of the time I just stood behind the counter wavering between the mass of giants in the dining room and the one giant in the back.

Serves me right; I should've let him bus tables or something. By putting him in back, I'd taken away my only refuge.

Finally the busy night came to an end. When all was quiet, Fred came out of his office and volunteered to wash the griddle for me; a peace offering for his previous absence.

The kid came out to where I was and asked if he could help again. That time I tried to sound a little less miserable.

"No thanks, I'm almost done."

He must've taken encouragement from my sudden lack of hostility because he started talking to me.

"Is it always this busy on Saturdays?" he asked.

"No, this was unusually busy." I shot darting glances at Fred. The kid didn't say anything more.

Fred, hearing what was meant for him to hear, shot his head out the kitchen opening and addressed Joel:

"Good job again tonight, kid. You can come back next Friday if you want, five p.m. sharp."

Fred didn't even bother to look at Joel as he talked to him. It was all me, so I smiled back at him. His face fell and he quickly turned back to his work, so I wouldn't see how much that had upset him.

I turned myself. Only, I turned towards Joel. I was going to try to recover the situation with him, but he was already headed out the door. I sighed; it was probably best. I needed time to clear my head, time to think.

chapter sixteen/ awakenings

I tried being reasonable. I didn't like it.
   -Clint Eastwood

   Sunday was bizarre. I felt so restless. When I got to Fred's, I looked at the clock. When I did the prep work, I looked at the clock. When they started coming, I looked at the clock again, the restlessness inside me building higher and deeper. It wasn't an unpleasant feeling; more like excitement than anything. It'd been a long time since I was excited about anything, I almost didn't recognize it.

   And then the excitement was gone, just like that. Instead, I was flooded with an overwhelming disappointment. It was deep, it was debilitating. One minute I was riding about as high as I'd ever been, the next I was just about as low as a person could be; I even almost started frickin' crying. My eyes went to the clock one last time. Five-o-one.

   It wasn't until my hand stretched towards the air that I figured it out.

   "*No!*" I breathed and my brain picked that moment to display all the pictures that it'd taken of Joel during the two short days I'd known him, like it needed to convince me. I didn't realize how closely I'd been watching him, but after the fifth shot of his eyes I couldn't deny that I had been.

I turned and ran into the bathroom and stayed in there until I heard a not so quiet knock on the door.

"Are you planning on coming out any day soon?" It was Fred's voice. That helped. I focused on Fred's fat face as I tried to dry my puffy eyes. They were still red, but I didn't think anyone would notice. Not many people there bothered looking me in the eyes. *Only one, but he isn't here today. That's the problem.*

I opened the door and walked past a visibly angry Fred. I purposely didn't look towards the washtubs as I went back into the dining room.

Each day that week the phenomenon was repeated. I'd feel overwhelmingly excited right up until five, then, like a switch, the tears started coming. By Thursday I'd been through it enough that I went to the bathroom right before five. It even happened in there.

I didn't know what to do, and I had no one to talk to, certainly not Nathan. He'd never understand. *I* could barely understand, and they were my feelings. I couldn't deny what Joel was. There was too much certainty for that. But I also couldn't deny that he wasn't anything like the rest of them. And that I was attracted to him. And that, possibly, it was slightly more than attraction.

It was a really lonely week as I battled with myself and the thoughts I tried not to have. Nathan knew something was up. He kept pestering me. But how could I tell him? How could I say that I thought I was falling in love with a Nephilim?

chapter seventeen/ epiphany moment #1

He who only sees the obvious wins the battles with difficulty;
he who looks below the surface wins with ease.
-Mei Yao-Ch'en

They were bothering her again. They were always bothering her. I'd thought Seth was way out of line when he grabbed her arm, but after watching her with the rest of them, I could see that it wasn't anything new.

Just wash the stupid dishes and forget about it, the voice said. I nodded and picked up the rag again. There was a bang as the swinging door slammed into the wall. I turned to look at her red face as she started making another pizza.

I wanted to talk to her, but I didn't know what to say. By the time I thought of something, she was gone again. The wash space was right by the kitchen, so I could see her most of the night out the opening that ran along the length of the prep table beneath it.

I'd never noticed before that Fred's only customers appeared to be from Newstead. It wasn't that hard to figure out. Besides being huge, most of them were wearing the school uniform that I'd grown to know and love.

The uniform was the same, but the colors were different. For some reason I was always given a blue one, but I'd seen lots of different colors since I'd started there. It was never more apparent than it was at Fred's as I looked out at a sea of reds, blues, greens, yellows, oranges, and purples. There was no rhyme or reason to it. It wasn't based on grade level or anything else that I could see.

Rachel was standing next to a blue, red, and yellow when I saw one of them reach out and grab her. He pulled her down to the seat next to him and Rachel's eyes filled with fear. The cloth dropped from my hand as I walked towards the kitchen door.

Just as I reached it, it swung open and Rachel walked right into my chest. I put my hands on her arms to keep her from falling over. She was shaking.

"Are you all right?" I asked.

"I'm fine," she answered. She didn't look fine. She didn't look like she liked me touching her either, so I dropped my hands. She walked past me without another word.

For the first time that night, I left the kitchen. I needed to put some people in their places. They didn't see me until I was standing right next to them. Each one of them turned to look at me.

"You got a problem?" the guy in red asked as I just stood there.

"Not really. I just wanted to let you know I'm working here now and as long as I am, you're going to leave her alone. Got it?"

I recognized him from gym. I'd just kicked his ass in wrestling on Friday. He looked like he remembered me, too, as he silently nodded. I looked at him for another minute before turning to go back into the kitchen.

Later, when Rachel went back out there, I watched to make sure I'd gotten my point across. I must've, because they didn't bother her anymore.

After I washed the last dish, I went out into the dining room to see if she needed any help. She said she didn't, but at least she sounded nice about it.

I picked one of the lines I'd played with when I was trying to come up with a way to talk to her. "Is it always this busy on Saturdays?" I asked.

Her face flashed red. "No, this was unusually busy."

I nodded and took a step back. *Guess I picked the wrong one.*

Fred called to me from the kitchen and told me my schedule for the next week. I left before I could stick my foot in my mouth again.

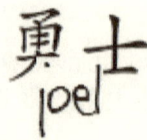

chapter eighteen/ epiphany moment #2

A wind that rises in the daytime lasts long, but a night breeze soon falls.
   -Sun Tzu, *the Art of War*

On Sunday, I woke up and stared at the ceiling. I already knew what Sundays were like at Newstead. Sundays were nothing days. I wished Fred had told me he needed me to come in, but he didn't.

Steven was still asleep, but Marcus was already gone. I forced myself to get up and shower. It took some effort; I really didn't see the point. I wasn't going anywhere.

Why can't you go anywhere?

I shrugged at the voice, but it was right. It's not like they owned me. I didn't have classes, or practice. I was free to do anything I wanted.

So I stopped back at my room and grabbed a few sheets of paper and a pencil, which I shoved into my jacket before heading out of Chapman. It must've snowed a lot overnight because the ground was covered. I had expected there to be snow up north, but that was the first day there was anything substantial.

That complicated my plan a bit. From what I'd seen of Weston, I doubted there were too many abandoned buildings to hide out in. I was going to go into the woods instead, but that was before the sky dumped two feet of snow on the ground.

I walked down the long drive and went towards Weston in case I was wrong about the whole abandoned building thing. I wasn't. But for some reason the snow wasn't as deep there. I walked through the town, then past the town towards another drive that looked remarkably like the one at Newstead, only without the gate. There was a sign there, too. It said "Lambert University," with small writing underneath: *Specializing in Horticulture.*

There was no snow there at all and their woods looked just as promising as Newstead's. They didn't have the Green Mountains on the edge of their forest, but they did have the West River running through it. I could hear it from the front gate.

No one stopped me as I walked down the long drive that felt remarkably familiar. It turned right twice, then left, before ending in a large, mostly vacant parking lot. It was the exact mirror image of Newstead's drive. And the similarities didn't end there. I looked ahead and saw twelve buildings all in a semicircle facing the parking lot. They weren't brick like the ones at Newstead. Instead, they matched the rest of the buildings in town; clapboard painted in a variety of colors. And they didn't have a fountain.

The gravel crunched under my feet as I made my way past each of the buildings to the forest that was just past the last one. The river sounded even louder there.

There were several marked paths, but I didn't feel like taking any. Other people were sure to be on them, especially since it was turning out to be a bright, warm day. The last thing I wanted was to have someone walk up on me while I was having some alone time.

So I headed straight into the woods and followed the sound of the river. Eventually I came out into a clearing that had the river flowing right in the middle. It was perfect.

The ground there was muddy, so I lifted a boulder that was on the edge of the forest and placed it right by the water. I took a deep breath. It felt like freedom to me. I don't know why. It wasn't like I was a prisoner or anything, but for some reason there was a difference.

I pulled out the pieces of paper and started writing. It took a while to get started, but eventually my hand remembered what to do. I was surprised at what it wrote.

What's up with Steven?

I sat and looked at the question. I didn't have an answer to that one. Without giving me too much time, my hand wrote another question. At least that one was easier.

What's up with Marcus?

Every school has a Marcus, a guy who everyone wants to hang out with, but no one knows why. In St. Louis, his name was Greg Raynor. He left me alone, but I was pretty much the only one. He was the most passed-to receiver on our team, behind me. He was the one who'd come up with the name Goliath for me. I hated Greg Raynor.

It figured that I'd end up getting stuck with his twin at Newstead. But at least Marcus treated me with the same respect that Greg had. I hadn't been so sure if he would, seeing that he was just as big as me.

My hand wrote one more question.

What's up with Rachel?

I sighed as I looked down at her name on the piece of paper. I didn't have an answer for that one, either. Instead, I folded the paper in half without writing anything. I lifted the rock and put the papers underneath it.

It was time to go.

I didn't have the river to follow that time, but I found my way easily enough.

Every night that week I went to my rock. I had to write with a flashlight, but I didn't care. It was better than hanging out in the rec room with a bunch of strangers, or in my room with Steven. The only night I didn't go was Friday. That was the day I walked towards Fred's.

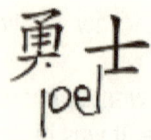

chapter nineteen/ misunderstood

Anger may in time change to gladness; vexation may be succeeded by content.
    -Sun Tzu, *the Art of War*

Her light footsteps stopped behind me. At first I thought she was busy doing something else because she didn't say anything. But when I turned around, she was standing there, wringing her hands, staring at her feet.

"Why does your mother need you to work?" Rachel asked, not looking up.

I shrugged, but after a minute I realized she wouldn't be able to see that, so I answered her out loud:

"It's complicated."

She looked up then and stared at me. I think she was expecting more of an answer, but I wasn't about to get into something like that, especially with her.

"How do you like it here?" she continued.

I shrugged again. That time I knew she could see me because her face started to lose some of its pleasantness, so I decided to answer her. There were worse questions she could ask.

"It's okay. A lot different from my school back home, though."

"What are you talking about?" She eyed me suspiciously.

What is she *talking about?* I didn't know, but I couldn't answer that one with a shrug. "Newstead is okay, but not like my old high school," I repeated slowly, emphasizing each word.

"I meant how do you like Fred's—why would you think I was asking about Newstead?"

"Fred's is fine." I shrugged. "I thought you were talking about Newstead because I just moved here."

She was a sight to behold; eyebrows deeply furrowed, her hand rubbing absently at her neck as she tried to grasp what was a simple concept.

"You just moved here?"

"Yes, I just moved here. Why is that so hard for you to get?" I had to give it to her, it took quite a bit to get me mad, but she seemed to be an expert at it.

"That's impossible. All of you start when you're fourteen. There's no way you just moved here." She looked smug, like she'd caught me in a monstrous lie.

I was speechless. What she'd said caught me off guard. *She's right. Why am I the only one to have started this trimester?*

I remembered my two days in the rec hall, and the reason I'd stopped going. They were all trying to one-up each other with their glory stories; the same ones, over and over again. I'd felt so out of place because I hadn't been there for any of them and the rest of them had. All of them.

It was suddenly obvious. No one else had started in their junior year. Just me.

Why is that?

It took me a minute to collect myself as I processed all of it. But I couldn't stand the pompous look on Rachel's face anymore, so I answered her, "Well *I* did. I just moved here from St. Louis last week. Didn't you notice you'd never seen me before?" I met her confused eyes with a defiant smile.

"How would I know? I never pay attention to you Newsteaders."

She said the last word with such revulsion it was hard not to be offended. I shook my head in exasperation and turned back to my work.

Neither of us seemed very interested in talking again that night, but she did get my mind working. For the first time, I saw the oddity of it. I started paying extra attention to conversations that week to see if she was right, even though I already had a pretty good idea she was.

It wasn't hard to get what I wanted. Everyone was more than happy to retell the same old stories. The hard part was looking interested. But by the end of classes on Monday, I'd asked enough of them to be certain. They'd all started in ninth grade. All of them, except me.

Why is that?

I didn't know, but I was determined to find out; it was time for me and my other roommate to have a little talk.

I waited until we were alone the next Friday night. It was a little after twenty-one hundred and I'd just gotten back from a very long shift at Fred's.

Marcus was out with his usual group of followers, leaving Steven and me alone in our eerily quiet room.

I decided to take the plunge; *what's the worst he can do—not answer?* I'd already been getting the silent treatment from him for a couple of weeks.

"Hey, Steven, I wanted to ask you about a few things." My voice sounded loud, especially when Steven didn't answer me. After a minute I heard another page turn.

I kept talking like I hadn't noticed, "I was wondering where you lived before you came here."

Still nothing from the upper bunk. Another page turned.

"I also wanted to know about *how* you came here. I mean,

what made you find out about this place?"

"Just drop it," was all Steven would say, not even looking up from the book he was reading.

But I didn't want to drop it. So I didn't.

"What did they tell you when they said I was moving in with you?"

His eyes flared as he held his book up higher, hoping I'd get the point. I played dumb.

"What's that you're reading?" I asked, not really caring.

Still not answering, he briefly raised the book up again for me to see before rolling over on his top bunk, back towards me.

I stared at that back for a while. He knew more than he was letting on; after two and a half years there, he'd have to. Now, I'd just have to figure out a way to get him to share that information with me.

Saturday at Fred's started out the same as Friday left off. I was washing dishes, and Rachel was ignoring me. It seemed to be the new routine of my life. Part of me would've preferred her talking to me, but it seemed like every time she opened her mouth she was either rude or angry.

I still wanted to be near her even if that was the last thing she wanted. So I did my part. I stayed quiet.

On the following Friday I heard the familiar footsteps stop behind me. I turned around and she was looking straight up into my eyes. Her face was flushed as she hesitated.

"What sports do you play?" she asked. She was almost acting nervous.

I smiled, knowing her agenda. She, like me with Steven, was choosing a safe topic. She was trying to start a conversation. But did she, like me with Steven, have a hidden agenda? Her face looked innocent enough.

"Everything," I answered.

She smiled. Her knowing eyes measured me. I could tell that was what she thought I'd say.

I took a deep breath and asked her a question of my own. "What do you play?"

Her face went white, like I'd just yelled at her.

"I don't play sports," she said before turning to walk away. She went straight to the bathroom and after a second there was a click as the door locked.

What'd I say? I shook my head and turned back to the dish in my hand.

I'd never felt so misunderstood in my whole life.

美人
rachel

chapter twenty/ you call this a date?

We are afraid to care too much; for fear that the other person does not care at all.
-Eleanor Roosevelt

…Fifty-eight, fifty-nine, sixty. I opened my eyes to check, but they were still red. Normally I would've gone out anyway, but it was a Friday, which meant Joel was there; Joel who looked me square in the face, Joel who never missed anything.

I shook my head at the reflection in disgust.

Look at me; locked in a bathroom, straddling a toilet. How did I end up sinking to such low levels? All I did was talk to him.

At first I did it to convince myself he was a jerk. The five-o-one heart palpitations were getting way out of control. But that had backfired on me in a big way, mainly because he wasn't a jerk. He was actually kind of nice.

So I switched gears; I talked to him for me. That was how I'd ended up in the bathroom. Again.

I looked in the mirror one last time. It was good enough, even for Joel. I pushed the door open, right into a glaring Fred.

Guess he noticed how long I was in here.

It must've been a while since I'd provided him with any entertainment because he grabbed my arm and dragged me over to where Joel stood by the washtubs.

Joel looked up and his face made me want to go right back into the bathroom. He looked very, very angry. Fred let go of my arm just as Joel dropped his cloth into the tub.

"I told Rachel to give you a chance at helping her bus tables tonight. It'll get you away from the sink for a while. How does that sound, kid?" Fred rocked back and forth with anticipation.

Joel took a deep breath and slowly let it out.

"Wherever you need me," he said, drying his hands on his towel and grabbing an apron to cover his saturated shirt.

It was soaked so that it clung to his chest and every line of his perfectly formed six-pack abs. I blushed and looked away, but not before both of them saw it. Fred's smile got bigger, but Joel looked upset again and started taking off the apron.

"Well, if Rachel doesn't want me to I'll just stay back here."

Fred's smile reached maximum proportions as he was, I'm sure, about to inform Joel that it really didn't matter what Rachel wanted. But I beat him to it:

"Actually, I could use your help for a while, if that's okay," I said before turning towards Fred. "Thanks, Fred. You're always looking out for me." I smiled sweetly at him, as his faded.

"Women," he muttered under his breath and went back to his office to mope.

I doubted Fred realized the favor he did for me that night. If he had, he never would've done it. Up until then, the only time I'd ever seen Joel was while he was in the kitchen washing dishes. But that night, Fred's intrusion gave me the missing piece I needed to start having faith in my judgment again.

Joel walked into the dining room and started clearing tables. He was just as quiet with them as he was with me. He never said one word as he put the dishes into the bin and carried it to the back, returning only a minute later to wipe down the tables. No one acknowledged he was there.

It was so different from the way they usually treated each other. It didn't matter if they were sitting together or not, they were all part of a group. Their exclusion of him was very evident. It wasn't just me who thought Joel didn't belong with them.

Strangely enough, I trusted their judgment more than I did my own. Because it wasn't long after Joel went into the back again that I tried one last time.

He was busy washing the dishes from the tables he'd just cleared. He didn't see me standing off to his side, trying to work up the courage to talk to him.

"Are you hungry?" I finally asked in a voice that didn't even sound like mine.

He looked up from his dishes, eyes bright. His soaked shirt was clinging to him again.

Damn.

"Starved." He smiled, his whole face lit up.

Double damn.

I swallowed hard before continuing, "I was just going to make myself a pizza. Do you want to split it with me?" I tried to ask innocently, but it still ended up sounding like I was asking him on a date.

"Sure. Can I help you make it?" He said it like he didn't notice my flushed face.

"No, I'm not really busy right now. What do you want on your half?"

Finally, we're talking without either of us barking at each other. I set about making the pizza, my side cheese and green olives, his side just pepperoni. I pulled a takeout box off the shelf above the ovens.

"Fred's Pizza" was boldly emblazoned on the box top, just above a picture of a jovial, Italian chef. The only resemblance between Fred and that man was the girth. If Fred was really trying to establish an authentic Italian pizzeria, maybe he should've tried a different name. But, the idiocy of it certainly appealed to my jaded sense of humor.

Joel got down a couple paper plates and napkins. He didn't seem to notice my sudden smirk at the pizza box.

He followed me as I went outside to the steps that were just past the back door. It was cold, so cold I could see my breath in the air. But that wasn't important; what was important was that Fred wasn't there. He never went out back.

I sat down on the top step and laid the box on my lap. It was pleasantly warm. Joel walked silently past and sat down on the bottom step, which put his face right at my level. Quickly, I lifted the lid and put a couple slices on a plate. I reached over the top to hand it to him.

The warmth of the box was fading as I sat there with the lid open, well past the point of ridiculousness. Carefully, I put the barrier down.

Joel smiled softly and picked up his first slice.

chapter twenty-one/ thoughts

If you can't make it good, at least make it look good.
  -Bill Gates

Neither of us said anything, at least not at first. When I was done eating, I took the box off my lap and put it next to me and leaned back on the railing to look at the stars. They were almost as bright there as they were at the trailer. I sighed contentedly, not realizing he was watching me until his quiet voice broke through the silence.

"Rachel?"

I turned to look at the face that was staring intently at me. His cheeks were reddened, either from the cold or from me looking at him. I should've taken the hint and looked away, but I couldn't. It was the closest I'd been to that face since I'd met him. His eyes were fixed on me as mine dropped to the sudden movement in his neck as he swallowed. Slowly my eyes lifted to his lips that were parted just enough to see his breath freeze as it hit the air. Even still, he looked warm. *Warm and soft and—*

"Rachel?"

My eyes darted back up to his.

"What were you thinking about just then?" His eyes were

narrowed, confused.

I flushed and looked away. "Nothing," I said, shaking my head, trying to clear it. The back door loomed next to me, tempting me more and more as the silence lengthened.

"How often do you work?" he finally asked.

That's random, I thought, turning back.

"Every day but Monday," I answered brightly, keeping my eyes safely above his hairline. *"That's the only day I have for me,"* I added under my breath.

He nodded, like he'd heard every word. "What do you like to do on your Mondays?"

"Absolutely nothing," I said, trying to keep it to a minimum.

"I know what you mean. On my time off I usually go hide. I'm always looking for hiding places," he said. There was a serious edge to his voice.

I exhaled. At least I wasn't the only one revealing things. "You hide?" I glanced down at his huge body and shook my head in disbelief.

"I didn't say it was easy." He laughed softly. "That's why when I find a good spot I tend to stick with it for a while."

"Have you found a place here yet?"

"Actually, just the other day I found a section of the West River deep in the woods. It just might work."

"And what do you do in your little spot?" I asked, drawing closer to him.

He looked away shyly, not answering.

"What? I want to know," I prodded. I needed to know something about him, something real. My hand reached out and touched his arm, just a graze, but he looked up when he felt it. My hand fell back onto my lap.

He shrugged. "I just sit and think."

My eyebrow rose, like Nathan's did when he knew there was more to be told.

"...sometimes I write," he continued, watching me, measuring.

"Can I read some of it?" I asked urgently. I don't think I've ever wanted anything more.

His face softened. "It's not really anything I let anyone read. It's just something I do to get things out."

"Someday, maybe?" I asked, not willing to let it slide.

"Maybe," he answered with a half-smile on his ruddy face as he leaned back on the railing and closed his eyes. He let himself rest for a minute before gracefully leaping up, gathering our plates in one fluid motion.

He hesitated with his hand on the door. "This was...good. We should do it again sometime."

"Well, you know where to find me," I answered, laughing, but he wasn't.

He held the door open for me as we both went back inside, but it must've slipped out of his hand because it banged hard enough to shake the glass.

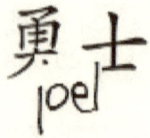

chapter twenty-two/ the recorder

If in the midst of difficulties we are always ready to seize an advantage, we may extricate ourselves from misfortune.
-Sun Tzu, *the Art of War*

In Tactics, we'd moved outside to the football field. We all gathered in a circle around the team leader. That day it was Marcus. Most days it was Marcus. He began choosing our positions for the mission that we were practicing that day. Being Tactics, all forty-two of us were there.

At first he chose quickly, confidently. But as the selection became sparser, he took his time looking over each one before assigning their roles. Finally, he turned to look at me. It was only Steven and me left to choose from. He paused, like he was having a hard time deciding.

"Joel, you be the recorder."

I nodded. It was the role he always gave me. If he'd known how much I liked to write he probably never would've given me that job.

As the recorder, I had some freedom of movement. I went from place to place and wrote down the stages of the mission. It gave me a chance to really see them.

Marcus had chosen his own posse for his commanders. They

followed him around, soaking up every word he said. He seemed to really get off on it. Next, I went to the enlisted men, those not fortunate enough to be of the elite, but still not as lowly as the ones who were doing the brunt of the work. They also were following around a central leader, hanging on his every word.

Lastly, I went to the laborers. They weren't hanging around a leader. Instead, they were busy looking at the higher-ups. Envy was clear on their faces. They looked like they would be willing to do whatever it took to be one of them. Whatever it took.

They were so busy watching them that they weren't getting anything done. I carefully wrote down their production level on the space in my log book. When that was done, I headed back toward Marcus; that's when I saw Steven.

He'd been the last chosen, so he wasn't one of the commanders or enlisted. He was a laborer and from the looks of him, he was the only one doing any work. I stood to the side and watched him.

He was moving the stack of sand bags to the far end of the field, setting up a barrier that would be utilized in future missions. He didn't look at anybody as he went back and forth. I tucked the clipboard under my arm and walked over to the huge pile of sandbags that were left. I slung five over my shoulder and carried them to the other side.

We carried them until the pile was gone, and then I walked over to Marcus to hand in my report.

He was still standing with his group when I approached him. He had a new guy with him, I'd forgotten his name, but I did recognize him. He was the guy in red who had gotten pushy with Rachel. He seemed to like the fact that he was higher in rank than me.

He turned and looked at me, like he was waiting for me to salute him. I knew I was supposed to, but I didn't. At first I thought he was going to call me on it, but something in my eyes must've made him change his mind.

Marcus turned to me and took my log without a word. I didn't salute him, either.

chapter twenty-three/ drowning

If it is to your advantage, make a forward move; if not, stay where you are.
-Sun Tzu, *the Art of War*

Fred tapped me on the shoulder and handed me an envelope. I took it, seeing cash as I looked inside. I looked down at him quizzically.

"You didn't think you were working here for free, did you?" He laughed as he headed back to his office. "See you next Friday, five p.m. sharp," he called, not bothering to look back.

Actually, I *had* forgotten I was getting paid. We'd never talked about my wages, and based on the small wad of dirty fives and tens in the envelope, Fred operated in cash.

Rachel looked up from wiping the tables as I came out from the back. I offered to help her finish up, but as usual she refused. Most of the time I just had to go ahead and do it without asking; she wasn't the type to ask for help, even if she was drowning.

"See ya," I said as I left. She didn't answer.

chapter twenty-four/ reflections

Move not unless you see an advantage; use not your troops
unless there is something to be gained; fight not unless the
position is critical.
    -Sun Tzu, *the Art of War*

Sunday was a void day at Newstead. Absolutely nothing went
on. No classes, no games. A lot of the guys got together and
watched hockey in the rec room, but that didn't interest me
much. So, I headed off campus and went to my new spot.

I settled down on my rock to write my mom a long overdue
letter. I was sure she was furious with me for not writing her
sooner. Cell phones weren't allowed on campus, so we'd
decided letters would be how we'd stay in touch. She'd made
me promise I'd write to her as soon as I'd settled in. It'd been
over four weeks, and I hadn't written even one line. I'd been
waiting for something positive to say.

I wrote briefly about my dorm, my classes, my teachers. I was
careful to avoid details that might end up in questions later;
questions I didn't want to answer. I knew she'd want to know if
I'd made any friends. That was always something she worried
about, my lack of friends.

I told her I'd taken a job in town where I'd met a nice girl. *Let her chew on that for a while.* I was sure my letter from her would be full of questions on *that* topic. But that was all right. At least when I was talking about Rachel I wouldn't have to lie. But as for the rest, how could I tell her the truth? That even though I was in a school with people who appeared to be my genetic match, I still hadn't found anyone I wanted to hang around with.

My classmates were all my size and they all liked sports, and I couldn't stand any of them, except for maybe Steven. But his rejection of me was also something I wouldn't be bringing up to my mom. Instead, I folded the single sheet—much shorter than I'd planned; much shorter than my mom would've liked—and tucked it into the envelope that already had the money from Fred.

I reluctantly headed towards town. I couldn't come up with any more reasons to stay in the woods. Besides, my body kept reminding me how cold it was in Vermont in early February. By the time I reached the post office I was running, trying to warm myself up. I put the letter in the slot marked out of town.

Marcus was in the room when I got back, which was quickly becoming more of a rarity. Steven was there too, reading as always. It seemed like that was all he did.

I sat on my bed and picked up my Western Civ. homework and started working on it.

My eyes drifted towards the one window in our room. I don't think Steven or Marcus realized that with our light on and it being dark outside I saw them as clearly as if I was staring at a mirror.

Steven *wasn't* reading. He was looking directly at Marcus with some of the same expression I'd gotten the first time I'd met him. Marcus, who was standing at the foot of the bed, met his glare with one of his own. My breath held as I watched them.

With his eyes never leaving Steven's, Marcus reached down

and grabbed his duffel bag.

"I'm going to the gym to work out for a while. Do either of you want to go with me?" If I wasn't looking at his reflection, I would've sworn his offer was serious. Steven slowly shook his head, his face still intense. Marcus smiled. I knew I needed to say something or they'd both wonder what I was doing. Even then I knew that would be bad.

"No, thanks. I've got to get this done."

"Maybe next time, then," Marcus said as Steven's face got even fiercer. "Next time," he repeated, giving Steven one last stare-down before walking out.

When the door closed, Steven's eyes raised to look directly at the window, and me. Neither of us dropped our gaze as Steven's breaths slowed.

He finally lowered his eyes to his book.

I glanced towards the door Marcus had just walked through. I didn't know which one was worse.

chapter twenty-five/ field training exercise

The clever combatant imposes his will on the enemy, but does not allow the enemy's will to be imposed on him.
    -Sun Tzu, *the Art of War*

There was energy in the air on Monday. I could feel it. Everyone was excited about something, but I didn't find out the reason why until Leadership.

We started class in the gym, but didn't stay there. That was pretty typical; we usually went outside to do outdoor exercises. But that day was special. We were told that was the day we were starting the annual training for FTX.

We assembled in two parallel lines, following behind our leadership instructor, Sergeant Foltz, and his assistant, Mr. Hall. They led us past the buildings to the forest that was behind it all.

About fifteen yards after the cover of trees there was another building, one I'd never seen before. I guessed that was the point. The back side facing the school was just a grass covered hill. The only difference on the other side was a thick steel door with a small, metal shed off to one side.

It was next to that door that Mr. Hall stood while Sgt. Foltz led the lines in. I was the last one on the right, so I was followed by Mr. Hall as he shut the heavy door behind us.

It was dark, real dark. I felt Mr. Hall's hands on my back, so I put my hands on the back of the guy in front of me. Far in the distance, I could see a dim light. We all walked towards it. It went left, we went left. It went right, we went right.

The place was like a maze. It made it hard to say how big it was, but if I had to guess I'd say it was pretty big. As we walked, the grade gradually got steeper, sloping downwards. I wanted to reach out to the side, to feel the walls I was walking past, but I didn't dare take my hands off the guy in front of me.

I felt him stop, so I stopped, too. Mr. Hall slammed into my back and it took quite a bit of effort to keep us from becoming like a row of dominos flicked by someone's finger. Mr. Hall grumbled to himself, like it was my fault he ran into me.

Someone turned on the lights and I realized we weren't in such tight quarters as I'd thought, at least not there. We were in a massive training room, at least twice the size of the gym. There were mats covering every inch of the floor and almost halfway up the twelve foot walls. But no windows. I tried not to think about how far underground we were.

Everyone followed Sgt. Foltz to the center of the room and sat in a circle around him. He remained standing and took a minute to rotate around so he could look each one of us intently in the eyes before starting his speech.

"As all of you know, this is February twenty-third, exactly eight weeks before you begin your annual FTX. Your training will start here. For the next two weeks, we will be meeting in this room to complete the initial portion of the Physical Endurance Display. After that we will move out to the training field where the FTX will take place. Any questions?"

I had a lot, but I was hoping someone else would ask them. They didn't. Everyone there seemed to know exactly what he was talking about.

"Mr. Hall," Sgt. Foltz said. Mr. Hall appeared by his side in the center of the mat.

"Mr. Hall and I will be demonstrating a maneuver that should be familiar to all of you." He turned to Mr. Hall and leaned in, like he was going to tackle him. And sure enough, that's just what he did. But he didn't just tackle him. He dragged him over to the other side of the room, far from the rest of the circle. We all turned to watch as Mr. Hall's face turned beet red as he was dumped on the floor. Sgt. Foltz walked back over to the rest of us and resumed his place in the middle of the circle.

"Now that, gentlemen, is what we call acquisition. In less than ten seconds I had my opponent captured, then placed. Speed is the objective here. In previous years we focused on other tactics, but speed is the only thing I want to see out of you today. Now let's see what the rest of you have got."

We were lined up along the far wall as he called us to the center circle, two at a time.

I didn't realize Steven had sat down next to me until he started speaking in a low voice, "FTX stands for field training exercise. It's something the underclassman do every spring."

I nodded without looking at him. It felt like the right thing to do, the way he was talking.

It must've been, because he continued, "This will be our third year, our last chance before we become seniors. They do something else, but you don't get to find out what that is until you're a senior. The last two years have been pretty similar. We spend a few nights out in the woods and try to get the other team's cylinder. There might be more to it than that, but from what I've seen, that pretty much covers it."

I nodded again and pretended I was looking at the two guys in front of us who were trying to take each other down.

"That's part of it, too," Steven said, gesturing his head towards the two I was looking at. "You need to capture prisoners of war. That way, there are less people looking for your cylinder. Plus, it lowers the number that can capture you while you're out searching for theirs."

"What's a cylinder?" I whispered under my breath.

"I don't know. I've never seen one. Only the platoon leaders get to see them."

I looked up just as Matt slammed Lucas onto the mat. He grabbed his arms and dragged him backwards towards the small grouping of guys who were sitting next to Mr. Hall. Lucas thrashed the entire way.

"That's part of the rules, too. You try to do whatever you can to avoid going into the prisoner of war camp. Because once you get in, you're not getting out until someone comes to get you out, and you can imagine how often that happens. It's like you're dead to them once you're captured."

The guys with Lucas looked completely dejected. They weren't even bothering to watch the center mat. They weren't looking at each other, either. It really was like they were dead.

"Cranston," Sgt. Foltz called from the other side of the room. I looked up. It was my turn. I stood and walked to the spot everyone else had gone to, right in the center of the mat.

"And Schultz," his voice called out again.

Marcus. Great.

Marcus stood and extended his arms over his head in an exaggerated stretch before twisting his neck to the left, then to the right. It cracked impressively.

I just stood there and waited for the timer to begin. With a loud buzzer, it did. Marcus crouched down and sprang at my mid-section. His head hit me right at my sternum. I reached down and grabbed him under both armpits. His head was pinned against my chest as I dragged him to the spot next to Lucas. It was done in three seconds.

I walked back to Steven and sat down. He was staring at me.

"What?" I asked. He shook his head. It was then that I noticed it was utterly silent in the room. I looked up and saw all of them looking at me, even Sgt. Foltz.

It took him a few seconds, but eventually he called out the next pair to go to the mat.

"Raynor and Robinson." His voice cracked. But maybe it had always done that and I only noticed it because no one else was saying anything.

Steven stood up and went to the center of the mat. He and Seth were friends, so I was surprised at how brutal it got. They circled each other and as they did the circles got smaller and they got closer. Seth swatted Steven's arm, but Steven continued his inward progress. He looked like a caged animal again, poised and violent.

Steven wasn't messing around with the useless jabs like Seth was. He went right for the throat. Literally. Both of Steven's hands wrapped themselves around Seth's neck. Seth dropped to his knees and still Steven didn't release him.

Steven dragged him that way to the spot next to Marcus. Only then did he let go. Seth gasped long and deep as Steven focused his attention on Marcus. I almost thought he was going to release him. I think Marcus thought that, too, because he had a hopeful smile on his face. Steven smiled, too, as he turned his back on him and walked away.

He didn't sit next to me again. Instead, he went to the other side of the room and sat by himself.

The exercise went on and I watched them. I'm guessing that was the real point, why they only had two of us going at a time. We were supposed to be watching each other, sizing each other up. Maybe that's why Marcus looked so mad when I beat him.

"Thank you, gentlemen. That completes our first round of the

Physical Endurance Display. We will resume tomorrow at fourteen hundred. Meet outside of this building and be prepared for the M.E.D," Sgt. Foltz announced as all of them groaned. That time, Steven wasn't sitting next to me to translate. I stood up and got in line. Steven and Marcus were nowhere in sight.

I put my hand on someone's back and felt another hand on mine as we made our way through the maze again. The door at the end was standing wide open with bright sunlight streaming in. No one was standing there, like before, so I took my time and looked at the small hill that was really so much more. The rest of the guys who had come out with me went on their way; none of them turned back like me.

I wondered if I would've been just like them if I'd started going there when I was fourteen, too. Maybe then I would've accepted it as the norm that we'd just spent the afternoon in a massive bunker, collecting prisoners of war. But I didn't start at fourteen. I wasn't slowly matriculated into the program. It was like I was that frog that was stuck in a pan of boiling water. I recoiled. *Something is seriously wrong with this place.*

chapter twenty-six/ the voice that got it right

Now in order to kill the enemy, our men must be roused to anger; that there may be advantage from defeating the enemy, they must have their rewards.
  –Sun Tzu, *the Art of War*

I pulled the pizza out of the oven and sliced it before putting it in the box. I already had the plates and napkins on the side, ready and waiting for Rachel to get done with whatever she was doing that was keeping her from our dinner.

"I'll be there in a minute," she called from the dining room. I smiled to myself; she must've known I was waiting for her.

Rachel pushed open the kitchen door and dropped off the last dishes for the night into my washtub. She dried her hands on her apron and then followed me outside.

I sat down in my usual spot, on the bottom step. Rachel went to hers, right at the top. It made it easier to see each other when we were talking. But that night she wasn't talking at all. She just sat there and ate her pizza and didn't say a word. That was typical behavior for her when we were working, but not out there. Out there we talked all the time.

She wasn't even looking at me. I tried to think what I might've done to tick her off, but nothing was coming to mind. I was about to ask her about it when she finally started. She still wasn't looking at me, though.

"Tell me about St. Louis," she said intently.

"It's a city in Missouri," I answered, internally laughing at the annoyed look that suddenly appeared on her face. Her lower lip practically disappeared inside her mouth. But at least she turned to face me.

"That's not what I meant."

"Then what did you mean?" I couldn't keep the laughter out of my voice.

"What was your life like there?"

"Pretty normal. I lived there with my mom. We have a small apartment on the lower west side. But I didn't spend much time there. Usually I was at practice or my place."

"Your place?"

"Yeah. I told you about that already, didn't I? My place in St. Louis changed a lot, but for the last few years it was a vacant apartment right across from my school."

"That's right; your hiding place. Did you write there, too?"

"Yes."

"And...?" She was starting to look frustrated; her hand was doing that thing it did, rubbing anxiously by her neck.

"And that's it. My life was pretty boring."

Her eyebrow went up, like she didn't buy it. She was right. There was a lot I wasn't telling her, like about the voice that kept me company most days in my hiding spots, both in St. Louis and at Weston. But Rachel Newell was the last person I was going to tell that to. I didn't need to lose the one friend I had by making her think I was crazy. I already saw how she looked at me sometimes, the hollow look that came into her eyes when she didn't know I was looking. I didn't need to give her more reasons to be afraid of me.

Her eyes narrowed slightly and then she fired off another

round.

"Tell me about your mother."

I tried to think of a smart-assed comment for her, but was coming up empty, so instead I just shrugged my shoulders. She didn't look like she was buying that, either.

"Come on, you lived with the woman for what? Sixteen years? And you can't tell me one thing about her?"

"She's short."

"And..."

"And I don't know." I was going to leave it at that, but Rachel looked like she wasn't letting that be an option. So I tried to think of something quick to appease her.

"She has just as many good and bad qualities as anyone, I guess. But she never seems to let things get her down. She's pretty strong that way."

Rachel nodded, then looked distant for a while, lost in her own thoughts. "What do you miss most about her?" she whispered.

I shrugged my shoulders again. I didn't know what to say. I mean, I did miss her, but honestly I hadn't given her much thought since I'd started at Newstead. It's not like I saw her that often at home, either. I didn't know how to explain that to Rachel without sounding heartless.

But I forgot how observant Rachel was, even more so when she was watching me closely like she was then.

"You don't miss her at all, do you?" She didn't even try to hide her disappointment in me.

"Sure I do," I quickly answered. "But you have to understand something about my mom and me. She worked all the time and I had practice all the time. That's just how it was in our family. So with us writing letters to each other, we're actually talking more now than we ever did."

"You write her letters?" Her face changed. It was brighter.

"Yes."

"Have you ever told her about me?" she asked quickly.

"No," I lied. But I shouldn't have, because during the course of our conversation Rachel had slowly moved closer to me, almost to the point of touching. That completely changed the minute the word was out of my mouth. She backed away and turned her face so I couldn't see it anymore.

What did I say?

Instead of wondering, I reached out and grabbed her arm.

"Hey, Rache, what's wrong?"

Is she crying? She had her back towards me, lifting her forearm quickly across her eyes. My arm spun her around mid-motion. She was crying.

"Nothing," she said as she turned back around and went into Fred's.

What's wrong with her? Why should she care if I told my mother about her or not? It's not like it's that way between us.

Maybe she wants it to be, the voice in my head said.

I stood there for a full minute as the words sank in. I didn't let myself think about Rachel that way. I was a self-preservationist and Rachel, I thought, had made her opinion of me quite clear. But what the voice said made me look at her reaction in a whole different light, look at Rachel in a whole different light.

I looked into Fred's and saw a shadow restlessly making its way around the kitchen. I smiled to myself as I made my way in to join her.

chapter twenty-seven/ humble pie

Nothing spoils the taste of peanut butter quite like unrequited love.
    -Charlie Brown

The door slammed shut behind me. I walked to the fryers and flipped them off and then went to the griddle and turned that off too. When I ran out of things to do in the kitchen, I went to the dining room and walked over to the window and flipped the open sign to read closed. Usually Fred did it, but he was still back in his office.

I glanced around the room, looking for something to do with my hands. I knew I needed to stay busy. That was the only way I was going to get through the next few minutes until Joel left.

I only paused for a second before grabbing the silverware tub, but it was long enough. Everything came crashing down on me in that one second, what I'd said, what he didn't. I'd always thought *I'd* be the one doing the choosing or rejecting, but that wasn't true at all. Joel didn't want me.

In all the schools I had gone to, I always sat alone. Me. My choice. But I knew that if I wanted it, it could've been different. I could have anyone, anytime I wanted. But was that wrong, too? Was I just the freaky new girl that no one wanted anything to do with? Was that why they always stared at me? Was I really that pathetic?

The thought was so overwhelmingly horrible that I quickly disregarded it. *No, that can't be it. No need to take Joel's rejection and turn it into a universal thing.* It was the one thing I was most sure of, that people either wanted to *be* me or be *with* me. I closed my eyes tightly as I tried to soak that thought into every fiber of my being. *I am wanted. I am wanted.* When I opened my eyes again I felt better.

The back door opened, and closed with a gentle bang. The faucet turned on shortly after. I looked back at the table in front of me and started rolling silverware.

Usually Joel left after he'd cleaned up his area. In the beginning he used to ask me if I needed any help with the closing work, but he hadn't done that in a while. He'd just mumble a goodbye and leave.

The faucet from the kitchen turned off and I waited to hear the front door close, but there was only silence. I glanced up.

I wasn't alone.

"What the...Joel you scared the crap out of me," I yelled, pressing my hand to my chest to keep my heart inside. Joel was standing by the booth, less than a foot away from me.

He moved to the other side and sat down and grabbed the silverware bin and started rolling. I sat frozen in place, watching him. He was rolling as intently as I had been. After a few seconds I went back to rolling, too.

When the bin was full, I stood up and carried it over to its place under the counter. Joel didn't move; he just sat there looking straight ahead.

"I did tell my mom about you." His quiet voice carried across the empty restaurant.

I let out a shaky breath and turned to look at him, but the booth was empty.

The bell above the front door rattled softly as it swung shut.

美人
rachel

chapter twenty-eight/ bad liar

Experience is simply the name we give our mistakes.
  -Oscar Wilde

Saturday was the first time I dreaded seeing Joel. On Fridays and Saturdays I only had the building euphoria, without the agonizing disappointment at five-o-one. But that Saturday I wasn't excited at all.

I couldn't even convince myself that he'd misunderstood my meaning when I'd asked if he'd told his mother about me. His words while he was sitting at the booth wouldn't let me. He knew exactly what I'd meant.

I didn't need his pity.

Thankfully, it was busy that night. My eyes only wandered to the clock a few times. Right at five he came in and walked directly to the back. I wasn't looking at him, so I don't know if he was looking at me or not. I did look in the kitchen window, but all I could see was his brown hair and his broad back.

"Did you get that?"

I turned back to the guy glaring at me from the booth. I nodded; I got it.

I went to the window and handed Sam the ticket for the two large pizzas, extra everything.

At eight I smelled pizza with green olives and a hint of pepperoni.

Is he for real?

I'd spent the whole night avoiding him and he was making our pizza like we were going to do what we always did, like everything hadn't changed.

"Rachel?" his voice called from the kitchen when I didn't go back. I still didn't.

What does he want from me? Does he want to gloat, rub my nose in it? But I couldn't avoid it forever, so I wrapped my arms around myself and pushed the kitchen door open. Joel was standing by the back door with our usual stack.

"Did more people come in?" he asked, like he was trying to figure out why I was still in the dining room.

I shook my head and walked past him to the stairs that we usually sat on. I just wanted to get it over with. He followed my lead and sat down and handed me my usual two slices, one of which I immediately shoved in my mouth. I was done with that one in three minutes and quickly moved on to number two. All the while, my eyes were fixed on the back door.

"Hungry?" I could hear the laughter in his voice. I turned to look at him. He had both his slices still on his plate. He was smiling at me. That was the first time I'd ever seen a smile reach someone's eyes like that.

I swallowed the wad that was in my mouth. "Not really," I answered, and I wasn't.

He laughed again and shook his head before picking up his piece. He ate very slowly, almost like it was deliberate. I'd finished before he was even halfway through with his first slice.

That's when he started talking to me. For the most part he didn't say anything too dreadful, but I should've known a set-up when I saw one. At least he didn't take too long.

"About last night," he said after the briefest of pauses. I knew that time he was going to get right to the point. His eyes looked too intense.

I quickly interjected, "Don't worry about it. I don't care either way." Not wanting to give him a chance to say more, I stood up and went inside. For the second night in a row, I closed the back door a little harder than I'd meant to.

"Watch it. You want to knock the place down?"

I walked around Fred and grabbed the broom. I started sweeping with a vengeance. I didn't even bother to flip up the chairs. As soon as I was done, I dragged the mop out. That was done with as much precision.

Then Joel came out. He grabbed the silverware bin and sat in my usual spot. He started rolling. I stopped my mopping and stared at him. *What is he doing?*

He could leave anytime. I almost told him that, and I would've if I was speaking to him.

He filled the bin much faster than I ever did. He carefully walked around the sporadic wet spots on the floor and put the bin back under the counter. He turned and looked at me.

"What else needs to be done?"

"Nothing," I answered as I watched him. Joel nodded and then sat down in one of the stools, still not leaving.

I walked past him to the kitchen to dump the dirty water and put the mop away. When I went back into the dining room he was still sitting there. I really should've cleaned the griddle, but I'd already told him there wasn't anything left to do. So I left it; Fred could worry about it in the morning. I didn't want Joel to think I was a liar.

I put on my coat and walked to the door. It was only then that Joel got up from his seat. He looked at me strange as I turned to leave.

"You walk home alone?" he asked suddenly.

I'd forgotten that he'd never closed with me to realize that's what I always did.

"Every night but Monday," I answered, trying to sound annoyed.

"What about your parents? Couldn't they pick you up?"

I paused. I wasn't used to Joel asking the questions. Usually I had an answer all ready whenever anyone broached that particular topic, but with Joel I was completely unprepared. So I told him the truth.

"I don't have parents. I mean, of course, I used to have them, but now I just live with my cousin and his mother, and they...," I paused, thinking of the right way to describe Nathan, "...don't get out much."

Joel's face did exactly what I didn't want it to do. If he didn't pity me before, he certainly did then.

"Is it a long walk?" he asked softly.

I was more prepared for it that time, so the lie came naturally. "Not really."

He still didn't look like he liked it. But what was it to him? I didn't turn back as I headed through Weston towards the woods that surrounded my trailer.

I wasn't thinking about Nathan when I walked into the trailer. Instead, I automatically turned and went towards my room.

"Excuse me, did you forget something?" Nathan's annoyed voice called out after me.

I stopped outside my door, but instead of going back to my nightly inquisition, I opened my door and closed it behind me.

chapter twenty-nine/ seniors

You must do the things you think you cannot do.
-Eleanor Roosevelt

I noticed the difference in them as soon as they walked in.
There were six of them, and they were some of the biggest
guys I've ever seen. I didn't need someone else to tell me what
I was looking at. I already knew. These were Newstead seniors.

We didn't often get seniors at Fred's. They preferred The Dry
Dock on the other side of town, a bar that didn't mind serving
the under-aged.

As soon as they walked in, the entire tempo of the place
changed. It was a nervous kind of quiet.

The group of them walked over to a table that already had
some people sitting in it. Without a word those people quickly
got up and moved someplace else. As the seniors sat down,
the noise level gradually increased.

I walked over to their table. Six pairs of eyes moved slowly up
and down my body as I handed them the worn menus. I gave a
tug on the back of my shirt, pulling the front up higher.

"Would you like anything to drink?" I began my typical line of
questions.

Six sneers was the only answer I got.

"I already know what I want," the boldest of them said, once again slowly looking up and down my frame.

I tried to ignore what he was implying and smiled my fakest smile. "Oh, then are you ready to order?"

He growled in disgust. "Yeah, we're ready. We want six fish fries, extra everything." He lifted the menus in my direction and let them drop to the floor.

I froze.

I knew what they wanted, what I'd have to do. They wanted me to pick them up, naturally, giving them a view of things I'd rather not have them see. I was just about to relent, when I saw Joel coming out from the back. He walked over to where I stood, and in one graceful movement, reached down and picked them up.

I quickly turned to leave, but not in time to miss Joel looking each one of my persecutors in the eyes. I didn't see his face, but I did glimpse their response to him. Each one held his gaze and then looked down, defeated. All but the ringleader; he refused to look down. He even smiled.

Joel sat down on one of the stools at the counter. He didn't say anything to me; he didn't say anything to anyone. He just sat there, with every muscle in his body flexed.

He stayed in the dining room until they left.

But he wasn't there the rest of the week when they showed up again. By Wednesday, I had started wearing turtlenecks.

chapter thirty/ a birthday to remember

What the ancients called a clever fighter is one who not only
wins, but excels in winning with ease.
    -Sun Tzu, *the Art of War*

I waited until I got to my room to open the package I'd gotten
from my mom in the daily mail call. It was another journal along
with a sappy card. I tucked the card in the inside flap and put
them both under a few layers of socks in my upper drawer.

Talk about the worst birthday ever; not so much as a single
person had mentioned it. I hadn't told anyone, but Erikson
knew. It was all over my files.

So I gave a gift to myself. I left and went towards Fred's
earlier than I usually did. It was around sixteen-thirty when I got
there, and Rachel was already running around like a crazy
person. She looked up when I walked in and smiled brightly. I
turned around to see if there was someone behind me. But
there wasn't; her big smile was meant for me.

Maybe this'll be a good birthday after all.

She was wearing my favorite shirt: a long-sleeved olive
colored thing that brought out the flecks of green in her brown
eyes and clung to her curves. The customers seemed to

appreciate her shirt too, especially a small group of huge guys in the far left corner of the dining room. I'd seen them there before, but that night they seemed particularly obnoxious.

I could understand their attraction to Rachel, of course. You'd have to be blind not to notice how beautiful she was, but there seemed to be more to it. A feeling of empowerment, maybe?

They looked like they really enjoyed making her uncomfortable. It was like watching a bully in a schoolyard. A bully who was really nothing more than a coward, picking on the smallest kid to make himself feel stronger. It was the most pathetic excuse of manhood I'd ever seen.

I decided I needed to talk to her about it. I waited until we were in our usual spot on the stairs.

"I don't like the way those guys hassle you in there," I said, gesturing with my head toward the restaurant where her torturers had just been. "Do you want me to do something about it?" I looked at her seriously.

"What could *you* do?" she asked, seemingly surprised I'd noticed.

"I can take care of myself." *And you too, if you'll let me.*

She laughed then, her mood lightening. "I'm sure you could." *Is she trying to pacify me?*

"I'm serious, Rachel. Those guys aren't fooling around like you think they are. I should know. I see their type every day."

"I know," she said gravely, dismissing the topic; dismissing me.

She stopped eating then, even though more than half her pizza was still lying on her plate. She looked forward, lost in her thoughts.

"Coming?" I asked as I stood and held the door open for her.

"I'll be inside in a minute," she answered, hugging herself with her arms, her soft brown curls gently framing her face.

Maybe she *had* been paying attention. After all, she looked serious enough then. I reluctantly turned and went to the pile of dishes that had stacked up while I was sitting in the dining room waiting for certain people to leave.

As my hands washed, my mind remained tense, alert. I'd been carefully listening for the sound of the back door clanging shut to let me know she'd come back inside. After a couple minutes of hearing nothing, I decided I needed to check things out.

I pushed open the back door. Rachel wasn't sitting where I'd left her. My eyes scanned the small lot behind Fred's.

Nothing.

I closed my eyes and tried to focus. That's when I heard it: the muffled sounds coming from behind the dumpsters.

I made it down the stairs in half a second. I made it to the dumpsters even faster, colliding into them before actually seeing what was going on.

His body pinned her to the ground, immobilizing her. One of his hands was over her mouth. Her mindless shrieks were the muffled sounds I'd heard. His other hand fumbled with his clothes and hers. Neither of them noticed me. She was too terrified, he was too determined.

I've never felt the same rage, the same surge of power that I felt at that moment. It didn't matter that the guy was half a foot taller than I was, or that he outweighed me by seventy pounds.

Even though I was seething, I was suddenly able to think calmly, rationally. The previous panic was gone. I began to analyze the situation and determine the methods I needed to obtain the outcome I wanted. It was like I was a machine.

In the fraction of a second since I'd seen them, I assessed my enemy, planned my attack, and implemented the strategy I knew would work, despite the obvious advantage my opponent had. I simply reached down and grabbed him from behind, revealing the crumpled form of Rachel beneath.

"Get inside." My voice was full of the fury I felt, but was somehow able to contain.

She scrambled to her feet, eyes darting from her attacker to me as she ran past us towards the back door.

I looked after her and waited for the door to shut, then I dropped him. He pulled himself to his feet and stood at his full height.

My fist was the first to make contact. It hit his jaw with a satisfying thud a second before he reeled backwards. I didn't wait for him to get up before I lunged at him. His face was my only target as I hit him again and again. He didn't fight back, he couldn't.

Eventually, I stopped. His limp body fell to the ground, a lump of disfigured flesh in the melting snow.

"Don't you ever let me see you here or anywhere near her again." I grabbed the hair on the back of his head to lift his face out of the slush that covered the ground. "Did you hear me?"

He nodded. He'd heard.

I left him to go check on Rachel. At first I didn't see her. And then I did. She was crouching on the floor by my rinse tub, arms hugging herself, head tucked in, her sobs rocking her small frame back and forth.

I waited by the door, trying to decide what to do. I didn't know her well enough to know what she would need from me. But the voice told me to go to her, so I did.

I walked over and knelt down, carefully placing my hand on her back, stroking it gently. Without looking up, she curled herself tightly against my chest. I continued rubbing her head, her hair, breathing in, long and deep.

After a little while, Rachel drew back and at first I didn't know why.

"I need to finish…Fred," she stammered.

Is she for real? Is she really worried about work?

"I'll do it. You just stay back here," I whispered against her head.

She froze. "No, don't leave me." Her hands clenched onto my upper arm.

"I won't," I promised. My voice was muffled by her hair. My hands were still gently running through it, my mouth pressed against it, not daring to kiss her.

chapter thirty-one/ wanted

The tragedy of life is not so much what men suffer, but rather what they miss.
 -Thomas Carlyle

I didn't see him until he was right there, standing next to me. My body didn't move, not when he grabbed my arm, not when he dragged me along the ground. Not that I had a chance against someone like him, but it was like I didn't even try. I was just a pile of Jell-O, pushed and moved however he wanted.

He let go of my arm when we were behind the dumpster. He just stood there for a second looking at me with a strange gleam in his eyes. And then I knew. He wanted me to try to scramble away, to make it more exciting for him.

So I did the only thing I could. I laid down on the ground and waited for it to be over. It was going to happen no matter what I did anyways, and I'd be damned if I was going to help him along.

But I forgot that I was dealing with a Newstead senior. He didn't need my help, not with anything. The look on his face told me that by the time he was done with me, I'd be begging for another chance to squirm away.

He crouched down and then sprung, catlike, landing directly on top of me. Every part of me was covered by every part of him. I don't know how I did it, but I managed to let out a weak scream before his hand slammed down over my mouth.

Part of me kept screaming and part of me closed my eyes and welcomed the fog that was threatening to overtake me. Fog was good. Fog was my friend. It kept me from thinking about what was going on as I was being crushed and stripped.

And then he was gone.

My body realized it before my mind as my lungs gasped for air. At first all they could do was cough and sputter, but, slowly, they blew off enough carbon dioxide for the fogginess to disappear.

I opened my eyes and found myself looking directly at his face; his face that was nothing but a twisted contortion of eyes and nose and mouth. His breath hit me again and again as he struggled. Against what, I had no idea. I was just lying there, as still as ever.

"Get inside," a rough voice demanded. It was Joel's voice. *What is Joel doing here?*

The eyes that were glaring at me went blank at the sound, and then I saw something I've never seen in the face of a Newsteader before. He looked afraid, terrified actually. Seeing him like that focused me. I carefully slid out from underneath him and once I was sure I was clear, I half-ran, half-crawled to the stairs that were behind Fred's.

Once I was inside, I stumbled to my knees, just at the door. *Too close.*

I crawled further in. *Still too close.*

I made it to Joel's corner and tucked my knees to my chin and hugged myself, blocking out everything except what reminded me of him.

The back door opened, then closed.

I tucked my head in further, knowing it was the end. I didn't care. I just wanted it to be over.

Heavy footsteps made their way over to me, stopping less than a foot away from where I was curled up in a ball. My breath held as massive arms wrapped themselves around me, only that time they felt different. I raised my head and saw a soaked white t-shirt.

It was Joel. He was sitting right next to me on the wet, dirty floor, and he was holding me, rubbing my back, my hair. I pressed my face against his chest and closed my eyes and breathed in. He loved me. That was all I could think about, all I'd let myself think about. He loved me. I breathed in again and smiled.

And then Fred walked by. I flinched back. There was no way I wanted Fred to see us like we were then, clinging to each other.

"...Fred," I said, trying to make Joel understand.

Even with my nonsense, he seemed to know what I was talking about, because he went to stand up.

I gripped his arm tighter, pulling him back to the floor. My scrambled brain wasn't processing much, but it did know that being away from Joel was a very bad thing for me at that moment. If I could've crawled *inside* him, I would have.

"Shh, I'm here. I won't leave you," he said as he started rocking me back and forth, rhythmically. After a little bit, he started humming lightly into my ear. It was the same song I'd heard that first day.

I'll have to ask him what song that is, I thought as I settled back onto his chest.

I could've stayed there forever. But I knew I couldn't, so when I was sure I wouldn't lose it again, I pulled back. Joel looked at me warily.

"I'm okay," I said. He didn't look convinced.

"No, really. I'm fine." And I was, sort of. I was at least fine enough to be able to form a rational thought, which was better than I was before.

He must've believed me because he let me pull away from him. I used the washtub as leverage to yank myself to my feet. Joel quietly stood by, waiting for my lead. I took a deep breath and went to the dining room to finish closing. Joel was always one step behind me, never leaving my side for the rest of the night.

As I finished mopping the last section, a new dread filled my mind. I'd have to walk the thirty minutes to the trailer in the dark, by myself. It was something I didn't think I could do, especially on *that* night. I almost asked Joel if he'd walk me, but I couldn't.

My next thought was Nathan, that maybe he'd come in the truck and pick me up. But I quickly disregarded it. Even if I gave Nathan a play-by-play of what'd happened to me that night, I knew he wouldn't come.

I closed my eyes and put on my most stubborn mask, knowing I'd have to do it alone.

But I was wrong about that too, because Joel was sitting at the counter holding out my jacket when I came in from the back, looking for it.

"I confiscated it, just in case you were planning on walking home without me," he said, smiling softly.

"Isn't that a little out of your way?" I asked.

"Someone once told me that your house was only a little way from here," he said, measuring me, seeming to know full well about my previous lie.

"Well...," I began.

"How far is it?" He smiled, helping me with my coat.

"About a thirty minute walk," I answered, avoiding his eyes.

A half grin abruptly appeared on his face as he shook his head. "We better get started, then. Lights out is at twenty-three hundred."

We walked towards the trailer in silence, not an awkward silence, just quiet. Neither of us seemed sure enough of ourselves to begin a conversation. Keep it light? Say the things that needed to be said? In the end we just said nothing for the first twenty minutes.

Finally Joel took the lead. "I'm sorry I'm not much of a talker," he said, looking ahead, not meeting my eyes.

"I don't mind," I said as I reached for his hand. If he could make an effort, so could I.

His hand was warm and his eyes were soft as he turned to look at me, searching my intent. I made no effort to hide what it meant for me. I'd already made up my mind; I knew what I wanted.

He smiled down at me, a knowing smile, and lifted our hands to his soft, full lips as he gently kissed the back of each of my fingers before letting them fall back down between us.

We continued that way in blissful silence until we reached the farmer's trail at the end of Markham Lane. It was no more than a frozen dirt path that after making a few turns along a creek led to my trailer. I slowed and Joel stopped.

"Something wrong?" he asked.

He bent over until his face was only a couple inches above mine. I don't think either of us was prepared for what being that close would do to us.

My hand lifted to his face and lightly traced along his cheekbones, up to his forehead, before circling back down to his jaw. My fingers hesitated by his lips.

His eyes burned bright as his head lowered. My breath held, waiting. But just when I would've sworn it was inevitable, his jaw tensed and he slowly shook his head. I don't know if it was to him or to me. His lips touched softly on my forehead instead, a light brush that was over before it began.

I sighed, disappointed, but I don't think he heard me because he straightened back up and took my hand and started walking towards my trailer again.

I'd never thought much about how we lived until that moment. Seeing it through Joel's eyes, I saw every imperfection in that shabby trailer as we approached it. *Is he surprised, disappointed—both?*

He didn't seem to be either as he turned towards me again, wrapping his strong arms around me. He bent down and gently kissed me on the forehead. I surprised myself and him as I tipped my head back, welcoming his mouth on my lips instead. Cautiously, he consented and then his lips turned into a smile as he kissed me again, that time meeting my lips on purpose. He pulled away, looking down at me as he did.

"This is a welcome surprise," he whispered, watching my eyes.

Something in them made him pause and draw back. "You don't owe me anything, you know." His face turned hard, unreadable.

"Joel, don't you know me by now?" If ever my feelings were displayed on my face, it was at that moment, when I allowed myself to be completely transparent.

He paused only a fraction of a second before his lips crushed down on mine with a sudden intensity that surprised me. It ended as quickly as it began as his hands reached up to cup my face. He gently pulled me away, lightly pressing his forehead against mine as he closed his eyes.

"I love you, Rachel," he whispered.

"I love you, too," I said out loud.

His eyes crinkled in the corners, even though they were still closed.

We stood like that: his hands cupping my face, mine cupping his, our foreheads pressed together.

My eyes never closed, though. I didn't want to miss one second of it. I was too much of a realist to think I could actually keep him forever. The here and now was all I had. So I enjoyed the here and now.

He finally pulled back, looking at me.

"I'm sorry…I have to go," he said reluctantly.

"Will I see you tomorrow?" I asked. My voice sounded as urgent as I felt.

He nodded reassuringly. "Tomorrow," he echoed as he backed away, not turning until he was out of sight.

I stood on the concrete stairs leading up to my trailer for a minute before going in. They were the only things permanent there. They'd been there before we came and would probably be there years after we left, a leftover from the migrant workers who came there every summer with their own trailers.

My heart ached for something stable, secure.

Six months. We'd already been there six months, a record for us. How much longer could I expect?

Forever, my heart answered.

rachel

chapter thirty-two/ just more

The best and most beautiful things in the world cannot be seen or even touched. They must be felt with the heart.
  -Helen Keller

Nathan was perched on my small metal folding chair by the front window when I walked in. He had the shades pulled over to one side with his face pressed up against the glass. I stood by the door and watched him trying to watch me. You'd think he would've noticed I wasn't outside anymore. I decided to give him a clue. I took another step in and closed the door, hard. The effect was instant and a little more animated than I'd pictured.

Nathan flew back and with that one motion both he and the chair toppled to the floor.

I smiled down at him. *Maybe that'll teach you not to spy on people,* I thought rather proudly.

He quickly got to his feet and sat down in his usual spot, like he actually expected me to give him his nightly report. I walked to my room and slammed the door.

Nathan's pounding on my bedroom door was what woke me

up the next morning.

"Rachel, come out NOW. I need to talk to you."

The pounding started again when I didn't answer. I glared at that door, knowing full well he wasn't going to give up. I took my sweet time throwing on my robe and pulling my hair back before finally pulling the door open.

There was no one there.

Foolishly, I stuck my head out into the hall just in time to see Nathan pause mid-step on his way back to the kitchen. I sighed. I knew what that meant.

He began walking again and didn't stop until he was sitting down at his usual seat.

So close. Why couldn't I have just waited two more seconds?

I stayed in my doorway and watched him as he pretended to ignore me. His fingers began tapping the table impatiently. It was then that I saw it: the metal chair, *my* metal chair, set up and waiting for me.

I'm guessing that means Nathan's giving me a do-over.

I almost went back to bed; that's what I should've done, but instead I walked towards Nathan and that stupid chair. My butt wasn't in it for half a second when Nathan began.

"Was that the Nephilim you work with?"

I don't know why I told him yes, but I did.

"Tell me what you know about him," Nathan continued, fully expecting me to answer him. I didn't.

"He's not what you think he is." He sat back in his seat and waited to see his words take effect.

"I think I know who and what Joel is," I answered, crossing my arms in front of my chest.

"Really?" he asked, eyeing me. "Do you really, Rachel?"

My face got warmer as I watched him. He knew something, something about Joel. It was written all over his face. If it was anything else, I probably would've let it drop, but it wasn't. It was about Joel.

I leaned forward. "Why? What do you know?"

"I know lots of things, lots more than you. Didn't you ever wonder why he is so different? Did it ever occur to you that maybe it's because he *is* different?"

"How's he different?" I asked, going down a road I never should've been on in the first place.

"You tell me."

I let out a deep breath, more exasperation than defeat. "What do you want to know?"

Nathan smiled. It turned out I wasn't that hard to crack, after all. You just had to know which buttons to push. And Nathan knew my buttons, better than anyone.

"Do you ever see him do anything unusual?"

"No more than the rest of them." I tried not to think about him dangling some three hundred pound behemoth midair with only one hand. I tried not to think about that, but Nathan's left eyebrow rose.

"And has he ever spoken to you about his father?"

"Who's his father?" I asked, insanely curious.

"Never mind. He's never mentioned him?"

"No. He only talks about his mom."

Nathan nodded, considering that. I took advantage of the pause and asked a question of my own. "Why is he different, Nathan? Please tell me."

For some reason, he did.

"He's not one of them any more than you or me are one of them."

"I don't understand," I said. And I didn't.

"His father's an angel, just not a *fallen* one."

For some reason that scared me more than anything else.

"What does that mean?" I whispered.

"It means that he's frightening and terrible and good and

cursed and blessed and..." He shook his head, as shaken as I've seen him. "I don't know what it means."

We both sat in a very loud silence as we looked at anything but each other.

After a few minutes, he asked me one last question: "Do you think the rest of them know what he is?"

I shook my head. I had no idea.

chapter thirty-three/ afraid

The heart is deceitful above all else.
  –Jeremiah, *the Bible*

Saturdays at Fred's were different than the rest of the week, except for maybe Sundays. On the weekdays, I'd have almost an hour to get things ready before the Newsteaders showed up. But not on the weekends. On the weekends, they were already lined up outside, waiting for me to open the door.

I rounded the corner right at eleven that Saturday, expecting to see what I always did: a bunch of loud, obnoxious guys making snide comments about hating to have to wait on a woman. They said the same thing every week. You'd think they'd just wait at their stupid school until Fred's actually opened if it bothered them so badly.

But that day was different. That day the sidewalk was completely empty.

I went in the back to start my prep work. After a few minutes the bell above the door chimed. I stuck my head out the opening to see who it was, but it was just Fred and Sam walking in together.

Neither of them bothered to flip over the sign. Instead, they just parked themselves on two of the swivel seats by the counter. I not-so-quietly stomped past them towards the front and turned the sign over, officially opening Fred's for business. I glanced out the window; there still wasn't anyone there.

So I went back to the kitchen and waited to hear the chime again. When it finally did, I was out in the dining room before the door could close, but there was only Fred sitting there.

"Sam went home," he said without looking at me. I nodded and sat down next to him. The seat was still warm from Sam's butt.

After an hour of no one showing up, Fred started to get mad. And when Fred got mad, he usually took it out on me. That day was no different.

He looked in my direction like he'd just remembered I was there or maybe not, because his next words told me he'd been thinking about me for a while.

"It's your lucky day, Rachel, because it's been way too long since this place has had a good cleaning." His smile was huge and cruel.

"What do you mean by that? I clean this place up every night," I said, slightly offended.

"Not the type of cleaning I'm thinking about." He smiled bigger as he stood up and walked to the kitchen door and pushed it open.

I stood next to him and looked, too. "What?" I asked. It looked all right to me.

It turned out that the cleaning he was thinking about involved the fryers being emptied and scrubbed, along with almost every inch of that kitchen.

Once I got started I could see his point. It was filthy.

The only part that didn't need almost a total overhaul was the washtub area. Joel must've cleaned it during any lulls he had because that was the only spot that wasn't covered in an inch of film.

Joel.

I closed my eyes and leaned back against the wall by his washtub. *What is someone like him doing here? Not just at Fred's, but in Weston at all. With me.*

Nathan's words that morning had rocked me to my core. But not just his words, it was more the way he'd said them, and the way he'd looked. Nathan was afraid of Joel, maybe even more than all the rest of them.

Fear I could deal with. I'd lived with fear every minute I'd been in Weston. But that wasn't the only thing I saw in Nathan's face as he looked at me; there was pity there, too. Pity was the one thing I couldn't take.

Nathan knew he was too good for me, too.

chapter thirty-four/ too close

Fear is stupid. So are regrets.
  -Marilyn Monroe

The bell above the door only rang one other time that day. I
looked up at the clock and swallowed hard. It was five.
  I was still in the kitchen. I'd been there all day, and that's
where he found me as his head peeked through the long
window that looked out into the dining room. I was by his
washtubs that were loaded with the dishes that'd gotten
contaminated during my cleaning.
  His smile was enormous when he saw me. He ducked his
head back and came in through the kitchen door. I had just
enough time to take a deep breath before he was standing next
to me.
  "Hey," he said. His eyes were warm and bright.
  "Hey," I answered just as he bent his head down and shyly
kissed me on my cheek. His head stayed down for just a
second as he leaned it on mine. I could hear his breathing, slow
and deep.
  And then I remembered. He loved me. It didn't matter that he
was some super-powerful angel's son. He loved me, and that
was enough. So that time when he pulled away, I was smiling,

too.

He grabbed the cloth from my hand and started washing the dishes. I didn't leave; there was no point. It wasn't like I had any customers to wait on. Instead, I stood by his washtub and dried the dishes as he handed them to me.

"What sports do you like best?" I asked after a few minutes of silence.

He smiled. "Football is probably my favorite. It's what my body size is suited for, besides maybe basketball. But I like them all the same. It feels like the only time when I can really be myself."

"Why's that?"

He paused, like he was really concentrating on his answer. In the end he just shrugged. "I don't know. It always feels like I'm kind of holding back. But when I play sports, I can just let myself go."

I nodded. That made sense.

"People must love to have you on their team," I continued as I dried the dish he'd just washed.

He had an answer for that one right away. "Not really. I guess I'm not a very good team player. I kind of get lost in the moment and forget that anyone else is out there."

"I've never played sports."

"Never?" He looked surprised.

"No," I answered and looked away. The silence stretched on for a few minutes while Joel looked at me. I knew he wanted to ask more, but he didn't. So I took advantage of the lull and asked the one question I was dying to get an answer to:

"Tell me about your father."

I watched to see his reaction.

"Never met him," he replied, looking uninterested. "What about your parents?" he asked.

I guess I deserve that.

"They both died in a fire when I was seven," I answered

automatically. I'd been used to giving the same explanation each time I moved to a new school.

"That doesn't tell me much about them," he probed.

I paused. No one had ever gone further than nodding acceptance. Occasionally an "I'm sorry," but no one ever asked more. The questions normally stopped, but not with Joel. He settled back and leaned against the washtub, waiting for me to answer.

"I haven't really thought about them for a long time," I said. It was true. I hadn't. I closed my eyes and tried to remember. After a few seconds a picture filled my head. It was of my mother, and she was beautiful.

Tears welled up in my eyes before I could stop them. I missed her so much. I hadn't realized how much that was until that moment. Maybe that's why I never let myself think about her. But I made myself think about her then.

"My mom was older when she had me. I guess she tried to have a baby for a long time. That's probably why she spent so much time with me." I swallowed hard and looked at Joel as he stood there, watching me.

"And your dad?"

"My dad was never there; he was always off starting churches somewhere. My parents were very religious, which was something I didn't seem to inherit." I laughed quietly to myself.

Joel wasn't laughing. He only looked at me with his soft hazel eyes, more green that night than brown.

"I haven't talked about them for a long time," I confessed. "Thank you, I needed that." I realized in that moment how much that was true. My life with my parents felt so distant, almost like it never even happened. But it did happen, and for their sake, as well as mine, I needed to remember that I'd had a real life once that didn't involve living in a decrepit trailer with two people who don't love me.

We went back to comfortable silence until Fred sulked out of his office, his belly peeking out a few inches below his tattered, stained t-shirt. No one would've guessed that between the three of us, he was the owner.

"What are you guys just standing around for? Clean this place up!" he bellowed irritably.

I jumped first. Joel had no idea how detail-oriented Fred could get. And I certainly didn't want a repeat of my earlier activities, once was more than enough. My skin was still crawling with all I'd seen that day.

I went to the dining room and emptied my tip jar on the counter. Some rolling change spilled out. I must've just taken the bills on Friday. Three quarters and four dimes. That was it. I hadn't earned so much as one penny all night.

As I was glumly refilling my jar, Joel came up behind me. Normally I could sense when he was near, but that night he took me completely by surprise as his arms wrapped tightly around my mid-section. I involuntarily jumped before I realized who it was.

"I'm sorry, I didn't mean to scare you," Joel said, pulling back. His face looked flushed, like he was thinking the same thing I was:

Just yesterday it had been other arms wrapped tightly around me.

"That's okay," I said, hiding a shudder. I'm pretty sure Joel saw it, though.

"Where's Fred?" I asked, trying to change the subject.

"He went home. He asked me to tell you to lock up."

I nodded. That sounded like Fred, always trying to get out of any work.

We both turned away at the same time, automatically gravitating towards whatever needed to be done. When we finished, Joel joined me in the corner booth to roll silverware into napkins.

"This is where I was sitting the first night we met," he declared suddenly, like he was trying to change the course of both our thoughts. It worked.

It'd been so long, I was surprised he'd remembered. I forgot a Newstead face as soon as I saw it and that's all Joel would've been to me then, a Newstead face. The only thing that stood out for me at all was when he'd asked for an application. That *had* taken me by surprise. Prior to that moment I had no memory of him. He obviously did as he seemed to enjoy retelling it.

"You were very busy. Sam must've called in because you were running the kitchen, too. You looked so annoyed at us." He laughed, looking off in the distance, like he was seeing it even then. It wasn't very flattering for me, but he didn't seem to mind as he continued, "I've never seen anyone more beautiful than you were that night, Rachel. Something just drew me to you. I had to get to know you, but it seemed like the more I tried to talk to you, the more I irritated you." He chuckled again. "Finally, on a whim, I decided to ask for an application, I really don't know why, I hadn't planned on working while I was here, but I'm glad I did," he finished quietly.

I didn't answer even though he had a look on his face that told me he wanted me to. I almost lied to him. How could I tell him the truth?

Great memory, Joel, but you meant nothing to me then; you were just one of the mutants I tried to avoid. So, no, nothing you just described rings a bell.

"You don't remember any of that do you?" He looked slightly hurt, but not surprised. He'd seen how I treated the many boys who tried to get my attention.

"I remember you asking for an application," I answered honestly.

His arms crossed themselves in front of his chest. "And?"

"And I was planning on throwing it away when you turned it in but you picked the one day I wasn't working to do it. Is that what you wanted to hear, Joel?" I asked, my temper rising, not at him, but at myself.

He looked surprised at my sudden venom, not quite knowing how to take it. I stopped my rolling and reached over for his hand, trying to take the sting out of my words.

"I'm really sorry for not noticing you, Joel. I wish I would have. But at least it didn't take me too long to realize how wonderful you were, right?" I looked at him, hopeful.

He didn't answer. He went back to work on the fork-knife-spoon combo, all wrapped in a cheap napkin. His eyes would occasionally flick to mine, then down again. He looked like he wanted to ask me something but couldn't bring himself to do it. It was almost like he was having an internal argument with himself. The side that wanted him to stay quiet must've won because he didn't say another word.

Instead, he went to the back and grabbed my jacket, holding it for me as I placed the bin we'd filled under the counter. I paused for a second before sliding my arms in. I wasn't used to having someone take care of me. It felt really good.

I locked the front door and slipped the key under the designated rock for Fred to find in the morning. Joel stood to the side and then turned in the direction of my trailer, like he was planning on walking me home again. I was surprised. I hadn't expected him to make a nightly thing of it.

I smiled as I considered what that meant. Joel would be with me by my trailer again. My face flushed warmly as I pictured it: Joel and me, alone.

My mind was so distracted with those thoughts that I didn't realize Joel was utterly silent. I looked over at him. He was at least a couple of feet away from me with his face tense and his arms stiff at his sides. Just as I was about to look away, his hands clenched into fists and then released.

All the pleasant thoughts I was having disappeared in that one second. Occasionally, I'd glance at him to see if he was still freaking out, and then I'd look away again. *Definitely freaking out.*

Finally, I couldn't take it anymore. I took a step towards him and reached for his hand and forced my fingers in-between each of his. It only took a second for his hand to relax, and with it, the rest of him seemed to relax, too.

He still didn't look at me, though, or talk to me. I was starting to panic the closer we got to my trailer. But he didn't let go of my hand; we had that connection, at least.

We rounded the last bend and he walked me right up to the concrete steps. He turned to look at me and his face was carefully controlled, looking vacantly down at me. But I knew a mask when I saw one, so I slid my arms around his waist until they met behind his back, and I molded my body to him.

At first he stayed remote, but only at first. After a few seconds, his head bent down and rested on top of mine as he breathed in deeply. That act seemed to dissolve whatever problems he'd been having. Soon, his body was molded to mine, too. And that time I didn't jump, or pull back.

We stayed that way for a while until I remembered the eyes that were probably watching us. It was easy to forget things like that when I was with Joel. I pulled back, and when I did, I saw something in Joel's face that I'm sure he never meant for me to see. His lips quickly pressed down on mine, to hide what was there.

I didn't mind the reason, as long as he was kissing me. He kept on kissing me, too, until he'd gotten whatever thoughts he was having under control.

When he did, his large hands cupped my face and pulled me

back. The intensity was gone from his eyes. Instead, he seemed at peace with himself, with me. He kissed me lightly; first on the forehead, then on the nose, finally, feathery light on my lips.

"Good night," he whispered, just inches above my face.

My head began to swim, having him so close. I nodded and slowly backed away towards the door. I stayed and watched him until he was out of sight, before turning to go to the inquisition I knew was waiting for me inside.

chapter thirty-five/ me

Rouse him, and learn the principle of his activity or inactivity. Force him to reveal himself, so as to find out his vulnerable spots.

-Sun Tzu, *the Art of War*

I walked quickly back from Rachel's to Newstead. It was very cold, even for the middle of March in Vermont. It seemed like winter was finally making its appearance, right before it was supposed to be ending.

Newstead was a fifteen minute walk on the other side of town, so my walk home from Rachel's totaled forty-five minutes. I didn't mind. I had a lot to think about.

All my life, ever since I could remember, I've had a voice in my head. I used to think everyone had one, until I answered it out loud once and people looked at me like I was insane.

So I ignored it. And I never, ever told anyone about it. I was enough of a freak; I didn't need to be a crazy freak, too.

That night, while I was beating up the guy who had attacked Rachel, the thin veil that was in my mind disappeared. I saw myself for what I was for probably the first time in my life. I realized that *I* was the voice, or it was me. It was like I'd looked in a mirror and saw that what I'd thought was my biggest enemy was really me, the part of me I tried to ignore that I was.

So I wasn't crazy. I was an even bigger freak than I'd first thought, but I wasn't crazy. I shook my head as I walked along.

Isn't it enough that I'm almost seven feet tall? Do I have to be able to use my mind like that, too?

I let out a breath. *I guess it isn't all bad. It let me help Rachel.*

chapter thirty-six/ quiet

All warfare is based on deception.
  -Sun Tzu, *the Art of War*

I walked into Chapman at a few minutes to curfew. It was completely quiet, which was strange for a Friday night. We were supposed to be in our rooms by twenty-three hundred, but that didn't mean people went to sleep. The noise usually went on until the morning.

But not that night; that night, there was absolute silence. That alone should've warned me, but I was too busy thinking about what I'd learned about myself to consider what I'd learned about them.

Marcus and Steven were both already asleep in their beds, or at least they looked asleep; their backs were to me. I quietly stripped out of my wet work clothes. Usually I took a shower when I got back from work, but I didn't that night. The silence was too thick. I didn't want to break it.

The creaking of my bed when I got in felt very loud, like everyone in the whole building could hear it. I smiled to myself as I laid as still as I could. It's not every night that you find out you're not crazy, you get in a fight and walk away without so much as a scratch, *and* the girl you love tells you that she loves you, too.

My eyes closed with that thought running through my mind. *Rachel loves me, too.*

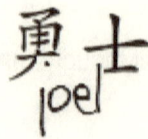

chapter thirty-seven/ cowardly lion

If the enemy leaves a door open, you must rush in.
-Sun Tzu, *the Art of War*

Marcus was gone by the time I woke up, but Steven wasn't. He was sitting up in his bed looking at me, like he'd been waiting for me to wake up. When I did, he just shook his head.

I looked at the clock; it was only zero seven hundred. I hadn't slept in—*why is he looking at me like that?*

He kept looking at me, too. I stood up and got my things and took the shower I didn't take the night before. When I came back in the room, Steven was gone.

I went to the mess hall and got breakfast. The guys there were looking at me, too.

Figures. I finally get over my hallucinations only to find out I'm paranoid. I guess I'm determined to be crazy in some way or another.

I sat by myself and ate as quickly as I could.

I'd meant to go back to Chapman for just a minute to grab the journal from my mom, but as soon as I stepped outside I knew I had to come up with a plan B. It was frickin' cold out.

The last thing I wanted to do was spend all day in my room staring at my clock, so I went down the stairs in Chapman instead of up. I paused as I stood outside the rec hall door. I hadn't been in there since my first week at Newstead. I had no idea if I was even welcome there anymore.

I thought it was completely empty until I saw the familiar form in a completely unfamiliar spot. Steven was sitting in one of the lounge chairs, reading a book. I walked over and sat down in a recliner by the TV. Neither of us said anything.

I flipped on the TV and stared at it as the hours slowly went by. I don't even know what I was watching. Other guys came and went, but Steven and I stayed there the whole day. It was like we were back in our room, only it was bigger.

Marcus came in at one point with his usual group. I looked up and our eyes met for a second. He looked past me, like I wasn't even there. He led his followers to a group of chairs by the air hockey table. It was as far away from me as they could possibly get. It even brought them somewhat close to Steven, closer than Marcus usually let himself to get. *I guess he thinks I'm worse.*

At sixteen thirty I left and headed to Fred's.

I stopped just inside the door and looked around. I'd never seen Fred's so deserted before. There was absolutely no one there. Not even Rachel. That thought bothered me more than I liked to admit.

I quickly walked to the kitchen door and pushed it open and did a quick scan. My heart didn't stop pounding until I spotted her standing next to my washtubs.

"Hey," I said as I walked over to her. She just smiled nervously.

"Slow night?" I asked the obvious. I took over washing the dishes that she was doing.

"Yeah, really slow."

I nodded. It sounded like the rest of my day. Something was really off.

That's when Fred came out from the back. At least *he* was acting the same.

"What are you guys just standing around for?" he yelled. I almost shoved the dish I was washing in his face, but I didn't.

I just kept washing, but Rachel dropped her cloth and made a beeline for the dining room. I'd never paid much attention to the interactions between Rachel and Fred, but I did then. Rachel was acting like she was afraid of him. But it was really Fred's smile as he walked back to his office that got my attention. He looked like he liked her fear. I dropped my cloth into the sink and followed right behind him.

Fred had sat down in his chair and quickly made himself busy shoving his mouth full of chips. Most of them didn't make it, though, and landed on his shirt instead. He tried to wipe them off, but only ended up leaving greasy smears on his already filthy shirt. I shook my head as I watched him. *Such a sloth*

I cleared my throat to let him know I was there. He looked up at me and, for the first time since I'd been working there, I saw the real Fred.

He looked like he was scared out of his wits. His eyes glanced behind me to the door, the room's only exit. *Does he honestly think I'm here to hurt him?* His panicked eyes told me he did.

"What do you want?" he yelled as he shrank back from me.

I just stared at him and shook my head. *What a frickin' loser. All this time I thought he didn't know how dangerous the guys from Newstead are, but that isn't it. He knows full well what's in his dining room every night. Of course he does; that's why he's always back here.*

Which just left Rachel, alone, with them. I took a step into his office. *He's just as bad as the guy I beat up.* I took another step. *Maybe he's even worse.*

Fred started whimpering. It was almost more than I could take. "Listen, you need to have at least two people on the schedule all the time. It doesn't have to be me, but you're going to stop leaving Rachel out there alone."

He must've decided I wasn't going to crack his skull open because he turned back into the Fred I was used to. He overestimated my level of control.

"Who do you think you are, coming in here, telling me how to run my restaurant?"

"Just do it," I demanded, disregarding his fist that was pounding on his desk.

But I couldn't disregard his finger that was poking me in the chest after he crossed the room and got right in my face, or at least as much as his five-foot-six frame would let him.

"What are you going to do about it?" he said, his chest puffed out.

That did it. I brought my fist down on his desk. Only mine didn't just make a dull thud like his had; mine cracked his desk right in half.

"I can do plenty."

Fred backed away from me again. That time it was him who was closest to the door. He scrambled for it and I followed him, right out the back door and then down the steps.

"You're fired!" he yelled as he ran down the alley away from his restaurant.

I turned back around to tell Rachel that Fred had gone home for the night.

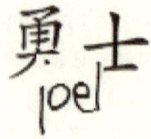

chapter thirty-eight/ meeting nathan

When fire breaks out inside the enemy's camp, respond at
once with an attack from without. .
    –Sun Tzu, *the Art of War*

That Sunday was even more bizarre than Saturday had been.
It was completely dead the entire day. Both Steven and Marcus
were gone by the time I woke up; everyone was. The mess hall
was empty; even the cooks weren't there. There was just a pile
of eggs on a heating tray and a stack of toast. I ate even
quicker than I had the day before.

At first I went back to the rec hall, but after a couple hours of
no one showing up, I went to my room. I kept looking at my
calendar to make sure I didn't have the dates mixed up, but it
wasn't between one of our trimesters.

Where is everyone?

My eyes went to the small hill that was right behind the edge
of the forest. I don't know how I knew they were there, but I did.
The big question was was why wasn't *I* there? Why wasn't I
included in whatever drills they were up to?

Something felt really, really wrong.

The howling wind was the only sound I heard as I left the

safety of my room and headed to the mess hall for lunch. I kept hoping against hope that it would be different, that someone would be there. At that point I'd even take Marcus. But it was just as empty as it'd been for breakfast, only that time there were PB and J's, a whole stack of them. I grabbed four and headed back to my room.

I skipped dinner.

At nineteen hundred I grabbed my jacket and left Chapman. By the time I got to the parking lot, I was running.

Rachel was sitting at the counter when I walked in. She was alone. The place was just as empty as it'd been on Saturday. She looked up when I walked in and then smiled when she saw it was me.

"Where's Fred?" I asked as I looked towards his office. The door was closed.

"He didn't come in today. I guess he's not feeling well."

I bet.

I grabbed the broom that was behind the kitchen door and started sweeping.

I could tell it'd been another quiet day. The place wasn't nearly as trashed as it usually was. Cleanup took less than thirty minutes with both of us working together.

I grabbed the silverware bin and headed to our table. It was still almost full.

"Slow night again?" I asked her as she sat down across from me.

"Yeah, I've never seen it this slow before."

"How long have you worked here?"

"Six and a half months."

"Did you always live here?" I asked, not realizing the hornets' nest I'd just stepped on.

"No, we moved to Weston about the same time I started working here. We've been all over the country, Nathan, his mom and me," she answered quickly, looking away.

"Tell me about your cousin," I said.

She paused mid-roll. "Describe Nathan; I don't think I've ever been asked that one before." She sat back onto the cracked vinyl bench to think about my question. "Nathan's well…almost a hermit. He's barely been outside the trailer in six years, except when we move. He's nineteen, but acts….I don't know if I can even begin to describe how he acts. You'll just have to meet him and decide for yourself."

"When can I meet him?"

"Tonight, if you want," she replied. "I'm sure he'd *love* to meet you," she added under her breath.

I didn't quite know what she meant by that, but I was soon to find out. A nineteen-year-old hermit who traveled across the country? It sounded like an oxymoron if I'd ever heard one.

We were soon done and on our way to Rachel's trailer to meet her cousin.

For some reason, Rachel stopped in the middle of the farmer's lane just before the final turn that brought her trailer into view. Her face flushed lightly as she turned towards me. I was a little dense, so it took me awhile to guess what she was doing. In fact it took her tilting her head back with her eyes closed before I figured out what she wanted.

The girl watched too many movies. It was actually kind of sweet. That one gesture told me everything I ever needed to know about her physical history. She was as inexperienced as I was. Probably more, if that was possible.

I paused briefly to make sure my control was in check before lowering my lips to her upturned face. My hands covered only safe zones: her back, her hair, gently stroking her face, as our kiss continued. I didn't dare go farther, no matter how much I wanted to.

But she did. She didn't seem to be concerned about going slowly as her nails dug into my back, pressing me closer, testing my resolve. When it came to the point where I didn't trust myself anymore, I pulled back.

She looked disappointed, but tried to hide it. Instead, she focused on fixing the mess I'd made of her hair. Soon she looked as beautiful as she had before my reaction to her innocent, upturned face.

She reached out her hand toward me and we turned together to walk to her trailer, and Nathan.

We didn't stop at the concrete steps like we had the night before. Rachel led me straight up and in, surprising the guy who was peeking out the window.

I snickered. *At least that explains the new stopping spot.*

The guy, Nathan, immediately jumped up from his metal folding chair, knocking it to the floor. He didn't even look embarrassed, like he should've.

Nathan wasn't what I'd been expecting. His long, scraggly black hair was tightly pulled back into a ponytail at the nape of his neck, hanging in greasy clumps all the way down his back. His clothes looked like they were the only ones he'd ever worn; a mismatched pair of dirty black sweats with a flannel shirt about three sizes too big. His skin was tight, like his bones were too big for his face; which made him look a lot older than what Rachel said he was.

The only thing that looked like Rachel at all was his coloring and his eyes. He had olive skin just like her; only on her it looked pretty. On him it just looked like dirt. His eyes were the same dark brown with green specks, but his shone with a brilliant intensity, almost a hunger.

Rachel introduced us, "Joel, this is my cousin Nathan; Nathan, this is Joel. Joel wanted to meet you."

He didn't seem like a hermit at all. *Don't hermits avoid people?* Nathan seemed very pleased to meet me, almost too pleased. His intense stare kind of gave me the creeps. It felt like he was dissecting my every move.

I stepped away from him and looked around Rachel's trailer. The furniture, besides being from a different decade, looked like something out of a dumpster. The place reeked like unwashed bodies and urine. I guessed the source of that smell to be the old lady sprawled out on the couch, oblivious to the rest of us. She looked like she was at least a hundred years old.

I couldn't see anything there that went with Rachel, not one thing. Strangely, they didn't seem to notice. I did my best to hide my disgust, but it wasn't easy. The place was revolting.

Nathan, oblivious to what was going on in my mind, bombarded me with questions. Some were incredibly personal, some just plain stupid. Thankfully, he didn't give me much time in-between each one to answer before going on to the next round. In the end, I don't think I told him much: Yes, my mother was very beautiful. No, I'd never met my father. Yes, sometimes I dreamed in color. Rachel soon saw how overwhelmed I was by all his questions and jumped in to save me.

"Nathan, Joel has to go now. He has to get back by curfew and he has a long way to walk."

Curfew. I forgot all about it. I thanked Rachel for reminding me, gave her a quick kiss on the cheek, and called over my shoulder that I'd see her on Tuesday before breaking into an all-out run, pausing only briefly to look at my watch.

22:45. *Forget running, I'll have to fly.*

chapter thirty-nine/ something wrong

Do not linger in dangerously isolated positions.
  -Sun Tzu, *the Art of War*

I set out from Rachel's and didn't stop until my foot hit the steps outside Chapman. I flung open the door and took the stairs two at a time, opening the door to my room just as the clock flipped to twenty-two fifty-nine. One minute to spare.

I half-expected the room to still be empty, but it wasn't. Marcus and Steven were lying on their beds, turned away from me again. *Guess that means whatever exercise they're doing is over.*

I went to bed, but not to sleep—at least not right away. It wasn't that I was winded, or that my heart was racing. It was that I was fine. I'd just run three-and-a-half miles in fourteen minutes and my pulse wasn't even over sixty. I stared at the ceiling with my index finger firmly pressed on my wrist and counted again. Fifty-nine that time. *There is something seriously wrong with me.*

I woke up that Monday to a day that would be one of the all-time worst in my existence. I never had much hope for it in the first place; I wasn't planning on seeing Rachel again until Tuesday.

On top of that, Marcus had planned a football game for later that day after a weather report had said it would be warm out. He'd tried to get away with not asking me, but I was in the rec room on Saturday when he'd been arranging teams. Even he couldn't be that big of a dick—to ask everyone else but me— and I'd reluctantly agreed.

I liked football as much as anybody, and if it had been anybody but Marcus—

I rolled out of bed, expecting to be sore.

Nothing. Damn.

I was hoping for an excuse to skip the game. A shower and a shave seemed to change my perspective, though.

It could be worse, I thought. Little did I know how true that could be.

chapter forty/ monsters

He who can modify his tactics in relation to his opponent and thereby succeed in winning, may be called a heaven-born captain.

-Sun Tzu, *the Art of War*

The abrupt turn in my day came during third period when the announcement over the P.A. informed me I was wanted in Dean Erikson's office, *immediately*.

I froze in my seat. *What can that mean? Did he hear about my three near misses with curfew? No, that can't be it. Other guys are cutting it close all the time.* Marcus was a perfect example of that, and I'd never, ever heard of him or anyone else being called to the dean's office.

The suddenly silent class all turned to look at me. Deep pity was on most faces, arrogance on a few others. I rose to leave. The teacher didn't even issue me a pass.

The receptionist seemed to be in the know, looking at me contemptuously for whatever heinous thing I'd done. He quickly ushered me into Erikson's office.

We weren't alone. A third person sat in the chair immediately inside the door. The chair my mother had sat in the last time I was in that office. His angry face looked defiantly at me as I came into the room.

I can't believe it.

Dean Erikson stood up when I walked in. He looked like he wanted to pop my head off.

"Sit," he said between clenched teeth.

I sat.

"It has come to my attention, *Joel.*" He said my name like it was a curse word. "That you are responsible for this." He gestured to the other chair and the person sitting in it.

I let myself look at him. That was obviously what Erikson wanted me to do with his exaggerated gesturing.

Did I really do that? The guy's face looked like a roasted marshmallow. He even seemed to be missing a tooth. *No, scratch that, three teeth.* And there was some wire in his mouth, binding it closed. *Guess he'll be taking his next few meals with a straw. At least that explains why he isn't talking.*

He scowled as I looked him over. I had to admit, I was a little ashamed of the way I'd left the guy. But if I had to do it all over again, I wouldn't have changed a thing. I'm sure I would've reacted that way if I'd caught him assaulting *any* woman, but he was lucky I could stop when I did.

Erikson looked at me expectantly, waiting for my groveling, my excuses.

"Yes." There wasn't even a hint of remorse in my voice or my eyes as they met his.

The floodgates broke. He began pacing, yelling obscenities that I'd never even heard of before. Finally, after several minutes of his tirade, he was in enough control of himself to address me again.

"What do you mean, *yes*?" he asked, standing behind me, clenching and unclenching his hands around the top of my chair. I think he was pretending it was my head.

"Yes, I was the one who did that to him." *What more does he want me to say?*

Evidently that wasn't the answer he'd wanted because he fell into his chair, utterly stumped about what to do next. I'm sure he was expecting begging and pleading at the very least. My honest admission wasn't what he'd planned on.

"And *why*, might I ask?" He addressed me with carefully controlled calmness, his real feelings evident in his fiery eyes.

"He was assaulting my female coworker," I hesitatingly replied; I didn't want to bring Rachel into it any more than was necessary. *I wonder if the jerk mentioned that part when he tattled on me.*

Erikson disregarded my statement with a wave of his hand.

"That is not the *why* I was talking about, Joel; the *why* I was referring to is why did you side with an outsider against your own brother?" He looked disbelieving at me, like he couldn't believe I thought he'd meant anything else.

I stared at him. *What would he have had me do? Join him?* I felt a shudder ripple through my body as I realized how close I was to the truth.

That new revelation brought the institution down to a whole new level for me. I was already suspicious and guarded when it came to their agenda, but if that was their stance on rape, what exactly did it make them?

"They're monsters," the voice in my head answered. I nodded in agreement.

I stood up, not sure if I could stand being at Newstead another minute.

"Dean Erikson," I said, completely disregarding the jerk sitting in the seat next to me. "That guy is not my brother. As for me, do whatever you want; I have a class I'm late for." I turned slowly, deliberately, out of his office, with the two of them staring at my retreating back.

If it wasn't for my relationship with Rachel, I would've opened the envelope addressed to my mother, taken out the last bit of cash I was getting from Fred, and purchased a bus ticket home right then and there. Even with Rachel in the picture, it was a serious temptation, but I couldn't leave her. So many other people had already done that. I wouldn't be added to the list. So I did it. I stayed.

chapter forty-one/ selected

When he (the enemy) keeps aloof and tries to provoke a battle, he is anxious for the other side to advance.
    –Sun Tzu, *the Art of War*

Leadership class was where I got my punishment for my behavior both on Friday and earlier that day, and it came in a most unexpected form. That was the day they were announcing the two team leaders chosen for the upcoming FTX. I was especially aware of the date because Marcus knew he was a shoe-in. He'd been sucking up to Sgt. Foltz all year just for that very reason.

The only question that remained was who'd be the other captain? No one really seemed to stand out any more than the rest. So there was still tension in the air when Sgt. Foltz called drills to a stop and gathered all forty-two of us in a loose circle around him. Marcus was already talking assuredly, informing those he intended to be on his team his plans, shunning those he didn't.

"We're doing things a little differently this year. Dean Erikson informed me just today that he intended to pick the team leaders personally."

Marcus's smile disappeared; a year of brown-nosing completely wasted. It was anyone's ball game.

"Chad Johnson," Mr. Hall read off the folded piece of paper in front of him. "You will be in charge of platoon Alpha. Please begin assembling your team and formulating your strategy."

Chad, a nobody before that day, was suddenly thrown into the spotlight. He was beside himself. Marcus was quickly forgotten as the throng gathered around him, hoping to be the first selected.

I knew what was coming before Mr. Hall opened his mouth. Dean Erikson was more astute than I'd given him credit for. Surely he must've known that would be the highest form of torture for me.

"Joel Cranston." Everyone stopped their clamoring at the mention of my name. "You will be leader of platoon Bravo. Please begin assembling your team and formulating your strategy."

No one moved, certainly not towards me. If anything, people slowly shifted towards Chad. They'd been holding out for the announcement of the second team leader, but now that it had been made they quietly made their way closer to him.

Chad quickly began selecting his group. Marcus was chosen first, of course, removing some of the sting.

Within minutes, Chad had the cream of the crop: the most athletic, most outspoken, most gifted students in the junior class. I didn't make a move as he quickly selected his platoon, afraid I'd try to snatch someone he wanted. By the time he was done, twenty guys stood in the center of the gym, un-chosen. The rejects. I had my team.

"Now that the teams have been chosen, the details of the competition will be discussed with the team captains. Everyone else is dismissed."

Chad and I followed Mr. Hall into a small office attached to the gym. We sat in two chairs as he fumbled through a stack of papers lying on his overcrowded desk. The entire room was disorganized, with files and papers spread everywhere. Finally, he found what he'd been looking for. He sat down on his chair and began reading the rules of the game.

"Two team leaders—that would be the two of you—must divide the class in half to form their platoons—that we just did." His dull voice droned on. "The exercise will take place in the outdoor training field, the last weekend before spring recess, from Friday zero nine hundred hours being completed by Monday at zero nine hundred hours. On the Monday prior, each team leader must submit a list of articles needed for his platoon no later than seventeen hundred. These requests will be made directly to the supply officer. No further requests may be made after that time. All supplies must be obtained and prepped on Thursday by twenty hundred, no exceptions."

He fumbled with some more papers on his desk, until he found the one he must've been looking for.

"Okay, here it is: THE OBJECT OF THE GAME. The primary objective is to obtain the opposing team's cylinder. These cylinders will be distributed to the team captains on Thursday evening by Dean Erikson to be returned to the Dean at zero nine hundred on Monday. It is your mission to guard and defend your team's cylinder, while at the same time attempting to acquire the opposition's. While this is the primary objective, it has never occurred in this school's history. Therefore, the winning team will be determined by the number of captured forces. Whoever is in possession of the most prisoners of war by Monday at zero nine hundred will be the winning team."

"What do we win?" Chad interrupted, his eyes blazing.

Mr. Hall paused for a second before reading the rest, "The rewards for completing the primary objective: to open the cylinder and retrieve the award that is inside, as well as a pizza party and an 'A' letter grade for the entire platoon. The prize for obtaining the secondary objective is the same minus the opening of the cylinder. Do you have any questions, gentlemen?"

Sir, no sir, I jokingly wanted to answer, just seconds before Chad actually did. I sighed to myself; *it's going to be a long six weeks.*

"Good luck, gentlemen. Plan well, plan wisely."

Mr. Hall saluted us as we left. I hoped the Dean was enjoying himself. I started to think about that envelope again, but my mind was made up; I would just have to live in my own personal hell.

Marcus was in the dorm room when I walked in later that night. I'd gone to the woods behind Lambert instead of going to his game. I doubt I was missed.

In fact, after that day, my absence was more than welcome, and not just by him, although he was the most obvious. He wasn't pretending anymore; his hatred was right there, out in the open, which was the way it was to be with us from then on.

Actually, it was a relief. I disliked him as much as he did me. It was better without the pretenses.

Steven was, as always, on his upper bunk reading. He'd had the misfortune of being one of the twenty guys left that Chad hadn't picked, which meant he was on my platoon. I felt sorry for him, for all of them. It wasn't fair that they had to be punished along with me. I was no leader.

chapter forty-two/ laying a claim

Mortal! That call'st the flowers of life, think not to escape the thorn.
　　–William B. Tappan

Nathan was beside himself with all the new data he'd gathered on his subject. I don't know how, but he'd even managed to get a piece of Joel's hair. He'd found an old microscope and was trying to examine it. I went to my room and tried to pretend we weren't related.

School on Monday started out normal. I had a paper due on Hamlet that afternoon, so most of my morning was spent working on it. My teachers were used to my silent silhouette in the back row, so I usually didn't have to worry about them calling on me. It was my way of making my own study hall.

Nothing appeared different until my sixth period Geometry class.

The class was full when I got there, which was typical. But my seat way in the back was empty. I made my way towards it and sat down. English was my next class, which meant I needed to focus. I leaned over and started working on my final draft.

My stupid hair kept falling in my face, so I reached into my pocket and pulled out a rubber band. I only looked up briefly to gather my hair back, but it was long enough.

Every single person in the room was turned in their seats, and they were looking at me.

"What?" I asked, to no one in particular.

"Do you know the answer or not?"

My eyes lifted to Mr. Bernard, my Geometry teacher. He was standing in the front of the class, staring as intently as everyone else.

It didn't even look like him. Mr. Bernard was your usual middle aged, overweight math teacher. He never said anything that wasn't boring and math related, at least not to us. But that day, as I looked at him, I knew math was the last thing he was talking about, no matter what he'd said.

"Could you repeat the question?" I asked, my voice cracking.

"It seems that Miss Newell has better things to do than pay attention in class. Isn't that right, everyone?" He wasn't looking at the rest of them as their heads bobbled mindlessly up and down; he was only looking at me. I felt myself shrinking back into my chair.

"Maybe Miss Newell has too much time on her hands. What do you think we should do about that?"

My mouth was suddenly dry. My mind raced, trying to calculate how I could possibly get past all of them. I wasn't very fast, or strong.

"We can be anywhere, Rachel. Remember that," he said before turning slowly back to the chalkboard. The rest of them turned around, just a second after he did.

My knees started shaking, then my hands. My eyes flicked around the room looking for something safe to rest on. I couldn't bring myself to look at them, even though I knew whatever it was, was gone. They'd given their message.

There was a window right by my seat, so I looked out that.

Usually, all there was out that particular window was the football field with the Green Mountains in the distance.

But nothing about that day was usual.

He was there, right outside the window, the one who had started it all. He waited until my eyes locked with his ice blue ones and then he smiled before turning to walk away. I heard a scream in the distance that sounded faintly like mine. And then everything went black.

rachel

chapter forty-three/ in-between

It is better to light a candle than curse the darkness.
    -Eleanor Roosevelt

It was dark. There was nothing there but a tick, tick, tick that kept going on and on.

Another sound came, louder than the ticks, "Rachel, can you hear me?" It was a woman's voice.

My eyes flicked open. I didn't realize they'd been closed. There was a woman standing over me; she looked worried. I wanted to tell her not to be worried. Everything was going to be fine.

"Rachel, I'm the nurse. Do you want to tell me what happened?"

Her words were very slow and repeated over and over again. *What happened?* I couldn't remember.

"Rachel, I think I need to call your parents."

My parents. That's what happened. My parents were in the church when the fire started. They didn't make it.

I heard her voice in the distance. "June, go get her file. Find out her parent's number."

My parent's numbers. November sixth was my mother's birthday. My father's was May eighth, but she was gone again before I could tell her.

rachel

chapter forty-four/ reasons

Don't be afraid to see what you see.
   -Ronald Reagan

"Rachel?"
I knew that voice. I opened my eyes.
Nathan.
He was standing over me. *What is Nathan doing here?* Nathan never left the trailer.
   "She's been like that for a little over an hour. Do you want me to call her doctor?" It was the woman's voice again.
   "No, I'll just take her home."
Nathan's arms slid under my shoulder blades as he tried to help me sit up. I took a deep breath in as I looked around the room. I was in the nurse's office, the same one I'd been at before, after I found out about the Nephilim.
   The Nephilim. It came back to me then, all of it.
   After I was sitting, Nathan wrapped his arm around my waist and tried to pull me up. He wasn't getting very far, so I stood up on my own. It was time to go home.
   We walked to the truck, his arms wrapped around me and mine wrapped around him, as everyone stared at us. If I looked

anything like Nathan, I could understand why.

He opened the door to the truck for me and I let go of him and slid myself in. He got in on his side and pulled out without saying anything. We drove through Weston, but I didn't see any of it. My foot pressed hard against the floorboard.

Go. Go. Go. The words ran through my mind over and over again.

But Nathan didn't go. Instead, he turned off the main road towards the lane that led to our trailer, and still my foot pressed on the floor.

It didn't ease up until Nathan parked the truck right by the trailer, like he always did. I grabbed the door handle.

"Wait."

I turned to look at Nathan, who was still sitting in his seat, staring out the window.

"What is it?" It wasn't like Nathan to linger.

"Was it bad?" He turned to look at me.

I could only nod.

He nodded too, and I knew he was thinking about his own time with them, in their woods.

"What happened, Nathan?"

For some reason, that time he answered me. "I was in the wilderness. It was beginning to get dark. The sun was setting and I was thinking about going home. It'd been almost a day since I had left and I still hadn't seen anything. Then I heard them. The drumming. They were a large group, but they were still a ways away from me, and at first they were too intent on what they were doing to notice me there. They weren't alone. There was a young girl dressed in white being carried by one of them. At first I thought she was asleep, or dead, she was so still. But then later…I knew she wasn't."

He closed his eyes. "The drumming got louder and then the screaming began."

"And then?" I whispered.

"And then it stopped. And then something else started. Something...Something no one should see. Ever."

"Please don't tell me about it." I didn't think I could take any more.

Nathan nodded and then looked away.

A thought occurred to me. "But didn't you say they knew you were there? How did you get away?"

Nathan's voice began again, a dead voice, "After they were done with the girl, the drumming started again and they turned towards where I was hiding, and I knew I was next. I don't know how I knew, but I did. I don't think I've ever been so scared in my whole life, especially since I just saw...." He stopped talking and looked at me. I shook my head.

"Anyway, it doesn't matter because I was moved before they could get to me. I was taken to the base of the mountain. That's where I spent my last night, and that's where I was told what they were."

"Who moved you? Who told you what they were?"

Before he said it, I knew he wasn't going to tell me. "I'm sorry, Rachel, but I was told not to tell anyone, not even you."

I nodded. "Then why didn't we move after that first night?"

"I already told you, we have a purpose here, and we're not leaving until it's done."

I nodded again and gripped the handle, pushing the door open before Nathan could say anything else. He might be staying because of his duty, but there was only one reason I was willing to stay: Joel.

chapter forty-five/ a decision is made

A kiss can be a comma, a question mark or an exclamation point. That's basic spelling that every woman ought to know.
   -Mistinguett

The door was locked. I pushed again, just to make sure, but it wouldn't budge.

What the freak?

I took a step back.

Fred's was completely dark. That wasn't all that unusual. Fred sometimes went back to his office and didn't bother with the lights. But he usually unlocked the door for me.

Unless he isn't here.

My eyes went to the rock where I'd put the keys Sunday night. *He couldn't. He wouldn't.*

He did.

The keys were still there, right where I'd left them. *Does that mean Fred wasn't here on Monday, either?*

I couldn't imagine that.

The door opened easily enough that time. The key helped. My first stop was Fred's office to see if my suspicions were right. His door was closed, and no Fred appeared when I knocked on it.

I backed away from the door. *What could've possibly happened to keep Fred away?*

I had no idea.

My eyes scanned the darkened kitchen, deciding. It would've been so easy just to back-up and leave; pretend I hadn't come in. *I mean if Fred can do it...*

I sighed and went to the fridge and grabbed a block of cheese. I wasn't working for Fred, anyhow.

When I was done with my usual prep-work, I walked into the dining room to wait for four-thirty to come. After the clock went there and then past, I sat down on one of the stools that lined the counter and thought about some things. Mainly, I thought about Joel and if I should tell him what I knew about Newstead. As far as I could tell, he had no idea about any of it. He didn't even flinch when I'd asked him about his father.

I decided he deserved to know; if there was something like that going on with my parents, I'd want to know about it.

美人
rachel

chapter forty-six/ indecisive

Indecision may or may not be my problem.
-Jimmy Buffet

The bell above the front door didn't ring until six-thirty. It was a long time to be alone.

I stood up as soon as I heard it and went to the kitchen to make our pizza. I knew it'd be better if I told him after he had food in his stomach. It was in the oven before he could poke his head around the swinging door to see where I was.

His shoulders were slumped over, making him look older somehow, and tired. Something was off. Joel never looked worn out like that.

"What's wrong?"

"That obvious?" he asked quietly as he pulled me into a light hug.

"To me," I whispered into his chest.

"Let's just say it's been a long couple of days," he answered, drawing back, attempting a smile that didn't reach his tired eyes.

"Want to talk about it?"

"Maybe later." He opened the oven door and spied the pizza I had baking inside. The smell had given my secret away. That time the smile reached his eyes.

"Rache, you always know just what I need." He pulled me close for another brief hug before walking past me to get our plates.

We both went to our new place, the small prep table by the fryers. Not that we couldn't have had our choice of any table in the dining room. It was completely empty; had been all night. I was beginning to think it was more than a fluke. Whatever the reason, I was grateful. It would be better if none of them were there when I told Joel.

I was about to say it, honestly I was, but something in his eyes stopped me.

"What happened?" I asked.

He hesitated at first, like he wasn't sure if he wanted to answer me. And then he did.

"I was chosen to lead an upcoming training exercise. It was completely unexpected and is much more challenging than I had first thought," he said robotically, not meeting my eyes.

There was something he wasn't telling me. I was about to call him on it, but he turned to me, and his tired eyes were pleading. So I didn't talk about that, either. Instead, I pretended to look interested as I asked him about his training exercise.

His face brightened; I'd clearly chosen a safe topic. "Have you ever played Capture the Flag or Eagle's Nest?"

"Never heard of either," I replied, waiting for him to continue.

"They're both the same, just with different names. It just depends on which summer camp your mom sent you to. Basically, each team is given a flag or an egg in the case of Eagle's Nest. The object is to try to capture the opposing team's flag, or egg." He saw my confused face and dumbed it down for me. "Mostly it's just an excuse for a bunch of guys to spend three nights out in the woods and play war." He laughed lightly.

I shuddered. "What does that mean?"

Joel's laughter cut off. "First, I had to pick my team of twenty guys. Now, I need to somehow plan a strategy to get their flag without losing mine. It actually could be a lot of fun, if there wasn't so much pressure attached to it." He looked away again, avoiding my eyes.

"When is this happening?" *Nathan needs to know about this.*

"The end of April, right before the two week recess."

I swallowed hard. "Two week recess?" The thought of their war games slipped completely from my mind.

"Yeah, after every trimester the school breaks for two weeks for us to go home to see our families." His eyes narrowed at the sudden blankness on my face.

"You're going home?"

Understanding slowly spread across his face as he realized what he'd been saying. The tired look came back, with something more, something like dread.

"I have to go, Rache. It's only for two weeks. My mom would kill me if I didn't go home. It's all she can talk about in her letters."

He ducked his head down so he could look at me, but I turned away and picked up my pizza again. After a few seconds, he picked up his, too.

There was plenty of dead air space for me to bring up Newstead, but I didn't; if I told him then, it would sound pathetic—a weak attempt to keep him there.

If he even believed me in the first place.

"Where's Fred?" Joel asked as I picked up our plates and carried them over to the sink.

"I don't know," I answered.

We walked out of the kitchen together and both of us looked around the dining room. It was as empty as it had been when I'd first walked in.

"Are you still going to stay open until eight?"

"I don't know," I said again. Joel looked at me briefly, then walked over to the sign and flipped it over.

"Do you have any closing work left to do?" he asked.

"There's really no point; it's just been me here."

He nodded and went into the kitchen again. A little while later he came back out with my jacket and backpack.

"Let's go."

chapter forty-seven/ unsure

Fear is excitement without breath.
    -Robert Heller

Joel stopped suddenly. I only knew that because I was jerked backwards when the hand I was holding wasn't moving forward anymore.

"What?" I turned back around to look at him. He was staring intently at me.

"What do you want from life, Rachel?"

It took me a minute to reorient myself. "I don't know. I guess I haven't given it much thought. Why?"

"What about us? What is it you want to come out of this?"

"I haven't given that much thought, either." I paused and then said *some* of what had been filling my brain for the last half hour: "I know I love you and I don't want you to leave me."

His face went white.

I reached out my hand to his arm. "Are you all right?" He didn't look all right.

He swallowed hard. "Never better."

He grabbed my hand again and started walking straight for my trailer. I stumbled for the first few steps as my legs tried to keep up. Joel didn't seem to notice as his arm just dragged me along.

He stopped again, only that time it was at the slight bend in the lane before my trailer came into sight. I knew the drill. I turned to face him and waited for my kiss.

I'd just stopped when his arms wrapped tightly around me and his lips came crushing down on mine. It was a frantic, needful thing that was over as quickly as it started.

"Will I see you tomorrow?" I asked breathlessly when he released me.

"Yes, you will," he answered, in a voice that I didn't recognize.

He turned to leave, not even bothering to walk me the last hundred feet to the trailer. I stood still and watched him go until I couldn't see him anymore.

And still, I stood there. The forest felt very dark and not very empty as I looked where Joel had gone. *We can be anywhere, remember that.* That's what he'd said. My hands went to my mouth that was still warm from his kiss.

But what if it wasn't his kiss?

I turned and ran to the trailer.

chapter forty-eight/ locked

There are times when fear is good. It must keep its watchful place at the heart's controls.

-Aeschylus

I sat on the stairs and waited. I tried to hurry it along. I even took a few deep breaths, but there was no rushing it. I knew I needed to be completely calm before I went inside. I wasn't ready yet to tell Nathan about my suspicions.

My hands went to my mouth again. *No, it was Joel; maybe a part of him I've never seen before, but it was him.* I nodded my head as I tried to convince the rest of myself. By the time I opened the door to my trailer I was almost there.

Aunt Beth slammed into me and I stumbled backwards. We both ended up on the steps, her on top of me, scrambling to get past. Her eyes were frantic, wild, darting here and there, but always looking in the same direction; the lane that led back into town.

Nathan appeared a second later and grabbed her by the waist and dragged her back into the trailer. She thrashed like a wild animal, but Nathan's wiry arms held firm.

She got like that sometimes. I have no idea why.

"Need any help?" I asked as I pulled myself up.

"No, we're fine," Nathan called out breathlessly. He'd gotten her to the couch.

I walked towards my room, staying as far away from them as I could, but her legs still managed to get in a few good kicks.

When I got there I flipped on the light and changed into my pajamas. There were a few bangs followed by the trailer swaying slightly. I pulled down the covers and climbed into bed. Another bang followed by a dull thud. I reached up my hand and locked my bedroom door.

Silence.

My hand reached up again to check, to make sure it was really locked.

chapter forty-nine/ the shunning

In war, practice dissimulation, and you will succeed.
  -Sun Tzu, *the Art of War*

I walked home from Rachel's very slowly. I didn't want to get back to Newstead before I absolutely had to. The last twenty-four hours had shown me that wouldn't be a good idea.

I woke up that Tuesday to the noise level I'd grown used to at Chapman. It actually sounded good to me. The quietness of the weekend had gotten to me more than I wanted to admit. Even Monday had been quiet, but thankfully, it felt like on Tuesday things were getting back to normal, at least the Newstead normal.

I got out of bed and showered and shaved. It didn't dawn on me that I was being ignored until I walked into the mess hall. I'd gotten there before most of them, so there were still plenty of tables to choose from. I filled my tray and sat down at one that had a few guys sitting at it. As soon as I was sitting, they stood up and went to another table.

My face burned. I tried to focus all my attention on my tray and pretend I didn't notice, but that was impossible.

I watched as the last few stragglers made their way in, to see what they would do. There were no more seats left, except for the seven empty ones right around me. Without missing a beat, they filled their trays and walked out of the mess hall to eat somewhere else.

I turned back to my eggs.

After about half the guys had left the hall, I stood up and threw out what was left of my breakfast and headed to my first class. Each class was like the mess hall all over again. I sat down, people moved. The teachers didn't even mention it: the sea of empty desks that surrounded me.

In Leadership, we'd moved to the training field, where the actual FTX would be taking place. It was a dense forest, a little over four hundred acres that butted right up to the Green Mountains.

I waited for the rest of my class by the bunker, which was where we were supposed to meet that day, or at least that's what they'd told me. After fifteen minutes of no one showing up, I headed into the forest to find out where the rest of them were.

I didn't see anyone, at least not at first. There was nothing but a lot of trees and the normal things you'd expect to see in a forest.

"Get down," my voice suddenly said. I dropped to the ground and belly crawled behind a tree.

Nothing happened at first, and then I heard voices coming from a bush that was just a few feet from where I was crouching.

"Do you see him?" one of them asked.

"No. I told you, he's probably still back at the training building."

"How long are we supposed to wait here?"

"Until he comes by."

"What makes you think he's coming?"

"They've set it up so he will."

"Okay, and then what?"

"You know what."

It was utterly silent for several minutes. My voice didn't need to tell me they were talking about me; I'd already figured that one out all on my own. I dropped to my belly again and crawled along the ground until I was some distance from the bush with the voices.

As soon as I was out of the training field, I walked to the bunker to find out what they were planning on doing to lure me into the woods.

There was a group of six guys standing right where I'd been just ten minutes before. They looked up when they heard me.

"Joel, there you are. Sgt. Foltz wanted us to wait for you," one of them said. His name was Anthony.

"What for?" I asked.

"For class, what else?" He started laughing, but it was a nervous laughter.

Five sets of eyes looked up as we heard more footsteps approaching in the distance. Only me and Anthony didn't look; we were too busy staring at each other.

"Joel."

I turned first. It was Steven's voice.

"Yes?"

"Come with me."

I paused a minute to see if my voice had an issue with that, but after nothing but silence I turned and went with him. He didn't lead me to the woods. Instead, I followed him back to our room. He climbed onto his bed and picked up a book like he normally did. I stood at the door and watched him.

"What was that all about?"

There was only silence from the upper bunk.

"Steven?"

Still nothing. Then very quietly I heard him whisper, "Don't go to Leadership for a while."

I nodded; I don't know if it was to him or to me.

That day I discovered one thing: Whatever plot there was against me, Steven wasn't in on it.

chapter fifty/ the art of war

So in war, the way is to avoid what is strong and to strike at what is weak.
-Sun Tzu, *the Art of War*

The next morning was no better. I purposely set my alarm late to avoid at least one of my roommates. Marcus was gone by the time it went off. Steven was still there, but he'd gone back to being silent.

I went to the mess hall and grabbed a few boxes of cereal before heading back to my room. For lunch it was the same thing, only sandwiches.

I half-expected to be called into Erikson's office again for skipping Leadership, but nothing was ever said to me. It went along with everything else my life had become. It'd taken a while, but Goliath finally found me. I was invisible.

Western Civ. was my second to last class of the day. When it was over, all of us stood and walked out in a line towards the training field for Leadership. I followed as far as the fountain, and then turned to go towards my room. A couple guys at the end of the line turned to look at me. It was the first time that day anyone had made eye contact. I stood by the fountain and waited, watching them. There was disappointment there, and something else, something I'd get to know much better in the coming days. They both shook their heads in unison and turned to catch up with the rest of them.

I watched until they were past the bunker and then started for my room again. My foot had just set down on the landing at Chapman when my voice decided to make an appearance.

"Go to the library," it said. So I did. I didn't have any better ideas, and it was still too early to go to Fred's.

I'd never been in Newstead's library before. I'd never been in *any* library before. Right away, I noticed the difference from the rest of the buildings there. The furniture was still scaled large, but not the rooms; they were all small and there were lots of them. It was almost like a maze.

I made my way through it, not really knowing what I was looking for. The voice hadn't said anything, just that I should go. Eventually, I came to the last room. It had big windows overlooking the training field. I sat down in one of the leather chairs that lined the rectangular table in the center of the room and looked at that field. In about five weeks it would be me out there.

Even though I couldn't see them, I felt them, all of them, as if they were looking right back at me.

That's ridiculous. But even as the words were running through my head, my eyes shifted away from that window to the bookshelves that lined the walls. They were filled with identical brown ledgers, all of them, except one. My eyes narrowed in on a small black book wedged in-between the sea of brown. I could just reach it from where I was sitting.

I pulled it out and thumbed through it. It was a paperback copy of the Art of War. I glanced back at the field. I knew where I needed to go and what I needed to do.

By the time I passed the fountain, I was running.

The river was loud again. It wasn't always, but it was that day as I sat on my rock and read every page of my book. For the first time since I'd been assigned as the captain of team Bravo I started to get excited.

chapter fifty-one/ blacklisted

How victory may be produced out of the enemy's own
tactics—that is what the multitude cannot comprehend.
        -Sun Tzu, *the Art of War*

Rachel was standing outside Fred's waiting for me.

"What's up?" I asked, worried.

"It was slow again, so I closed early," she said as she took my
hand.

"I'm sorry. You weren't waiting there long, were you?" I didn't
want to picture her standing out in the cold, alone.

"No, I just locked up a few minutes ago," she replied lightly,
beginning to pull me in the direction of her trailer.

"Do you need to get home right away?" I asked as a thought
suddenly formed in my head.

"What did you have in mind?"

"Would you like to go on a date with me?" I asked, trying not
to sound too stupid.

She smiled.

I pulled her back towards town as we checked out our options.
The town only had three other restaurants besides Fred's. One
was a snobby place for rich people, and the other two were

dives just like Fred's was.

We tried the first one—Janice's Diner. For some reason crappy restaurants are always named after people. It was packed. Rachel and I looked quizzically at each other before moving on to the next one. Green Mountain Family Restaurant, right across the street, was also crowded. A guy who was waiting outside told us it would be about thirty minutes. We kept walking.

That left The Bistro, the richy-rich place just before you left town. *Maybe we can share an appetizer.*

The place was as empty as Fred's had been. We sat down at a table and looked at the menus the waitress dressed all in white had handed to us. I shifted uncomfortably in my seat until she came back and told us about the specials. They were better.

The dim candlelight on the table flickered gently as Rachel rubbed her arms in discomfort; we were both very underdressed. Luckily, there was no one there to compare ourselves with.

"Why do you think Fred's was so dead and those other places were packed?" It was the obvious question that was baffling both of us, or so I thought.

"Seeing that huge guy back there scared me. I thought it was *him,* but then he turned around, and I knew it wasn't. That's when I realized I haven't seen a Newsteader besides you since..." She flushed, then continued, "Last Friday night."

At first I thought she hadn't heard me, or was trying to change the subject. Then her meaning became crystal clear. Not only had she answered the what, she went one step further and answered the why.

Usually, Fred's was swamped with overbearing, obnoxious guys: Newstead guys. But not since my birthday; not since that night.

Has Fred's been blacklisted?

I suddenly felt way over my head. There was too much going on that I didn't know, that I didn't *want* to know. My hand hovered over my pocket that had the cash in it. It would be so easy to just go, and at that point I think they would've let me. Not later, of course, but at that point I was still relatively clueless. That was the problem.

"It's not time yet."

I don't know why my head snapped up to look at Rachel. The voice wasn't hers. It wasn't anyone's. It was a waterfall at full force that somehow formed words.

It was a voice of dreams, or nightmares, rather.

chapter fifty-two/ insane

The onrush of a conquering force is like bursting of pent-up waters into a chasm a thousand fathoms deep.
  -Sun Tzu, *the Art of War*

Crazy is a state of being. In that moment, I was certifiable. Either the memory of the water voice or the voice itself—I really don't know which one—filled my head over and over until I was swimming in it. My hands went to my head to hold it all together, but it wasn't enough. I was coming undone.

Somehow in all that chaos, I heard it: a soft pulling in of a breath. I listened very carefully for it to be let out, and after a couple seconds, it was. I focused on those breaths and as I did, the voice faded to the background. I lowered my hands from the sides of my head and forced them to lie flat on my legs. Only then did I open my eyes to look at the girl staring warily at me from across the table.

I knew I needed to say something, anything that would distract both of us. It worked too well. By the end of the night, the last thing I was worried about was that voice.

"What has Nathan been up to?" I asked slowly, carefully. I thought I'd picked a safe topic, but Rachel's eyebrows furrowed closer together as soon as the words were out of my mouth.

"Nathan has been very busy with his mother lately," she answered vaguely.

I tried to remember the old woman lying passively on the couch and wondered what trouble she could possibly cause. Unless incontinence was trouble, which, in its own way, I suppose it was. The way the place smelled I could hardly believe it was something new for her.

"How's that?" I continued, despite the absent look on Rachel's face.

"I really don't know what's wrong with her. She's never acted this aggressive before, at least not for this long. But it's been going on for almost two days."

"Aggressive?" My head started to pound again.

"Yes, aggressive. Not violent or anything." She looked away. "Just unsettled; Nathan doesn't know what to make of it, either."

Rachel began rubbing absently at her neck with her free hand, but she still wasn't looking at me, so I couldn't tell if she was telling me everything or not. She spent the next couple minutes staring at her glass of water, so I decided to do her a favor and change the subject.

"What makes you guys move around so much? Haven't you found a place you like yet?" Surely moving had to be safe; it was something she did often enough.

"Nathan just likes to move," she said cautiously.

"And...?"

"And every three to four months he just decides it's time to move, that's all," she answered smoothly, lifting her intelligent eyes to mine.

"But didn't you say you've already been here for a little over six months?" The discrepancy confused me.

"Yes, I did," she answered.

"Then you think you'll be moving any time now, don't you?"

She looked away, giving me all the answer I needed. Rachel would be leaving anyhow. I couldn't think of any reason left to stay, except a nagging in my gut that told me I needed to.

The waitress came back and dropped off our meals. She put my plate in front of me and I looked down at it and thought about it being perfect timing or something like that, something about being glad I had time to think things over. It must've been about Newstead; if I should stay or go; that's the only explanation for what happened next.

Pounding, like drumming, filled my brain, going faster and faster until it became one huge explosion. My hands went to my head again as my eyes slammed shut, expecting pain, but that's not what it was at all.

It was like being born. That's the only way I can describe it. Who I was before wasn't lost. I was still me, but after that final beat of the drum I was plunged into air and I breathed in long and deep.

I had begun.

My mind race forward, gathering data to answer the question I must've asked: Should I stay at Newstead?

Completely analytical, my mind did not have room for emotions as it weighed the benefits versus the costs. Rachel was the only thing on the benefit side, but there was an asterisk next to her name, signifying she was only there temporarily.

"There are more reasons than just Rachel," the water voice added. It was clearer than before; less water, more man. I could listen to it without feeling like my brain was getting scrambled.

"And they are?" I asked back in my mind.

"You forgot about the Cylinder; you'll get all the answers you need from that."

Where have I heard of a cylinder before? I wondered as my mind surged forward. In a fraction of a second I had an answer: FTX.

I was about to argue the impossibility of it, when I heard the water voice one last time. I will be with you it said.

Great, I thought. *All I need is another hallucination hanging around.*

I opened my eyes and looked at Rachel. She lifted her fork to her mouth and slowly chewed and then swallowed her food. She picked up her glass of water and took a sip and placed it back on the table. I wondered what she was thinking.

Chapter fifty-three/ aunt beth

Courage is resistance to fear, mastery of fear, not absence of fear.

   –Mark Twain

It was dark in the trailer when I walked in. Aunt Beth was lying on the couch with Nathan snoring on the floor parallel to her. I closed the door quietly and as I did, Aunt Beth sat up and looked straight at me. I didn't like the way her eyes looked.

Those eyes followed me as I quickly made my way to my room. I locked the door behind me. Then I pushed my small dresser in front of it for good measure.

I sat down on my bed and listened. It was completely still. And then I heard it: my knob scratching against the back of my dresser as it turned first to the left and then to the right.

It clicked as the lock released.

I jumped up and placed both hands on the door to brace against it.

My feet slid along the carpet as the door inched open until there was no carpet left.

Time for plan B. I wedged my feet against the wall for leverage and pushed with all I had.

The door slammed shut.

I left one hand on the door and gripped onto the dresser with the other. In my mind it was so simple; I'd swing the dresser around and push it up against that door thereby blocking her way in.

Things in life are never as simple as they are in your mind.

The door flew open, knocking the dresser and me to the floor.

She stood in the opening and the brightness in her eyes was the same as before, only this time she wasn't looking out towards the woods. This time she was looking at me.

I scrambled to my feet and scanned the room, looking for something, anything.

There was a window along the wall. It was small, but so was I. Her eyes flicked towards it, like she knew what I was thinking.

But it was the only chance I had, so I took a step in that direction, hoping she wouldn't notice. She smiled and took a step of her own. That was repeated a few times over, not as many as you might think; there's only so much space in my room. Her eyes shone with a brilliant intensity as I took my last step, the one that had me pressed up against the wall, with only her looming in front of me. I stood still, waiting, knowing it was inevitable.

But I was wrong.

Arms; thin, beautiful, wiry arms gripped around her waist and dragged her backwards out into the hall. She thrashed the entire time, but those arms never let go. My door slammed shut.

"Stay in there, Rachel." It was Nathan's voice.

I wasn't sure if he meant not to go out into the hall or not to go out my window. I did neither.

I lifted up my dresser and put the drawers back in. I picked up some of the clothes that had spilled out. I did a lot of things, but really, I was listening. It was strangely quiet. But eventually I heard a sound, and it was coming from right outside my door. It was a sound I instantly recognized: Nathan's soft snoring. He'd repositioned himself on the floor in the hall, right outside my room.

I fell asleep that night listening to that sound.

I woke up to a different one. It was Aunt Beth, and she was shrieking. She almost didn't sound human.

There was a loud knock on my door. I looked towards my window.

"Rachel?"

I walked over to the door, ready to brace it again.

"Yes?" I whispered. I don't know why I bothered; it was a small trailer. I'm sure Aunt Beth could hear me no matter where she was.

"I'm going to open the door. Have your clothes ready and go right into the bathroom."

I didn't know what he was talking about, and then it hit me. He still expected me to go to school, like it was just any other day, like we didn't have a deranged lunatic in our trailer.

"Rachel, did you hear me?" He sounded worried.

"I heard you. Just give me a minute to get my clothes together."

I opened my drawer and grabbed whatever was on top. I had no idea if it even matched, but at least it was clean.

"I'm ready," I said, but really I wasn't. I never wanted to go out that door again.

There was still yelling, but it sounded like it was coming from the other end of the trailer. My bedroom door abruptly opened, and Nathan yanked me out of my room and pushed me into the bathroom across the hall. The door closed the instant I was in. The screams didn't sound that far away anymore.

I turned on the shower and tried to drown them out. Singing helped, a little. But I couldn't stay in the shower forever, especially because our holding tank was only forty gallons. Our water heater was even smaller, so after a couple minutes, the usual cold water replaced the warm. I knew it was time to get out.

"Are you ready?" he asked after giving me a couple minutes to brush my hair and teeth.

"What's your plan?" I asked. I doubted he could pull the same maneuver that had gotten me into the bathroom in the first place. The trailer wasn't huge, but the front door was pretty far from the bathroom.

"I'm going to hold onto her and I want you to make a run for it. And Rachel?"

"Yes?"

"Don't look back."

I nodded, but I knew he couldn't see that.

I gripped the door handle and it spun in my hand. I dried my palm on my jeans and tried one more time. The door swung open.

Nathan was nowhere in sight; neither was Aunt Beth. I took a deep breath in and ran for the front door, and I almost made it. Her hand shot out of the darkness and grabbed onto my shoulder. Thin arms appeared around her again, but she didn't let go; if anything, she gripped harder as her nails dug deep into my flesh. Nathan pulled back and her nails tore along my arm as she gave up her hold on me.

"Go!" Nathan yelled. I went. It wasn't until I was outside that I realized I'd forgotten my jacket.

I looked at the trailer door. *There's no way in hell I'm going back in there. I'd rather freeze.*

And I did, all the way to school.

rachel

chapter fifty-four/ alone/not alone

Fear tastes like a rusty knife and do not let her into your house.
-John Cheever

It was still early when I got there. The parking lot was empty and the school looked dark and deserted. Normally I would've waited outside, but normally I would've had a coat on. So I tried one of the doors, just in case someone had forgotten to lock it. It turned easily in my hand. Without thinking about how strange that was, I went inside.

Weston High School is made up of five old buildings all connected by long hallways. They just stuck a gym on one end and called it a school. It's known to the locals as the Haunted Mansion, and that's exactly what it felt like it as I walked past all the ornately carved doors that for some reason didn't look anything like they did with the lights on.

I stopped to peek in my Biology classroom, mainly to assure myself that's what it was.

All our desks were just how we'd left them. I could even picture Mr. Haynes at the front with his slide projector. It was just a classroom.

A foot quietly stepped down somewhere behind me. My breath held, but a second footstep never came. I ran.

chapter fifty-five/ crushed

Throughout life people will make you mad, disrespect you and treat you bad. Let God deal with the things they do, cause hate in your heart will consume you too.
    -Will Smith

All buildings come to an end, even those that have five of them stuck together.

It came to an end for me at the front door, the main entrance. I ran right up until I slammed into that door, gripping the handle, clawing it. Pulling with all I had.

That one was locked.

I slowly turned around, expecting to see someone right behind me; there wasn't; just shadows. For some reason that felt worse.

My eyes went to the large staircase in the middle of the hall. Going up was my only option.

I slid along the wall, staying in the shadows. Every few seconds I stopped to listen. There were no more footsteps. I couldn't decide if that was a good thing or not.

And then I heard it: a soft creak of a floorboard and then a pause. Someone else was listening, too.

I wasn't going to make it up those stairs. My eyes scanned the room for a place to hide.

Nothing.

And then I saw a small opening at the base of the stairs. The majority of the space under them had been converted into storage, but not the few feet that were directly underneath the first three steps. Without thinking about what I was doing, I dove headfirst into that small opening.

I closed my eyes and held my breath and waited.

It was completely quiet until it wasn't. Another floorboard creaked, that one was directly over my head.

I opened my eyes. The stripe of light that filtered down was interrupted by one large shoe. That shoe didn't move.

The floorboard sunk deeper until it was pressing on my forehead.

I closed my eyes and tried to quiet my breathing as the board pressed lower and lower, crushing me.

A low moan escaped my throat. *I'm going to die*.

There was quiet laughter as the shoe lifted off the step and the floorboard sprang back up. The footsteps went the rest of the way up the stairs.

I let out a very long, very deep breath.

chapter fifty-six/ remembering

Trust, but verify.
   -Ronald Reagan

As soon as the footsteps had faded, I shimmied around until my feet were where my head had just been.

I could live without feet.

Not that I thought he was coming back. I knew he wasn't. If he'd wanted to kill me, he would've done it.

No, he's saving that for Joel.

I closed my eyes as that traitor thought made its way in. I'd promised myself I wouldn't think about it, but it was inevitable, even if I wasn't forced into it with all the extra time I suddenly had.

It started when Joel took me out to dinner. It didn't go very well. Not the dinner, that was fine, it was more the way Joel was acting. He was all right at first, a little confused about what was happening at Fred's, but there was nothing really new about that.

It wasn't until I told him about us moving a lot that the change took place. His eyes that had been looking at me suddenly weren't. They didn't even look like his eyes anymore. They were cold, hard; everything about him was.

I slid my chair back away from him, but he didn't look like he'd noticed. His lips were moving rapidly, but he wasn't talking, at least not to me.

It was the first time he'd looked like a Nephilim.

I already knew from my time with them that they could sense fear. So I did my best to pretend I didn't notice the change in him. It only worked while I had my eyes down, looking at my plate.

By the end of the meal, Joel's murmuring was no longer internal. I don't know if he realized he was speaking out loud or not, but the dialog that abruptly came from his mouth was enough for me to slide my chair even further from the table. I knew I needed to get out of there, but I stayed. Listening to him was both fascinating and horrifying at the same time.

"It isn't time to go yet, I've already told you. We still have to stay and analyze the changes in Beth," he mumbled, his lips moving rapidly. It didn't sound like Joel's voice. It was deeper, almost raspy.

"We will, but right now I need to make sure Rachel doesn't figure out what's going on," he answered himself; that time it sounded like Joel.

That was the last thing he spoke out loud, but it was more than enough for me. I stood up and put on my coat. I was leaving.

I don't know if he followed me or not. I didn't look back to see. I almost ran, but didn't. If he was becoming one of them, then that was the worst thing I could do. I forced myself to go slow.

When I walked into my trailer last night, I discovered firsthand what Joel had been talking about. Aunt Beth certainly had changed. She'd never acted like that before, never.

My finger went to the gashes her nails had made. I didn't want to go back there. I didn't think I *could* go back there.

I could leave, I thought. There was nothing keeping me there anymore, especially if Joel was becoming one of them. I had a little bit of money saved up. Not a lot, but enough for a bus ticket somewhere.

Only one thing made me pause, and, strangely enough, it was something Joel had said while he was talking to himself. He'd said he had to keep an eye on Aunt Beth.

Last night Aunt Beth had proven herself to be my enemy. If Joel was watching her, then what did that make him? My savior?

It would make sense; someone like me deserved a lunatic for a savior.

chapter fifty-seven/ dead anyway

I am trying to find myself. Sometimes that's not easy.
   -Marilyn Monroe

The person who suddenly stepped on the stairs had really bad timing. My heart jumped as clouds of dust settled on my body. But it was just someone passing by.

I looked around me. I couldn't hide under the stairs forever. And as tempting as the idea was, I knew I wasn't going to leave. Ironically, it was my teacher's words and my aunt's behavior that convinced me of that. I was going to stay because no matter what I did or where I went, the end result would still be the same. And I was beginning to believe what Nathan had said, about me having a purpose here. Why else would they want me dead so badly?

They'd gotten into my school. They'd gotten into my trailer. And maybe they'd even gotten into Joel. I was dead no matter what.

The big question was: Was I brave enough to face Beth, Newstead, even Joel?

I laughed as I glanced at myself, crouched under the stairs, hiding from everyone and everything. I hardly looked like someone who was brave. And I wasn't.

But it doesn't matter if you're brave or not if you're dead anyway.

Once I'd made my decision, I knew it was time to leave the spot I'd found. I was done hiding.

chapter fifty-eight/ facing it

History is the version of past events that people have decided to agree upon.
   -Napoleon Bonaparte

I walked slowly towards Fred's after the last bell rang. It was freeing, knowing you're dead. It made life much simpler. There are a lot of things you don't worry about anymore, like what you're afraid of.

I knew Joel was going to be at Fred's that night. I knew that it might not be him at all. But I also knew that with Joel it would be over a lot quicker than with the others. I knew how strong Joel was.

Once I got there, I tried to keep myself busy, but no matter what I found to do with my hands, my mind kept wandering back to the same things: Joel, Newstead, Beth. Nephilim.

But at least none of them showed up again that night. Only a few locals came at a little after five. I wish they would've stayed longer. It was good to not be alone.

They left at six. After half an hour of nothing, I almost closed early, but I knew I was just being a coward. I sat on one of the swivel stools and waited for the end.

It was then that I heard the bell above the door ring one last time. I knew it was him before I looked up. I didn't want to look. And what I saw didn't make me feel any better. He was the same as he'd been the night before: hard as flint.

He didn't talk to me. He didn't look at me. Instead, he walked to the sink and washed the few dishes that were there. It took a minute, but I was able to pick up the broom and start sweeping. *I guess I'm stronger than I thought I was.*

He came out when he was done and grabbed the silverware bucket and started rolling. He was done by the time I'd finished mopping. Without a word, he waited for me by the door. He didn't even mention that I wasn't wearing a coat. He stood by as I locked the door and placed the key under the rock.

He became my very large shadow. If I walked fast, he walked fast. If I walked slow, he walked slow. His steps stayed right in line with mine. He stayed that way the entire walk home, not speaking, only glaring straight ahead.

That's why it surprised me when he suddenly stopped. I stopped, too, and turned to look at him. It was his eyes that made me walk the few feet back to where he was standing. They were Joel's eyes again. They were soft eyes.

"Joel?"

"Rachel?" he flippantly responded. His smile was bright and full.

He soon erased the few inches that were separating us by pulling me tightly against him.

"I missed you," he whispered into my ear.

I looked up at him to see if he was joking; he'd been with me for the past two hours. But he didn't look like he was. It looked like he'd meant it. It was then that he kissed me urgently, like he knew our time together was short. And it was.

His lips hardened against mine. I opened my eyes and saw that his were wide open and as cold as the ice we were standing on. His jaw was clenched, just like his hands, which, up until that moment, had been running up and down my back. He placed them firmly on my shoulders and pushed me away.

He didn't have to say a word, and he didn't. I already knew my Joel was no longer there.

He'd placed me a couple feet away from him, but that didn't feel like enough, not with the way he was looking at me. I slowly backed away and then ran the remaining hundred feet to the trailer.

I stood on the steps for several minutes with my head pressed against the door, listening. It was quiet. But I knew that didn't matter; it'd been quiet the night before, too.

I'm dead anyway, I repeated to myself several times as I opened the door.

chapter fifty-nine/ insane

I've been so afraid, afraid to close my eyes. So much can slip
away before I say good-bye.
  -Tenth Avenue North, "Hold my Heart"

Nathan was awake, sitting on the couch, waiting for me. I
glanced around the room. There was no Aunt Beth anywhere. I
looked at Nathan expectantly, waiting for my instructions.
  "She's not here."
  I hadn't realized how on edge I was until he said those words
and I felt myself relax.
  "Where is she?"
  "I drove her over to the hospital in Springfield today. She got
her hands on the knives..." He trailed off. He didn't need to go
on. I'd seen enough in the last two days to imagine the rest.
  "How long will she be there?" I sat down next to him on the
couch.
  "I don't know. They have her pretty sedated right now."
  I only nodded. I didn't want Nathan to know how relieved I
was.
  "What do you think's wrong with her?"
  He looked away. He didn't want to answer me. He didn't have
to; we both knew what it was.
  "Nathan?" I asked as I stood up to go to bed.

"Yes?" He looked at me. He looked tired, too.

"I know she's your mother, and I'm sorry about that, but thank you; for last night, and then again this morning."

"Go to bed, Rachel." His eyes wouldn't meet mine.

So I did.

The next day started off better. I woke up at seven and took a shower without having to hear my aunt screaming in the background.

Nathan even took a shower, too. He was going to the hospital to visit his mother. I wisely didn't comment as he told me where he was going.

He walked out of the trailer with me. It was strange seeing him outside.

"Do you want a ride?" he asked awkwardly.

"No, thanks. That would get me there too early." I didn't plan on walking into school even one minute before eight from then on.

I waved to him as he drove away. *Better you than me.*

The school didn't look as threatening in the daylight. I was even able to climb the stairs in the main hall without looking at that first step. By the time I went to Fred's, I was in a relatively good mood. Things were looking much better than they had just twenty-four hours before.

Maybe everything is going to be all right, I thought as the Newstead crowd stayed away for another night. I was just beginning to believe it until the door opened and Joel walked in, or at least his shell did.

He didn't say one word to me as he did an exact repeat of the night before. He walked to the back; he did a few dishes.

I sat on a stool and watched him. He still didn't look like the rest of them, but he didn't look like Joel either.

I didn't know what he was.

I put on my coat and waited by the door for him to come out

from the back. After a few minutes of nothing, I decided to make sure he hadn't fallen in someplace.

I opened the kitchen door; he was standing by his washtub, staring out into space. He didn't even blink when I walked in.

"Ready?" I tried to sound more patient than I was.

He glanced down then, but I still don't think he saw me. He grabbed his jacket and followed me out into the dining room and then out of Fred's.

The silence was normal. I expected the silence. And I even expected the pause before it came. I felt my heart begin to race as we walked along, as we neared the bend in the lane. I stopped just one second before he did.

"Rachel?" It was a question, like he didn't know if it was really me or not.

"I'm right here," I said as I walked over to him. I put my hand on his arm. He seemed a bit disoriented. He shook his head quickly and then smiled the smile I loved, the one that made his eyes all crinkly.

"What are you doing way over there?" he asked. I was standing right next to him.

He reached his arm around my waist and pulled me tightly against him, still smiling. As long as he looked like that, it was okay. Anything was.

He lowered his face until our foreheads met, then his lips softly brushed against mine. When they came down again they were hard. I opened my eyes and saw him staring intently at me. I took a step back and the arms that had been holding me fell to his sides. I took another step back and then I turned and ran to the trailer. Again.

I stopped on the steps and looked back to see if he was still there. He was. He stood frozen in the exact position I'd left him, arms at his sides, head bent over.

I almost walked back to him, but I couldn't bring myself to do it. Instead, I turned and opened the door to the trailer.

rachel

chapter sixty/ the list

Experience: that most brutal of teachers. But you learn, my God do you learn.
     -C.S. Lewis

Aunt Beth was asleep on the couch when I opened the door. I knew that she'd eventually come back, but I had no idea it would be that soon. Part of me had hoped she'd never come back at all.

I wanted to turn back around and run in the other direction. But Joel was out there, with his hard eyes and his harder soul. Nathan must've sensed the course of my thoughts because he walked over to where I stood by the door with my hand still on the handle.

"She came home earlier tonight. They said she just needed some medicine."

I looked towards the passed-out woman on the couch and let go of the handle. She definitely looked like the least threatening between the two. I went to my room and locked my door. But I couldn't get to sleep until I heard Nathan's soft snoring on the other side of it.

The next day was a Friday, so I knew Joel would come earlier to Fred's. I didn't know what I thought about that. I kind of wished he'd stay away and just meet me in the lane by my trailer. I didn't know if putting up with the new Joel for four hours was worth the few minutes that I had of the old one.

But that Friday was better. When he walked in, he didn't immediately start working. Instead, he walked over to where I was standing by the prep table, cutting up a pizza for a take-out order.

"Hey, Rachel," he said, and it almost sounded like him.

I looked up to watch him. He wasn't quite what he used to be, but at least that vacant look wasn't there.

"Joel."

"Do you need any help with that?" His eyes were trying to meet mine, but I wasn't quite ready for that yet.

"No, I'm almost done."

He just nodded and went to the sink and started washing. He stayed away from me for the rest of the night. I don't think it was because he wasn't himself, I think it was more because of the way I was acting.

During the walk home, I tried to lighten up. I even talked to him.

"I had a test on Animal Farm today," I began hesitantly. My voice sounded strange in the silence. He turned to me and smiled. I guess he sensed my effort. He made his own.

"I've never read it before."

"It's good for an allegory. Normally they're not quite my style, but I didn't mind it."

For the first time that night, I looked at his face, his eyes. It was Joel, but there was still something off.

He just nodded. We went back to the silence. I didn't know what to say to him. The last time I spoke candidly with him, he turned into a whole different person. I hated walking on eggshells around people. I hated that it had to be that way with Joel.

"You look tired," he said after several minutes of nothing.

"Yeah, Aunt Beth got home from the hospital last night. We have to give her medication every few hours or she acts up. Nathan must've slept through the overnight dose because she woke up at a little after four and I couldn't get back to sleep."

Joel's face froze. Whatever gains we'd made that night were gone; he was more frightening than ever. I backed away from him and he didn't stop me.

I began compiling a list that night; things I couldn't bring up to Joel. Poor crazed Aunt Beth took slot number two, right below us moving.

He stopped at the bend like he always did. I almost didn't. I was getting tired of the drama of it all. But one look at his face and I changed my mind.

"You look tired." That time it was me who said it. He'd just gotten done pulling me close to him and for the first time I saw him up close. He *did* look tired.

He nodded.

I guess there's things he isn't going to bring up, either.

That night, I pulled away before he reverted back to whatever it was that took over him. It was better that way, to leave on a good note. He still didn't follow me to my trailer, though. It was like Aunt Beth's shrieks were too much reality for him.

Each day got a little better. I was learning what not to say, and he was trying to keep that gleam out of his eyes. It still wasn't like how it used to be. Except in the lane.

At first I thought he was becoming like the rest of them. But it had been so long since I'd seen any Newsteaders that I didn't know how wrong I was.

It wasn't until the first week of April that I realized my mistake.

美人
rachel

chapter sixty-one/ a reminder

I don't know what I want so don't ask me. Cause I'm still trying to figure it out. Don't know what's down this road. I'm just walking trying to see through the rain coming down.
    -Taylor Swift, "A Place in This World"

We were starving. Not figuratively, but literally. I had to admit to myself that there was at least one good thing about the Newstead crowd that used to engulf Fred's: they always left me tips. No Newsteaders, no tips. No tips, no groceries.

It'd been almost two weeks since I'd brought home any food. Usually I went to the store every Monday on my way home from school, but it was Sunday and I still hadn't gone yet. Not that I didn't need to go. I just didn't have any money.

Our cupboards in the trailer were bare. Even my secret stash had been emptied. My little security net, the small fund I'd kept hidden from everyone, was gone, too. It's what I'd used to buy groceries the Monday before the last one.

Nathan had even threatened moving. Not that he'd rescinded his philosophy about us having a purpose in Weston. He knew we were starving, too.

So that Monday after school I headed into Weston to look for a second job. I couldn't quit Fred's. It was the only time I got to see Joel's shell. But I also couldn't let us starve. So I figured I could squeeze a few more hours in. I had my Mondays.

There weren't many places to work in Weston, at least not with my skills. I walked past the auto repair place. I considered the store. Weston had a great general store. But I needed to make some good money quick and nothing's quicker than waitressing.

Besides Fred's, Weston had two other possibilities. I wasn't classy enough to work at the Bistro. I was more suited for the other two that I stood in front of. They were both directly across the street from each other. I looked from one to the other, trying to decide which one to go into first.

In the end I turned left and went towards Green Mountain. I liked its name.

It was laid out similar to Fred's, only reversed. It was cleaner, too. There was a waitress there who looked as busy as I used to be. There was a cook, too. *That's a plus; at least if I worked here, I won't be expected to do everything.* I sat on a stool at the counter and waited for the waitress to finish what she was doing.

Eventually, she made her way over to me. I recognized the frenzied look on her face. It changed as soon as I asked for an application.

She handed it to me with a pen and insisted I fill it out right then. From the look on her face, I might be able to start that very day.

I began filling in my information, intently concentrating on what to list and what to omit for my work experience. That's probably why I didn't see him there.

"Rachel?"

I froze. I knew that voice and who it belonged to.

"I thought that was you." His voice sounded pleasant, like we were old friends, but I knew better.

"Are you going to work *here* now?" he continued, ignoring my ignoring.

Finally, I turned and looked up at the large man standing inches away from me. I backed as far from him as the counter would let me. He didn't look like he noticed my discomfort. Or maybe he did; maybe that was the reason for the smile on his face.

It was amazing how close my nightmares had come to the real thing, even down to the ice eyes and hair so light it was almost white. His teeth in his huge smile were the same color.

I stood up, leaving my unfinished application on the counter. Starving was a better alternative.

I couldn't believe I'd been so stupid. It was like I'd forgotten Newstead was even there, that their students still roamed free. For three weeks, they hadn't plagued Fred's, and in those three weeks I'd forgotten so much.

Blondie boy reminded me as his eyes raked up and down my body as I tried to squeeze out of the tight space between him and the stool. He didn't move an inch as his legs and other parts of his body brushed up against me.

"It was good seeing you again, Rachel; next time, don't stay away so long," he called after me as I walked out the door. At least I waited to shudder until I was on the street.

Seeing him again made me look differently at the changes in Joel. In that one moment I knew he wasn't becoming like them, with their aggression and pride. It was something else, something opposite.

It was like he was becoming more protective, almost violently so. But the question was—who was he protecting, and what was he protecting them from?

The second question was surprisingly easy to answer. Newstead, what else? But why the sudden change in Joel's attitude towards them?

He never used to mind talking about Newstead. But I'd had to put Newstead at the very top of the banned list. His jaw immediately tightened; his eyes became like flint at the mention of them.

The first question was tougher. I knew that as far as Joel was concerned *I* was safe. I'd never told him about what had happened at my school, or how close it had come with Aunt Beth. I didn't want to find out what *that* information would do to him.

Surely it couldn't be *him* who was in danger. If that was the case, he could just leave any time. It's not like he wouldn't have a home to go to if he went back to St. Louis. If he was in trouble, what could possibly be the reason for him to stay?

My heart tried to tell me he stayed for me, but I ignored it. It couldn't be possible. People just didn't do that for other people, no matter how much they loved them. They didn't leave themselves in harm's way just because their girlfriend was there. It was such a ridiculous concept that I quickly disregarded it.

I was stumped. I had no idea who or what Joel was protecting. And I had no hope of finding out. Joel never said anything to me that mattered anymore.

I slowly made my way home from Weston. I was hoping to surprise Nathan with the good news that I'd gotten another job. Instead, I had to tell him I was too much of a coward to even try. My growling stomach didn't help any.

I usually had at least one meal a day when I worked at Fred's. But it was a Monday, so I hadn't eaten since late Sunday night. That was still better than poor Nathan and Aunt Beth. It'd been a couple of days since they'd eaten anything.

I looked back towards town one last time before heading down the path at the end of Markham Lane.

"A little help here!" I yelled to no one in particular. Just as I did, my knees started to get wobbly. I didn't know if it was from hunger or exhaustion, maybe both. Either way the end result was the same; they buckled underneath me and I ended up in the mud on my butt. I stayed there for a while, sobbing. My only comfort was that there was no one there to see me.

Eventually I forced myself to stand and finish the walk to the trailer. Nathan met me at the door, and the look on his face wasn't what I'd expected. He looked happy. In his hands was a basket of fruit. Fruit wasn't something I usually associated with Nathan.

"Where did that come from?" I asked as I made my way inside.

"Someone dropped it off a few minutes ago," Nathan said, still smiling.

"Someone dropped it off?"

He nodded.

"All the way out here?"

His smile faded. He hated being the one who had to give the information. "It was your boss. He came out here looking for you. He said he was dropping it off because he felt bad."

"What would Fred have to feel bad about?" I sat down on my side of the booth and peeled a banana. It was mushy, but it helped with the pain in my stomach.

"I don't know. He only said he felt bad that he fired everybody else but you."

"He didn't fire everyone. Joel still works there." I started working on an orange.

"No, he doesn't. Fred said he fired him a while ago. I think that's what he felt bad about. He said he was glad you didn't quit after he fired your boyfriend. He said he was glad you kept coming into work. I guess he's going out of town and he wanted to make sure you're going to keep coming in."

At least that part made sense. Fred was bribing me to make sure the place would keep running in his absence. The part that didn't was Joel. He hadn't said anything to me about getting fired. But it's not like Joel was saying much of anything to me those days. He still came in, just like he always had.

Whatever. I'm done trying to figure out Joel.

I gave all my attention to the basket in front of me. I didn't care if it was just fruit. It was food. I filled myself full of it. Nathan had left quite a bit for me. I don't know if he was being nice or if it was because it was fruit, but I pretended it was because he was nice.

It wasn't until later that night as I was laying in my bed as full as I'd been in weeks that something occurred to me. Nathan had said Fred came a few minutes before I got home. There was only one lane going to and from my trailer, and I'd spent the better part of ten minutes lying right in the middle of it. I never once saw Fred, coming or going. And of course, there was the fact that I'd never told Fred where I lived.

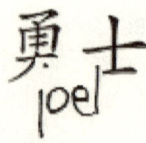

chapter sixty-two/ walking through the valley of the shadow of death

Do not press a desperate foe too hard.
  -Sun Tzu, *the Art of War*

0400. My eyes darted over to the bunk bed. Marcus was already gone. That meant it was time for me to go, too. Steven shifted slightly in his bed as I slid out of mine. My uniform was right where I'd left it the night before, tucked under my pillow. I grabbed it and went to the shower room. I only had a few minutes.

I washed as quickly as I could and dressed even quicker. Within five minutes, I was headed out of Chapman.

I'd learned pretty early on to just go and not look back, so I have no idea why on that day my eyes went to the grassy hill past the tree line. There was nothing there but trees and dark.

There are six of them, with Marcus in the center, my voice informed me. *Fourteen feet past the oak that stands by the bunker door. They're in gas masks.*

Gas masks, I thought. *That's a new one.*

Steven? I asked.

My mind surged forward and did its thing. After a fraction of a second, I had my answer.

Their position indicates they plan on luring you out, not doing anything to your room that would cause injury to Steven.

I nodded and turned towards the drive that led out of Newstead.

There were times I was tempted to start a fire, just a small one, just enough to let off a little heat, but that would've been like waving my arms in the air and announcing to the world where I was. No one knew about my hiding spot behind Lambert, and I was determined to keep it that way.

I sat on my rock and pulled my jacket tighter around myself and let my eyes close.

The warmth from the sun hit the back of my head and I opened my eyes and looked around. It always took me a few seconds to figure out where I was, even though I'd been waking up in the woods behind Lambert every day for the last three weeks.

Time for breakfast, I said to myself as I slid off the rock and headed towards the river. My stomach did a nose dive. It wasn't fooled; it knew I was just going to stuff it full of the nasty greens that grew along that part of the river.

It's better than nothing, I told it, but I don't know who I was trying to fool, the stuff sucked.

At zero seven forty-five, I left the woods and headed back towards Newstead.

Weston was just waking up; even from the road I could smell the bacon and eggs, sausage and coffee. I walked faster, not that I was late, I wasn't. I just couldn't stand it. But that wasn't the worst. The worst was going by Fred's; dark, deserted Fred's. My mouth filled with saliva as it mistakenly thought it was getting its one meal of the day. I broke into a run.

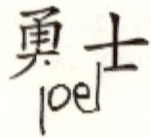

chapter sixty-three/ getting beat

On dispersive ground, fight not. On facile ground, halt not. On contentious ground, attack not.
  -Sun Tzu, *the Art of War*

The gate to Newstead was still wide open. I kept waiting for the day when it would be closed. Everything else they did told me I wasn't welcome there–why not the gate, too?

But it wasn't. It was open, daring me to walk through it.

I only paused a second before doing what I did every other day at that time; I walked through the gate towards Newstead and my own private hell.

My Algebra class was already half-full when I walked in. I automatically went to the seat in the far back corner of the room and sat down, waiting for the rest of them to show up. They came in groups of twos or threes, all but Marcus and his clan. All seven of them walked in at once and sat in the very front row of the classroom.

Class didn't start until they were sitting, even though the second bell had already rung a few minutes earlier.

I felt my eyes close and I didn't try to stop them. It was safe there, at least as safe as Newstead could get. Or maybe I'd just convinced myself of that because no one had tried to kill me there, at least not that I knew of.

My voice woke me up right as class was ending. I waited for the rest of them to file out before standing to go to my next class. That time, my eyes stayed wide open.

I headed towards the gym, some distance behind Marcus and his group. I knew better than to follow them too closely. When I got to the locker room, I stood outside and counted to sixty, three times. That was usually long enough to miss most of them. The ones who were left were too focused on not being late to mess with me.

I pushed open the door and went to the far corner and quickly changed out of my blue uniform into the standard grey shorts and t-shirt. We all looked the same for gym.

I walked into the gym right as the first bell rang.

Guys were in various groups, stretching or running in place, while they waited for Mr. Pomeroy, our gym teacher, to show up. I stood off by myself; Steven wasn't in my gym class.

"All right, gentlemen, I want to see some laps," Mr. Pomeroy shouted as he walked in. He put down his coffee so he could blow his whistle.

Running. That was good. They couldn't do anything to me with running, or at least I didn't think so. I'd been surprised in the past with what they'd been able to come up with.

I waited until the last one ran past before following behind in a slow jog. I carefully kept my pace; fast enough to not get passed, but still slow enough to be by myself. It was a delicate balance; Marcus could run pretty fast.

The whistle blew again. "Double time; come on now, girls."

I picked up my pace to match the rest of the guys. It was a little harder that time; some of them were falling behind, getting tired. I had to pass a few. It was either that or get passed by Marcus and his gang.

A few guys dropped to their knees, breathing heavily. I passed them, too.

"Again, faster." More whistle blowing. I ran faster. More guys dropped out.

I almost stopped, not because I was tired. I wasn't. But from one quick look over my shoulder, I could tell it was just Marcus and me still running. I knew that he didn't like to get beaten, especially by me.

The whistle blew one final time. I looked back and Marcus was on his knees right behind me. I ran another couple yards before I stopped.

Mr. Pomeroy was glaring at Marcus, shaking his head. I guess that meant he didn't like that I'd beaten him, either.

"Class dismissed," he called as he went over to Marcus. He helped him up and dragged him to his office. I saw my chance and ran for the locker room and changed before he got done with him.

I didn't stop running until I was sitting in my seat for Biology.

For some reason, we hadn't been learning about Biology for a while. The last thing even resembling science I could remember learning in that class was when we'd done the unit on evolution. Apparently what we'd moved on to was a more in-depth version of that: the study of different races and kinds, and how some were superior to others.

I didn't get what they meant at first; Newstead had lots of different students, from lots of different backgrounds. It wasn't until that meeting with the dean after Rachel got attacked that I figured it out. They meant us versus them, and them was everyone else but us.

We were the superior race. *We* were the ones who deserved to take whatever we wanted, no matter who it hurt. It didn't matter, because they weren't as evolved as us.

Each day, Biology class got a little bit deeper into their deranged philosophy. I could finally understand why that jerk had thought he could just take Rachel; he'd been programmed that way. She was nothing more than an animal to him.

I paid very close attention to everything my teacher said, and the books he showed us to try and prove his point. I knew Leadership class was the place where the weapon was formed, but it was first created right there, in Biology.

I stood when the bell rang. Lunch. I hated lunch. There wasn't enough time for me to go to Lambert, so I had to go to the mess hall and just endure it.

I walked in and sat at my usual spot. In the beginning, I would fill my tray, but it'd been several weeks since I'd done that. Not that I wasn't hungry. Watercress wasn't much of a breakfast, let alone enough to hold me to dinner. But I had to.

Three weeks before, I'd been sitting in that exact spot and was about to take a bite from the pile in front of me when my hand froze. It was mid-air on its way to my waiting mouth when it happened. I literally couldn't move it. I raised my other hand and pulled the frozen one back down to the table.

The fork fell to the plate and landed in the pile of mashed potatoes with a surprisingly loud sploshing sound. I looked around to see if anyone else had heard it, but no one had; they were too busy ignoring me, as usual. Just as I was looking down again, I caught Marcus's eye. He was watching me, but doing his best to make it look like he wasn't.

He quickly looked away, but I didn't. He was rocking back and forth with nervous energy, talking rapidly with the guys sitting next to him. After a couple minutes his eyes lifted to me again. I was still watching him, so he quickly looked back down.

Marcus was waiting for something and it was something to do with me.

I automatically lowered my hands to my lap. It wasn't until they were there that I realized I could move my right hand just fine. I flexed it once to make sure, but it was just like the left one.

My eyes went back to my plate of food and the fork that was sticking out of it. I lifted my right hand again to finish eating and it wouldn't move.

"Do not touch it."

I'd heard the rushing water voice often enough by that point that I was pretty sure my face didn't give anything away, especially since it appeared that it was more than just Marcus who was occasionally glancing my way.

"Wait five minutes, then stand and throw it in the garbage. Do not eat any of the food prepared at Newstead from this day forward."

I nodded slightly as I looked back down at my plate.

So I did what it said. I threw out my lunch and never ate anything there again. It made it easier that none of them sat with me; I don't think I could've gotten through lunch hour if I actually had to watch other people eat.

chapter sixty-four/ by the fountain

Let no act be done at haphazard, nor otherwise than
according to the finished rules that govern the land.
   -Marcus Aurelius, *Meditations*

Marcus looked up at me again. That was twice that lunch hour
already. The only time Marcus looked at me was when they
were going to try to pull something. I laughed to myself. I
doubted Marcus knew how often he gave their stupid attempts
away.

His eyes locked with six others at adjoining tables. They
nodded slightly at him. *Seven of them; hell, that's a cakewalk
after some of the stuff I've been through.* Marcus gestured with
his head towards the clock on the wall. *It'll be soon, right after
lunch.*

My eyes flicked to Steven, who sat two tables away from me.
He looked like he was watching the exchange, too. His eyes
lifted to mine briefly, then went back down to his plate. He
wasn't eating his food, either.

Steven won't be there to help me this time. Sometimes he
was, but I made sure none of the rest of them knew that. I didn't
want Steven to have to deal with what I was going through. His
was more of an informative role, like a spy. Occasionally he'd

show up and act like he didn't see them there and drag me away, or he'd just warn me ahead of time.

I didn't like that he wasn't eating his food, either. Maybe they were beginning to suspect that Steven was helping me, or maybe he just wasn't hungry; either way, his lowering eyes told me what I needed to know: Steven wouldn't be there to save me that day.

I took a deep breath in and stood up to go to my Literature class. I just wanted to get it over with.

Seven other chairs scraped across the floor as they followed me.

Instead of walking directly to the building my class was at, I went over to the fountain. It was still dry, even though it was probably warm enough to not have to worry about the pipes busting.

One was standing by Chapman, another two stayed by the mess hall. That left just four, who stopped about ten feet behind me. I didn't turn around or make any indication that I knew they were there, although they must've known. It's what had kept me alive that long, my ability to see them coming.

The first bell rang; the one that told us that lunch was over and we had five minutes to make it to our next class. I turned around and looked Marcus right in the eyes. They were lined up like bowling pins; Marcus in front, two slightly behind him off to either side, with the fourth a little behind all of them, towards the left. The last three stayed in their positions.

I moved to walk past them, and the group shifted to move with me. It was almost like a dance. But it didn't take long for the dance to break up. It only took Marcus's hand reaching out and touching my shoulder.

Without thinking about it, my hand reached up and grabbed his, twisting his arm backwards. I felt the pop as it came out of the socket. The guys around us only heard the scream.

I let go of his arm and walked past them. Marcus stood, with his left arm dangling at his side, "Hey! I'm not done with you yet."

I turned back around to look at him. His ice eyes became a fire. Without a word, I turned and continued on my way. The rest of the guys were too stunned to carry out whatever their plan was.

The fact they didn't care that I was standing in the exact middle of the campus told me a lot. Dean Erikson wasn't concerned about secrecy anymore.

I think he was finally beginning to see what was right in front of his face. He'd made a huge mistake when he selected me as captain of team Bravo. At the time, he was probably only doing it as a joke, a way to show me my place. He expected the shunning, but as the weeks wore on and I proved I was capable, he had to face the final outcome of his foolish act:

I could win.

To Erikson, that was completely unacceptable. So he did what all power-hungry dictators do; he tried to have me eliminated. As the weeks wore on and I remained alive, he only grew more desperate.

If he was dealing with the Joel Cranston who had first come to Newstead, he probably would've been successful a hundred times over. But he wasn't. Whatever I had been was buried so deep, even I couldn't find him. Instead, I'd become the voice, or it had become me; either way, the end result was the same. Joel David Cranston didn't exist anymore.

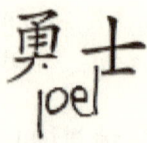

chapter sixty-five/ joel's list

He who exercises no forethought but makes light of his opponents is sure to be captured by them.
   -Sun Tzu, *the Art of War*

Literature class slowly filled, but the seat front and center remained empty, even past the second bell. Marcus didn't show. The teacher didn't even look like he noticed. Instead, he picked up right where he'd left off the day before.

I wasn't paying attention to him at all. Instead, I was measuring the mood in the room. I hadn't decided if I was going to Leadership class. It was a touch and go thing. Some days I went, some days I skipped. It all depended on what I determined, how acute the threat was.

That day I couldn't tell. They'd already tried once, but that didn't necessarily mean I was safe. It would be foolish to think that.

No one did anything to make me alarmed; it was more a gut feeling. So right after the teacher handed out the reading assignment for the night, I stood to leave, before the rest of them had a chance to get outside.

I headed down the long drive that led out of Newstead. The

gate was still open, so I went through it and began walking down Lawrence Hill Road. I got about a hundred feet closer to Weston when I abruptly turned to go into the forest.

There was a slight thinning of the shrubs where I entered. I pushed through them and began walking quickly back, parallel to the road I'd just walked down.

I looked at the ground. A path had developed where my feet had passed countless times. I knew I needed to find a different way the next time I came there. The last thing I needed was for them to suspect anything.

I could see the tops of the buildings through the bare branches. *It probably wouldn't be a bad idea to find a different route, anyway. With my blue uniform on, I'm anything but camouflaged.*

I sank to my knees and crawled until I was past the buildings. Once I couldn't see them anymore, I stood up. I was in my territory now: the training field.

In the past four weeks, I'd walked every inch of those four hundred acres. I knew every rock, hill, and tree formation. Sun Tzu advised that you know your ground, and I knew my ground very well.

But scouting wasn't on my agenda that day. I needed to see if my instinct had been right. I headed through the woods to the slight rise just inside the forest edge—the bunker. I crouched behind a thick maple and carefully positioned myself so that one eye could see past it to the scene below.

Sgt. Foltz was standing by the open door, scanning the horizon. I could feel his eyes looking for me. Groups of two or three went past him into the bunker. He put his arm on each of their shoulders as they went in, like he was counting them.

Marcus approached alone. His left arm was in a sling. I watched him grimace as Sgt. Foltz's hand clamped down on his shoulder just like he'd done with the rest of them. Only with

Marcus, his hand stayed there. His fingers dug deep into his left arm. The rest of my class walked by the two of them as they stared at each other.

Sgt. Foltz didn't look like he'd said anything, but Marcus nodded slightly before turning to go in. Sgt. Foltz went to the door and turned back to the forest. His eyes did one last sweep of the training field before he turned around and went in, closing the door behind him.

The bunker. I hadn't set one foot in the bunker since I'd been assigned as platoon leader. I didn't need either voice to tell me that would be a bad idea; I'd figured that one out all on my own. The only time I went to Leadership class at all was when it was in the gym or at the football field. Which meant I hardly ever went.

I stayed behind the tree for a full three minutes and then I turned and went back through the forest towards town.

Fred's was still dark when I walked by. Fred, the frickin' loser, hadn't been back since I'd confronted him. I must've scared him more than I'd meant to. *Guess it's okay to have threatening guys in his restaurant as long as they're not threatening him. What a dick.*

I turned towards Lambert and my hiding place.

After stuffing my mouth full of more greens, I sat down on my rock to write my mother a letter. It started out normal enough: me lying about my job, me lying about my school, but then, without warning, the letter turned honest.

You're probably wondering why I haven't sent you any money lately. It's because I threatened my boss and he fired me.

I looked down at the words my hand had written and then I started writing more, I started writing it all.

I still go to work, though. Mainly to get away from the guys at my school who are trying to kill me. But that's not the only reason I go. I go because there's a girl there who knows me and actually wants to spend time with me. It doesn't hurt that she's smoking hot and likes to dig her nails into my back when I kiss her neck.

Well sorry to make this so short, but I've got to go eat my one meal of the day that isn't coated in rat poison.

Your botched abortion,

Joel

I looked down at the words my hand had written. *Talk about keeping it real.* After a few minutes of silence everywhere, including inside of me, I crumpled up the paper and started over.

Mom,

School is going well. I'm doing good in all of my classes. I don't have a lot of time right now to write; I have to get to work. We'll catch up later.

Your son,

Joel

I pulled out the last letter I'd gotten from her. She was planning on picking me up for the two week break and going on some kind of vacation. We'd never been on a vacation before. It just wasn't something we could afford. Maybe my mom was saving extra money with not having to feed me.

I'd asked Steven what his plans were and he surprised me by telling me that he didn't have any. He, along with everyone else at Newstead, would be staying behind during break. He didn't stay out of choice; he didn't have any place else to go. His mother had apparently died a few years back. He said it was hard at first when everyone else would go home during break and he was stuck there alone, but that hadn't happened since his freshman year.

Now they had all kinds of activities planned for them; business as usual, minus the classes. When I acted surprised at this, Steven just shrugged his shoulders and told me it'd been like that for a while. For some reason, all of them had cut ties back home, never visiting, rarely calling or writing.

I shook my head as I put my mom's letter in the envelope. *I guess that's another thing to put on the list of how I'm not anything like the rest of them.* It was getting to be a long list.

My growling stomach reminded me what time it was. I stood and went back into the woods. I knew Fred's wouldn't be dark that time.

chapter sixty-six/ good ground

All armies prefer high ground to low and sunny places to dark.
  –Sun Tzu, *the Art of War*

Everything changed in one day; not even one day, really; it was more like one minute. I was walking through the training field like I usually did; only that time it was a Saturday in April. Time was running out.

It was a clear day. The sun was bright and warm, so warm that I wasn't even wearing a jacket. The snow was gone, but it was still early enough in the spring that the trees only had the beginning of buds. It left the woods looking rather brown. The mud on the ground was brown, the trees were brown.

That was probably why I could see them when they were still a long way off.

They were fifty yards in front of me, but they were busy working on something, otherwise I'm sure they would've seen me, too.

What the hell are they doing in the woods on a Saturday? It was bad enough that they overran the place during the week. Saturdays were mine.

I pulled myself behind a big maple and waited to see if I was wrong about them not seeing me. After two minutes of nothing,

I knew that they hadn't.

I looked down at my clothes. I was wearing a white t-shirt and jeans. Normally, that would've been fine, but it would be like a neon sign to them.

I glanced around to see if there was anything I could use. My eyes rested on the mud at my feet. Quickly, I reached down and scooped it up by the handful. In five minutes, I was just as brown as the rest of the forest.

The smart thing would've been to turn around and come back later, when they weren't there. But I didn't feel like being smart that day.

Almost all of the Leadership classes were held in the bunker, so I had no idea what types of things they were being trained in. I decided it was time to find out.

I crouched to the ground and inched my way closer to them. At a distance of eleven yards I stopped and slid behind a tree. I was close enough.

There were twenty of them and they were setting up a large, open-air tent. It wasn't going well. Probably because everyone was too busy telling everyone else what to do and no one was actually doing anything.

Not one of them was in a uniform, even though I could tell they all went to Newstead. Instead, they were all wearing camo fatigues and combat boots and had as much mud on their faces as I did.

It was then that I realized what I was seeing. It was the freshman's weekend for FTX.

I don't know how I missed it. There were tents, smaller ones, set up already and coolers stacked by the tent they were working on. It must've been their makeshift mess hall.

I looked at the sun in the sky. It was about zero nine hundred. They were twenty-four hours into their campaign and they were still setting up tents.

I slowly moved around the perimeter of their home base to see how they'd laid things out. It was all pretty simple: ten tents off by themselves, an empty prisoner of war camp, and the big tent that they were working on.

Twenty-four hours into it and they didn't have even one prisoner of war.

I was familiar with the spot they'd picked. It was one I'd thought about, too. It was slightly elevated and had good cover.

But after that day, I saw a major flaw. I'd gone around the entire ground and no one had seen me, which meant it had cover for the enemy, too.

After two hours I almost walked out from behind the tree I was crouched behind and helped them set up their stupid tent. They were still struggling with it. Instead, I decided it was time to find the other platoon.

The training field was four hundred wooded acres over a variety of terrain. I knew they could be anywhere. I also knew it was imperative that I find them before they spotted me.

I put more mud on my arms and face and went deeper into the woods.

Every few seconds I stopped and listened, my eyes scanning the horizon. There was movement on the ridge seventy-five yards from my position. I looked to the left, then to the right.

Is it possible they're that stupid?

There were only two truly elevated positions in the training grounds, and they were directly across from each other, separated by a valley about a hundred yards long. And that's where the two platoons had set up their home bases, only a football field away from each other.

The western elevation was the better ground. Its front three sides were steep walls of rock, with only its rear being approachable.

I crept back into the cover of the forest and made my way

towards a path I'd grown familiar with.

Their camp was eerily quiet. The movement that I'd seen in the valley was gone. I planted myself in an overgrown bed of cattails and waited for them to come back.

They had tents set up, just like the other platoon had. Only they'd been able to get the mess tent up, too. Their POW camp was also empty.

I pictured the looks on the guy's faces down at the other camp when they were captured. There they were setting up their stupid tent when all the while the other platoon was out hunting them.

Fifteen minutes passed and still, I heard nothing. Twenty minutes. Nothing.

Finally, after thirty minutes, I decided to leave my shelter and go in search of a missing platoon.

I followed the cattails deeper into the forest that ran behind the western elevation. It offered good, thick coverage when at that time of year coverage was hard to find.

The thing about cattails is that they're usually next to water. And those cattails were no different. I found myself huddled next to a small stream, surrounded by the missing platoon.

They were fishing. Not capturing the enemy that lay oblivious at their doorstep, not trying to locate the opposition's cylinder. No, they were fishing. All twenty-one of them.

I didn't stay with them as long as I had stayed with the other platoon. There was no point; they weren't showing me anything other than how big the trout in Vermont get.

I followed the cattails away from the stream and back towards their home base.

The rules of FTX say the cylinder has to be somewhere in your home base, which meant the cylinder was there, completely unguarded.

I could take it.

Why bother with waiting for the juniors' weekend? For all I know, I won't even survive that long. But for some reason, it didn't feel right. It almost felt cowardly.

The temptation was strong, though. So strong I knew I had to get back into the woods and away from the focal point of my obsession for the last four weeks. But I was thinking about it, a lot. That was probably why I walked right into the edge of the mountain. Nothing brings you back to attention like a mouthful of rock and blood gushing down your face.

"Great. Just great," I said out loud. I think I said it to the mountain, like my bleeding face was its fault.

I carefully placed the flap of skin that was dangling over my eye back into place and sat down on the dirt and leaned back against the mountain. I pressed harder, waiting for the bleeding to stop.

While my right eye was closed tight, my left eye was wide open. The ground I was sitting on was covered in brown pine needles; it was actually rather comfortable, a lot better than the swamp that most of the training field was.

My legs were extended out in front of me. They were angled down at a slight grade, maybe ten degrees. I was surrounded by pine trees, the ones responsible for the soft cushion I was sitting on. Pine trees offer good cover, even in the early spring when the rest of the trees haven't grown their leaves yet.

There was a clearing in the middle of the pines, about a ten yard by fifteen yard spot. It was good ground.

I sat back and waited for my head to stop bleeding. I sat back and watched the sun get higher in the sky. I sat back and started to plan.

chapter sixty-seven/ nothing

There are roads which must not be followed, armies which must not be attacked, towns which must not be besieged, positions which must not be contested, commands of the sovereign which must not be obeyed.

   -Sun Tzu, *the Art of War*

Rachel didn't look up when I walked in. I stood there for a while, thinking she just hadn't heard the door. But after nothing for a full minute, I had to admit she knew I was there.
How long has that been going on?
I went to the back and kept myself busy washing dishes while I tried not to think about it. *I know I haven't been myself in a while, but....* I picked up a dish and washed it again.
I could hear her, her soft footsteps going anywhere but back by me. I leaned against the wall and took a deep breath in and then let it out. The kitchen door swung open.
I jerked forward, like I was going to ask her about it. Instead, I settled back against the wall. I knew I didn't want to hear her answer.
She wasn't there to see me, anyhow. She just went to the fryers, threw in a dozen wings, and then went back out into the

dining room again.

I took another deep breath and pushed on the swinging door. She was standing behind the counter. Just standing there. She wasn't busy. She wasn't waiting on anyone. She just wasn't with me. She looked in my direction but her eyes didn't go above my chest.

And all that time I thought I'd have to come up with a lie about what happened to my face. She didn't even ask about it.

I turned and went back into the kitchen and leaned against the wall again. I knew things weren't great between us, but I'd at least thought they were fine. But the look on Rachel's face told me we were far from fine. It was like it was already over for her.

The kitchen door swung open as Rachel went back to the fryers. I looked at her face and saw nothing.

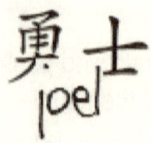

chapter sixty-eight/ not ending it

All men can see the tactics whereby I conquer, but what none can see is the strategy out of which victory is evolved.
-Sun Tzu, *the Art of War*

I walked towards her trailer. I knew she was behind me; I could hear her footsteps, but I didn't turn around. When we got to the edge of the forest, her footsteps stopped.

I turned to look at her and she said the first words she'd said to me all night.

"Joel?" She said it like a question, like she wasn't sure if it was me or not.

I almost kept walking. I didn't want to give her a chance to end it. She took two steps closer and I saw her face. She didn't look the way I'd thought she would.

"Joel." That time it wasn't a question. She reached her hands out and pulled me the last few inches towards her. I didn't fight her.

Her hands that had been on my shirt reached up and pulled my head down. She started kissing me like it was the most natural thing in the world, like she hadn't spent the last six hours completely ignoring me.

At first, I didn't kiss her back and she pulled away and looked at me again. She looked confused, but then pulled my face back down. I kissed her back that time.

chapter sixty-nine/ recon

If the enemy leaves a door open, you must rush in.
  —Sun Tzu, *the Art of War*

  With me not wanting to leave things that way with Rachel, I
ended up getting to the training field later than I wanted to. It
was twenty-one thirty before I was headed in that direction.
  I stayed close to the ground, using the bramble as cover. In
the distance there were bright embers glowing. I took two more
steps and crouched behind a tree. Slowly, I peered past the
tree and its branches. It was a fire.
  A small, contained fire illuminated the night and the people
sitting around it. I stood at my full height to get a better look at
it. There were five of them sitting around what appeared to be a
campfire. They even had marshmallows.
  I couldn't believe it.
  A few more of them joined their numbers as I made my way
closer. They had three fires blazing, with guys going back and
forth between them. They were making no attempt at stealth,
nothing like it. It was almost like a party.
  In the distance, up on the western hill, I saw the gleam of
more fires.

I crept close enough to both home bases to see that both POW camps were empty. I didn't get it. Wasn't the whole point to capture the enemy and reduce the number of people trying to get your cylinder? It was thirty-six hours into their exercise and no one had done anything, except set up a tent and catch a few fish.

I went to the edge of the mountain again. It was a good spot, about three hundred yards behind the western elevation. After one hundred yards I couldn't see them anymore; after two hundred yards I couldn't hear them.

I sat down and thought about what I'd discovered that weekend, seeing FTX with my own eyes. It wasn't even close to what I'd expected. True, I'd been considering the same locations as the freshman had picked, but that was the only similarity.

What I was seeing was nothing like what Steven had told me. I couldn't believe he was even talking about the same thing. Only one thought made sense, something he'd said about the prisoners of war.

He'd said it was part of the rules that you could rescue a teammate who had been captured, but no one ever did. He'd said that once they were prisoners of war, it was like they'd died.

Because at Newstead, if you weren't one of them, you *were* dead, and if you were captured, then you weren't one of them.

Is that why they don't risk it? Is it better to lose than be captured?

Why *would* you? If venturing out meant possible capture, and capture meant exile, then why risk going out into the other platoon's territory when you could just accumulate captures on defense?

To them it was better to lose as a team than individually. A team could be exonerated–but an individual? Never.

I remembered Sgt. Foltz's hand on Marcus's shoulder, the one that was in a sling. No, it wasn't good to stand out, especially if you were beaten.

What absolute and utter foolishness! By initiating that mentality, they'd completely undermined all their training, everything.

If only they were a real team who looked out for each other, then maybe someone would get off their ass and actually do something. Instead, they just sat around and waited for the other team to make their move. Why even bother with things like leadership training and tactics in the first place? No one there was using either.

In my mind, I imagined how it would happen, year after year. The faster team got to the higher hill first, gaining a strategic advantage. The second team would relent and take the smaller hill. They'd both just sit there and stare at each other, waiting for someone to get enough balls to make the first move.

And then someone would, because it was still all about a cylinder, and there was still one out there. And then they all would, and the upper hill would take twice as many as the lower just because of their location. Then it would be over, they'd each go back to their own home base and lick their wounds, just happy that they'd avoided capture.

No one would get rescued and no one would find a cylinder. Zero nine hundred on Monday would roll around and each team leader would hand Dean Erikson back his precious prize, another year wasted.

It was the stupidest thing I'd ever seen.

chapter seventy/ freshman

In the wise leader's plans, considerations of advantage and of disadvantage will be blended together.
-Sun Tzu, *the Art of War*

I spent as much time as I could in the training field that Sunday, between curfew and work. It happened just like I thought it would. A stray guy from the western elevation triggered it all. He went a little farther than usual to take a leak and the eastern side must've gotten wind of it because they lined up their forces and charged the western hill.

Then utter chaos ensued. People were being captured left and right, with the team on the western elevation dragging off twice as many as the other. I didn't bother staying to watch after that; I knew they'd just be spending the rest of their time guarding the prisoners of war that no one was going to rescue.

I turned to go back towards my trail. I didn't bother with the mud that night or staying towards cover. But I should have.

There was a full moon out that night which made it almost as bright as the daytime. I was busy smiling to myself over what I'd just seen, too busy to notice the two guys who were watching me.

The first indication I had that anything was wrong was the

sound of a twig cracking, that was all. I turned my head towards the sound.

Ten yards behind you, to the left, my voice whispered.

I quietly lowered myself to my knees and listened again. Another crack; that one was closer. I looked around to see what would provide the best cover. I knew I didn't have much time. Two trees and a large bush. That was all. I took the better of the two options and dove into the bush just as I heard the voices that went with the rest of the noise.

There were two of them and they were dressed just like the rest of the guys I'd seen that weekend, in camo and war paint. The only difference was that they looked like they were taking things seriously.

"Did you see where he went?" one of them asked.

"No," the other answered. He didn't sound too happy.

"Do you think they've got guys out, too?"

"No. You saw them while we made our rounds, they were all there, except for the ones we've got. It was probably just someone going to the bathroom again. Next time try to be a little quieter and maybe we'll actually get one."

Definitely not happy.

"How many do we need to get?"

"We need two more to tie, three to win."

The first guy didn't say anything else as the two of them traveled further into the woods. I watched them as they went. I had to admit, it was the first thing I'd seen that weekend that impressed me. I wanted to follow them and see if they got anyone, but I didn't have time.

Quietly, at a few minutes to curfew, I slid back towards town to re-enter Newstead from the main gate.

chapter seventy-one/ plans

The general who loses a battle makes but few calculations beforehand. Thus do many calculations lead to victory, and few calculations led to defeat: how much more no calculation at all! It is by attention to this point that I can foresee who is likely to win or lose.
    –Sun Tzu, *the Art of War*

As soon as school let out on Monday, I headed back to the training field. I wanted to look at the carnage first hand.

The tents were down, but that was about it. There was trash thrown everywhere. I didn't stay there long; it was too quiet. I didn't trust it. Someone would have to come back and pick the place up, and knowing my luck, it would end up being Marcus.

I knelt down and looked at the footprints in the mud. The majority of them were around the home bases, but there were some in the valley. I went back to the spot where the two guys had found me and followed their tracks. Twice they'd come across someone else. I don't know if they got them or not, but I hoped they did. Either way, it wasn't enough for them to win.

It turned out I was right to be wary about the home bases. Just as I was heading back in that direction, I heard voices as the clean-up crew got busy. But I wasn't ready to leave yet, so I turned back around and went in the opposite direction.

I sat down by the mountain and pulled out the piece of paper that I'd shoved in my pocket. I started writing down a list of the provisions and equipment I would need.

On Thursday, right after lunch, I silently stood near the table where I'd sat by myself for the past five weeks. Slowly, the noise in the mess hall stopped as all eyes were drawn to me.

Inexplicable hate was on most faces, poorly concealed as they all tried to stare me down. Marcus wasn't looking at my eyes. His glance went a little higher, to the large gash that went from my right eyebrow to my hair line.

I requested a meeting with my team immediately after lunch to discuss my plans for the upcoming FTX. There was no need for me to raise my voice; everyone there heard me. I watched carefully for their reactions. Most were surprised, but some eyes became darker as sideways glances were made between private parties.

It was exactly what I'd anticipated. I didn't expect loyalty. My past experience told me not to count on that.

I was quickly able to discern fourteen people assigned to Bravo platoon who seemed overly pleased with the new information. Fourteen who'd like nothing better than to turn traitor. Hadn't Erikson made it clear where their loyalty should be?

But I hoped at least some of them would want to win enough to make some attempt. My plans depended on it. Six men, including Steven, looked directly at me with no evil intent in their eyes.

My real team had been formed.

All twenty met me at the specified location as I informed them of our plans. We'd attempt to gain the higher ground, just like they all expected me to say. They knew the way it worked. After all, they'd been through it twice before. If Team Alpha was able to obtain the higher ground before us, we'd go to our secondary location: the smaller eastern hill just past the valley. They were all familiar with that location as well.

"What kind of supplies do you think we'll be needing?" I asked to no one in particular.

That seemed to wake them up. They all clamored around me, trying to make sure I wrote down their requests. Only Steven remained quiet, looking disgusted with me.

My earlier observation of them had been correct. The fourteen traitors gave themselves away again and again with sideways glances, shooting elbows, and the most grandiose list of needs. I ended the meeting promising I would do my best by them.

The following day I was summoned to Dean Erikson's office for the second time since my arrival to Newstead.

I walked in, knowing Erikson wouldn't be nearly as easy to fool as my teammates.

He was at the door, waiting for me.

"Come in, Joel," he said, gesturing to a chair. I walked over and sat down.

His voice came from behind me. "I've been told you've had a meeting with your team."

I turned around to look at him, but he was already walking towards his desk.

"Yes, sir. I was discussing our strategy for the upcoming FTX."

He sat down so that he was relatively eyelevel with me. "Good. I'm glad to see you're finally coming around."

I didn't need to ask him what he meant by that; it was the whole purpose for me being there, for the meeting with my team. Erikson, all of them, had to believe I'd become just like the rest of them.

"You, of course, will disregard our previous treatment of you," he said. It wasn't a question.

I nodded. I didn't trust myself with an answer, especially to that.

"You must understand that it was necessary; we don't want any weeds in the wheat, if you know what I'm saying."

I nodded again and looked out the window while he went on with all the rest of his justifications as to why it was all right to have me killed. It wasn't until he mentioned Rachel's Aunt Beth that I turned back.

"What did you say?" I asked.

Erikson smiled. "I said we'll end our surveillance there, with Beth."

He saw my sudden confusion and disregarded it with a wave of his hand. "We have our ways, Joel, of being anywhere we need to be. Since you were never here, we had to be there."

"I never saw anyone there," I answered, still innocent at that point, still unaware of exactly what I was dealing with.

"Of course not, Joel. You only saw Beth, but that didn't mean others couldn't see you. We have many weapons at our disposal. Occupation of others is only the beginning of what we're capable of." He chuckled at my naiveté.

The muscles on my face formed a smile that I hoped was believable.

What exactly is occupation of another? I asked as Erikson watched me, gauging my reaction.

Instead of answering me outright, my brain replayed all that Rachel had said about her aunt.

Was that because of them? Were they really there, inside of her?

Yes, my voice answered simply.

Erikson smiled, seemingly satisfied with my reaction. He sat back in his chair and, with his eyes still watching me, proceeded to give me a play-by-play of the last five weeks from his perspective. I did my best to hide my horror as he described in graphic detail each and every attempt on my life. I didn't know about half of them. He stopped at several points, waiting for me to explain myself, but I just shrugged my shoulders. I had no idea how I was still alive any more than he did.

Why is he telling me this? I wondered as he went on and on.

I finally decided it was either because he really believed my sudden conversion was genuine, or he just wanted to gloat. But now that I know Erikson better, I know that neither of my assumptions were correct. He was just testing me to see how deeply in I was. My fearful eyes and fake smile must've convinced him that I was still relatively harmless.

With that same smile still firmly fixed on my face, I stood to leave. He rose with me and held out his hand. I shook it. His eyes, like Marcus's, went to the healing wound above my eye. He smiled big and bright as his other hand clapped down on my shoulder. I left and didn't look back. The smile stayed on my face for the rest of the day.

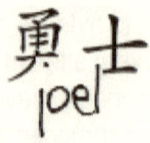

chapter seventy-two/ facades

He will conquer who has learnt the artifice of deviation.
  -Sun Tzu, *the Art of War*

  I went to Leadership class for the first time in three weeks.
And for the first time in three weeks it was held outside. We
were doing simple drills, very basic. Too basic.
  I couldn't help but think it was all for my benefit. It was like I
was a doomed spy they were using to carry false information
back to the opposition: me. They wanted me to think that's what
they'd been doing all along while they were hiding in their
bunker. I went along with it; it was better that way. It was better
if they thought I didn't know about them.
  I smiled as I jogged to the pylon, picked it up, and carried it
back to my home base. They smiled at me too, even Marcus,
who'd conveniently forgotten that the last time we'd had drill
together, I'd kicked his ass.

chapter seventy-three/ fear

Soldiers when in desperate straits lose the sense of fear.
  -Sun Tzu, *the Art of War*

I walked out of Chapman at a little after nineteen hundred, took a deep breath, and willed myself to feel the relief; the shoot-to-kill order had been lifted. Not one attempt had been made on my life since I'd left Erikson's office.

It was strange feeling things again. It took a little while to get used to it. Feelings took too much energy, and until that moment, all the energy I had was spent keeping myself alive.

The facts and figures continued to run through my head as I walked towards Fred's. I was walking twenty yards parallel to the path I'd carved in the woods; there was no one else on the road I was on; a skunk family fifteen yards to my right was coming out of hibernation.

I acknowledged all of it; it was all true, but I had to admit that there was more, a whole aspect of life I'd been ignoring. I forced myself to go where I didn't want to. I forced myself to feel.

The first feeling that came was fear. It hit me like a freight train. I doubled over right where I was standing as my mind begged me to put an end to it, but I didn't. Not fearing made me careless. Not fearing made two guys see me while I walked through their woods. I needed to fear, so I pushed harder and let myself feel the burn.

I cringed as scenes flashed in front of my eyes, all the things I had to fear. The last one was Rachel's empty face. I feared that more than anything.

So I pushed further. And the feeling of love, raw and deep and hurtful and real, filled me. And I felt the burn of that, too. It almost knocked the wind out of me. I saw then all the nights when I thought I was loving Rachel and I wasn't. I saw Rachel's eyes grow more and more vacant as she watched me disappear right in front of her. It wasn't her who'd left me; it was me who'd left her.

My eyes stung as I squinted them closed. *It's not too late. It can't be.*

chapter seventy-four/ spring

The principle on which to manage an army is to set up one standard of courage which all must reach.
    -Sun Tzu, *the Art of War*

Fred's wasn't empty when I walked in. There was a couple in the far corner and a four-top somewhere in the middle. The door to the kitchen was swinging back and forth, going progressively slower and slower. Rachel must've just gone in the back. I turned to go in that direction, too. She was bent over, reaching deep into the fridge. She looked up when I walked in. And then she looked again.

I hadn't thought the change had been that drastic, but Rachel seemed to think so.

"Hey," I quickly said, trying to distract her. She straightened up and blinked twice, but didn't say anything. I waved my hand in front of her face. She blinked again and then seemed to come back from wherever she'd been.

"Oh. Hi, Joel. I was just..." She paused and looked at me again, long and hard. Her hand was still on the open fridge.

"You were just what?"

"Oh, nothing. I was just getting more cheese to grate." She lifted the block in the air, like she had to prove it.

I took it from her frozen hand and went to the cheese grater. I could still feel her watching me and then I heard her walk away. The kitchen door swung loudly, whacking into the wall. I swallowed hard. It would've been so easy to revert back and feel nothing, but I didn't. Instead, I forced myself to turn around and face the most frightening thing of all.

I grabbed a juice glass and filled it halfway with water and took the flower I'd found by the road on my way to Fred's and put it in the glass. I took one deep breath and called to Rachel. When she came back in the kitchen she was looking at me with those probing eyes again.

"Look, this means it's spring," I said to her.

chapter seventy-five/ rest

The good fighter will be terrible in his onset, and prompt in his decision.
-Sun Tzu, *the Art of War*

Rachel closed the door. From the look in her eyes she had lots of questions, none of which I felt like answering right at that moment, especially when there was someplace else I needed to be.

I turned and started walking, but soon my pace got quicker until I was in an all-out run. I shouldn't have gone into Rachel's trailer; it took too much of my precious time. I only had two more hours until curfew. Only two hours to see if the sophomores would turn out to be as predictable as the freshman. But I needed to. I needed to make sure Aunt Beth was being left alone, and from the look of her, she was.

At twenty-one ten, I stepped onto the training field. I had a good idea where both teams would be just based on the freshman campaign, but that was only an educated guess on my part. I knew they could be anywhere.

The woods were dark and quiet as I slowly made my way through them.

It was exactly the same, even down to the fires. I didn't stay very long; there was no point. No one would be doing anything before Sunday night.

Steven was in the room when I walked in. He didn't look up.

I laid down on my bed and fell asleep as soon as my head hit the pillow. There was no zero four hundred wakeup call that night. Instead, it was the sun shining through the window down onto my face. I looked up at the clock: zero nine hundred. I'd slept for eleven hours straight.

For the first time in over a month, I didn't feel tired. I stretched out my long limbs, completely at peace. The place was quiet; I was probably the only one left in bed.

I propped myself up on my elbows and looked out the window. All I could see was woods. But I knew there was more. Even though I couldn't see them, they were out there.

I was showered and shaved in two minutes, a personal record for me. In less than five, I was heading out of Newstead, down the long drive.

There were no campfires that morning, or marshmallows. But there was no indication they were on a mission, either. Most of them were still sleeping when I got there. *Must've been a late night.* I watched as they slowly came out of their tents, awkwardly stretching out their kinks. The only ones who bothered being quiet were the ones fishing in the stream.

On Sunday night the tide turned. There was no more fishing, no more fires, but there wasn't anything different, either. As a group, team Bravo descended the upper ridge, and team Alpha, also as a group, came out to meet them.

There were no two guys trying to pick up stragglers that time.

rachel

chapter seventy-six/ new joel/old joel

If you live to be a hundred, I want to live to be a hundred
minus one day, so I never have to live without you.
  -AA Milne, *Winnie the Pooh*

By the third week of April, I'd become used to the routine of
things. We weren't starving anymore and I still had my Mondays
to myself. And I didn't even have to wait on people that terrified
me the rest of the week. Life was good, sort of.

Joel still wasn't himself. He was better than before, but it still
wasn't the same. I'd had what it could be, and even though
things were better, I remembered the difference.

Until that night.

Joel showed up right at five, like he usually did on Fridays. I
noticed the change in him almost immediately. It was something
like hope. I tried not to get too excited, tried not to read too
much into it. But that was impossible.

He patted my head as he passed me on the way to the
kitchen. I turned, stunned at the transformation. He was actually
whistling as he started to wash the mountainous stack of dishes
waiting for him.

Whistling? I'd never heard him do that before. I followed him
into the kitchen and stared at him.

"What happened?" I asked before thinking, stunned at this new/old Joel. I was seeing firsthand why I'd fallen in love with him in the first place.

"What do you mean by that? Can't I whistle while I work?" he asked, smiling. He changed his tune to the childhood classic. His sweet, simple humor made me smile in spite of myself.

He took a finger overflowing with dish bubbles and placed it lightly on my nose and laughed playfully as I tried to swat it off. His light laughter continued as he gently kissed where the bubbles had been. The tenseness was gone. Any and all fear of him had passed. Who could be afraid of a big teddy bear?

At that moment I could've forgiven him anything, and I did. I consciously forgave him for all that he'd put me through for the last month. It would've all been worth it, even if the change was only for that moment.

But it wasn't.

"Hey, Rachel," he called from the back as I was clearing off a couple of tables.

"Yeah?" I asked as I stepped past the swinging kitchen door. He was standing by the prep table, making our pizza.

"Come see this," he said excitedly.

I walked over to where he was standing. In his hand was a juice glass with a crocus stuck in it.

"This means it's spring."

I looked at the flower, then back at him. It was all too much. I'd gotten used to Joel the way he was. Sure, it wasn't great, but it was better than it had been. Fear ran through my veins, but it wasn't the same kind. It was the fear of hoping too much. What all Newstead hadn't been able to do, Joel could with that one little flower.

I wanted to ask him about it, but I didn't, mainly because I didn't want to see that cold look in his eyes as he reverted back. He put the glass with the flower in it on the prep table and put our pizza in the oven. I stood back and watched him. Even his movements were different. He was more fluid, less robotic.

I could tell he didn't like me staring at him, so I tried to make myself busy. I got our plates and went to the dining room to turn on the radio. The pizza was out and cut by the time I came back into the kitchen.

"How's Aunt Beth?" he asked easily, as if asking about the weather, as if talking about Aunt Beth wasn't banned.

"The same," I began hesitantly, not daring to say how truly bad it'd gotten. But his mood didn't seem to change. There was no hardened jaw and cold eyes, just sympathetic concern.

"How's school?" I asked, taking the plunge. It was the question I'd wanted to ask for the last five weeks but had never dared to get the words out.

To my surprise, his mood seemed to elevate even further as he told me about the training exercise the following week.

"Great, actually. Next week is that FTX I told you about. I've finally finished getting ready for it; it should be a lot of fun."

He said the words lightly, but I sensed there was still more to it he wasn't telling me. But at least he was telling me something, and I was grateful for that.

Is that what his moodiness has been about? He hasn't felt ready for his training exercise, his Capture the Flag? And now that he has it figured out, all's well with the world? He couldn't possibly be that shallow, could he? No, the intensity in his eyes, that protective grimace couldn't possibly be about a game.

And then I remembered. It wasn't about a game. It was about a war.

"Tell me more," I encouraged, hoping to set myself at ease, to silence my growing fear.

"Pretty much every class we've had for the last two months has been focused on this exercise. They take it very seriously. We learned the other day that you can drink your own urine to survive if you have no water. Did you know that?" he asked.

I busted out laughing. That wasn't what I'd expected him to say at all.

"I don't know why they'd think we'd need that one. We're only going outside for three days and water is one of the supplies we're allowed to take with us. But I thought it was kind of fascinating, something you'd never think of, right?"

"I'd never think of it," I said as I tried to get control of myself. If you'd told me earlier that day I'd be talking with Joel about drinking pee, I'd never have believed you.

He'd gone back to being a goofy seventeen-year-old; he'd gone back to being just...Joel.

He frowned, already moving on to another thought. "It kind of reminds me about how intense Coach Feurch would get before playoffs. I really like football, as much as any sport I play, but he acted like it was a matter of life and death. That's how they are about FTX here. It means everything to them."

I nodded, but didn't answer. It looked like this FTX was important to him, too.

Too important.

Another memory flashed into my mind before I could process that thought. It was someone else telling me about it, someone other than Joel. Nathan, in hushed tones and wayward glances, had told me about it, too. Only he hadn't called it FTX, he'd called it training their army.

He'd said it long before Joel had even come to Weston. Nathan had been in their woods and he had seen things, things he wouldn't tell me about, things I refused to know. I already knew too much. I'd already seen them, what they were training them to become.

And now they were training Joel.

I swallowed hard and forced myself to forget about it, at least for right then. I'd already learned how quickly *my* Joel could disappear. For all I knew, those short minutes were all I had with him. Instead, I listened as he talked about his spring break with his mother. It was a good distraction from what my mind kept going back to.

She'd be picking him up a week from Monday. Apparently, she was surprising him with some vacation. Joel didn't have a clue what her waitress salary could afford, but he was excited anyway.

He wasn't talking for a while before I noticed it. Instead, he was watching me with a strange look on his face.

"Why are you looking at me like that?" His confused eyes were trying to read mine.

Reluctantly, I asked the question I'd been dreading since I'd first noticed the change in him that night.

"What's been up with you lately? And then tonight, for no reason, you're back to being yourself again. Do you want to let me in on it?"

His face clouded momentarily. *Great. Why can't I just leave well enough alone? Why do I always have to know the reasons behind everything?* But it was only for a moment. Joel's face returned to normal as he thought about my question.

"Rachel, I know this sounds like a copout, but really, the less you know the better. You're right; things weren't going well there for a while. I can't give you more details than that, but earlier this week things started looking up. I'm sorry I put you through hell this month, Rache. It should be over now, though." He ended his speech with a bright smile that almost reached his eyes.

I only hear one word: *should.* He'd said things should be over, not that they were. His cautious eyes confirmed my rising doubt.

This new Joel was for my benefit, a way of making up for the last five weeks.

Sometimes I wished Nathan's inquisitions hadn't made me so observant. I truly wanted to believe everything was going to be great, to believe every word Joel had said, that suddenly life was grand. But I just couldn't; I wasn't wired that way. For his sake, though, I also would pretend that somehow one week had changed everything. My fake smile was placed right back on my face.

We left at a little after seven-thirty, but it was still light out, another sign of spring. We got our last one as we were walking along the farmer's lane. It was a complete mud pit. I clung tightly onto Joel's arm as I cautiously made my way along. Joel quietly laughed every time my feet slid out from underneath me. His never did.

For some odd reason, Joel didn't stop at the bend before my trailer. Instead, he walked with me up the concrete steps, and even asked if he could come inside.

I paused briefly to hear if Aunt Beth was unusually rowdy. All was silent, so I nodded to Joel, who was looking expectantly at me. I wasn't sure what we'd find there. Nathan, exhausted from his mother's rampages, had been sleeping at odd hours, catching catnaps whenever Aunt Beth fell asleep.

To my surprise, they were both sitting on the couch, and they were dressed, like they'd been expecting us. I glanced at Nathan and as I did, he nodded slightly. But it wasn't towards me. I turned to Joel just as he was finishing a nod of his own.

Joel unfolded the metal chair that was leaning against the wall and seated himself opposite Nathan.

"How's she doing?" Joel asked, nodding towards Aunt Beth. His face was somber.

"Just fine now," Nathan answered. Neither one of them seemed to notice my eyes going back and forth between the two of them.

Surprisingly enough, Aunt Beth *did* look fine, as if whatever had been causing her behavior for the last five weeks was gone. She looked like herself again; better, actually. She looked clear and focused, not the lethargic aunt I'd grown used to for the last ten years. She looked like she did in all those younger pictures of her that lined the trailer walls, the pictures that were taken before Uncle Henry died, when she'd looked whole.

Joel only nodded in understanding to Nathan's answer as if he fully understood the reason behind the transformation. I alone was in the dark as Aunt Beth met Joel's gaze with a nod of her own.

Did I just imagine that?

Aunt Beth, who hadn't been able to put together a rational sentence in years, was somehow clear enough to nod to Joel before he quietly turned his gaze towards mine.

Joel stood up, the purpose behind his short, bizarre visit apparently accomplished. Nathan rose also, and reached out his hand towards Joel, a gesture I'd never seen Nathan do before. Joel took his hand willingly enough and shook it briefly once, twice, before turning to leave.

I followed him outside, hoping to get some kind of answers from him. Joel quietly took me in his arms as soon as we reached the bottom of the concrete steps.

He lightly kissed me on the lips before turning to stroll slowly back towards Newstead.

I turned, too, only I went into the trailer to talk to Nathan.

He was still sitting on the couch next to his mother when I walked back in. That time, it was me sitting on the folding chair. Nathan didn't seem to notice; he was too busy talking with her. I'd never heard them have a conversation before. It was rather fascinating.

They didn't talk about anything important; it was just that they were talking at all. Nathan was bubbling over with satisfaction every time his mother answered one of his questions. And he had quite a few.

I waited for over an hour for either one of them to notice I was in the room with them, but neither did. Or maybe Nathan was just avoiding the inevitable argument. I don't know, but that night I let him win. It was getting hard to watch them.

I stood and went to my room, unsatisfied.

chapter seventy-seven/ something like that

Just living is not enough. One must have sunshine, freedom, and a little flower.
    -Hans Christian Anderson

I got to work at eleven like I always did on Saturdays. Taking the key I'd placed under the rock after closing on Friday, I unlocked the door. No Fred again. I hadn't seen him in over five weeks. I hadn't known that when he'd told Nathan he was going out of town that he'd meant permanently.

After his visit, he started mailing my pay to the restaurant. Every week I'd find it there, shoved through the mail slot in the door. It was just mine, and even though it came through the mail, it still contained a small stack of dirty fives.

I wondered if Fred knew Joel was still working there. I'd never told Joel that I knew about him getting fired, and he never mentioned not getting paid.

It was kind of nice being alone as I began to do the usual opening procedures: turning on the oven, warming up the fryers, taking the dough out of the fridge from the previous night, lastly, turning over the sign to tell the world we were open for business.

Some of the locals arrived just then, seating themselves on two of the swivel seats by the counter: Stan and James, seventy-somethings, who'd become some of my regulars on Saturdays.

I poured each of them a cup of coffee without bothering to ask. I knew what they wanted. They each quietly opened their papers as I resumed my daily prep work, stopping on occasion from my cheese grating to refill their half-empty mugs.

At twelve, a couple other locals joined them, preferring the far booth; *our* booth. I took their order while delivering Stan's club, no mayo. (His wife had put a limit on his mayo consumption since his last heart attack. She had failed to dictate anything about the bacon, though). James was content with an order of toast.

Joel had been arriving earlier on Saturdays since the beginning of April. The large pile of dishes waiting for him when he came in at five must've shown him that business was picking up. So, I wasn't surprised that day when he walked in at two. The two men on the stools looked up briefly, nodding their acknowledgement.

Joel's bright mood had at least lasted more than a day; his smile was still radiating. Stan also seemed to notice, having only known the somber, sullen Joel.

"Did you win the lottery or something, kid?" Stan sarcastically asked, nudging his neighbor. Pointing to Joel, he continued, "Look at the kid." James looked up courteously before returning to his paper, unimpressed.

"Something like that." Joel smiled as he filled their cups before turning to go into the kitchen to finish whatever prep I hadn't started.

"What's up with the kid?" Stan asked me, as if I had some secret information.

I shrugged as I peeked into the kitchen. Joel was whistling

again.

He came out from the back and cleared the few tables I hadn't gotten to yet. As he walked past me, he leaned his head in and lightly kissed me on the cheek. My face enflamed. I quickly glanced at the two men who were sitting at the counter to see if they saw. They did.

Stan laughed, shaking his head behind his paper. "Something like that," he repeated, before turning away, giving us our privacy.

I glared towards Joel, but he'd already slipped back into the kitchen.

I tried to stay mad at him, but it was impossible. Especially when he spent most of the day with a big grin on his face, like he *had* won the lottery.

By six, it had started to slow down and I went in the back to make our usual pizza. He was already there waiting for me, with the pizza made and cut. There was a second flower in the juice glass.

"What are you doing on Monday?" he asked suddenly.

"Nothing," I answered, getting excited.

"I have this place I go to a lot, especially lately. I just wanted to show it to you." His playful face had suddenly turned very serious.

"Is it your hiding place?"

"Yes."

"And will I finally get to read some of what you've written?" I moved closer to him, until we were almost touching.

"Don't push it," he said, but his eyes were teasing.

"I'm not going to drop it, you know."

"I know," he answered, still smiling.

I guess I don't look too threatening. "But seriously, I'd love to go with you."

"It's a date," he answered, the matter settled. By then, I was smiling, too.

We made arrangements for him to meet me at my trailer on Monday, right after I got home from school. I began to wonder what kind of place he'd been spending his time at. It reminded me that there was a whole side of Joel, a secret life almost, that I was completely unaware of.

Like the bizarre exchange between Joel and Nathan the other night. I still wondered what my keen eyes had missed. Neither of them were offering anything, but that had never stopped me before.

rachel

chapter seventy-eight/ a miracle

Life is what happens while you are busy making other plans.
  -John Lennon

I didn't plan on skipping school that Monday; it sort of just happened. I was running later than usual. Aunt Beth had slept the whole night through, so the rest of us did, too. It kind of surprised me when I woke up and it was already past seven-thirty. It'd been a long time since I'd done that.

School started at eight, but it was a little after that by the time I was hurrying through town. I usually don't look in store windows, but even in my rush, I found myself drawn to Clancy's, Weston's one clothing store.

Maybe it was because I was already thinking about my date with Joel that night, or maybe it was just a really beautiful dress. Either way, I walked over and peered in the front window at a dress that looked like it had been made just for me.

I didn't own a dress, not even one. I don't know if I ever had. But for some reason I wanted that one. It was dark brown with long sleeves and a straight skirt that went about halfway down the mannequin's legs. I could see myself in it. It was simple.

I went to the door and opened it. Clancy's was the first real clothing store I'd been in that I could remember. Usually I just picked up what I needed from thrift stores. It would feel strange being the first person to wear something.

The dress was even prettier up close. I found my size and carried it to where the changing rooms were. I quickly pulled my rust-colored sweater over my head and put on the brown knit.

My bedroom at home didn't have a mirror in it and the bathroom only had a very small one right above the tiny sink. The changing stall that I found myself in had a big mirror, from the floor to the ceiling. I stood and looked at myself for the first time in forever. The reflection didn't look like the mental picture I had of myself. In that dress, I was a completely different person. In my dress, I felt beautiful.

I should've looked at the price first thing, then I wouldn't have gotten my hopes up. But too late, I glanced at the white tag dangling by my wrist. Two hundred dollars.

Even if I took everything I owned and sold it online, it wouldn't have added up to two hundred dollars. I carefully took the dress off and put it back on the hanger. It was hard to put my own clothes back on. I looked at the girl in the mirror one last time before pulling the curtain open.

There was a loud angry voice coming from the back of the store, by the registers. A woman was there yelling at a red-faced cashier. He probably wasn't too much older than me.

"It has an ink spot on it. Do you expect me to wear something with an ink spot?"

"What do you want me to do about it?" he asked as she continued to confront him. I stood back and watched the scene. It always amused me to watch someone make an ass of themselves.

"Take it back and give me a new one. I spent perfectly good money on this dress and I want a perfectly good dress in return."

"Let me see if we have another one. What size was it?" he asked anxiously.

"Size four," the woman stated incredulously, like she couldn't possibly be anything else.

They marched past me towards the front window and started looking at the rack that my dress had come from. I knew they wouldn't find a size four there because I was holding the only one. I almost told them so, but I waited instead. I was having too much fun to have it end so soon.

The woman didn't disappoint me.

"Do I look like a size six to you?" she yelled when the cashier suggested she take the next size up. Another person came from the back of the store to see what the commotion was about.

"Is there something I can help you with?" the new person asked. It was really getting good. By that time, the trio noticed me watching them.

The angry customer walked over to me and puffed out her chest.

"Would that happen to be a size four?" she asked. I could tell she was having a hard time keeping herself under control. I was, too. The look on her face was priceless.

"Why yes, it is," I said, smiling.

"And may I have it, *please*?" The control was definitely slipping.

"I haven't decided if I'm going to buy it or not yet," I lied. I'd decided the second I saw the price, but it was fun watching her face turn purple.

Both workers ran over to our side to break up any brawl that might take place. But the puffed-up woman had already looked me over and decided against that course of action.

"There's no need to be hasty. There are two dresses. You can both have one."

"I don't want one with an ink stain," the woman said between clenched teeth.

They both turned to look at me. They obviously thought I looked like the more reasonable one of the two.

"Well, I don't want to pay full price for a dress that's damaged, and has probably been stretched out." I looked down at the woman with a smile. She didn't miss my meaning.

"Fine, fine. We'll give you a really good deal on the stretched out...I mean the damaged one," the second cashier said. He looked nervously at the woman, who didn't miss that, either.

"What kind of a deal?" I began to get excited but did my best to hide it.

"How does twenty bucks sound?"

I paused to look like I was thinking it over. They all stared at me anxiously.

"Fine," I finally said, with more calmness than I'm usually capable of. I really wanted that dress.

I counted out four of Fred's dirty fives and handed them over to the cashier. From the look on his face, he noticed there was nowhere near enough money in my wallet to have afforded the original price.

I smiled as I walked out of the store carrying my new dress that had been neatly folded and wrapped in tissue paper before being placed in a real department store bag.

I crossed the street to the general store. It wasn't long before I found what I was looking for. I knew from years of experience buying things second-hand that hairspray would take out the tiny ink stain the woman was having such a fit about. On my way to the register, I grabbed a pair of panty hose. Having a full length mirror had shown me the necessity of that purchase.

It was only ten by the time I left both stores. I should've gone to school, but I knew I'd have to forge an excuse and I really didn't feel like going through the drama. So I didn't.

Instead, I turned in the opposite direction of the school and headed deeper into Weston. It was a part I'd never been through before. It wasn't on the way to either work or school, so there was never a need for me to go there.

There were no businesses in that section of Weston, only houses. They were lined neatly in rows with fences surrounding each one.

I didn't have a purpose to my walk; I was just walking. And then I saw him.

He was four, maybe five. His yard was one of the fenced in ones and he was playing in what used to be grass; only now it was mud, and he was covered in it. I watched him with the same amusement that I'd watched the irate woman.

Boy is he going to get it. And then he wasn't alone. A young woman came out and sat down next to him, in the mud. She didn't yell at him for destroying their front yard or make him go in and take a bath. She played with him.

She played with him.

I didn't realize I was crying until I felt the tears fall off my cheeks onto my sweater. The ache that was suddenly inside me had a heartbeat. I felt each thump as the words rushed through my head, my heart: family, love, acceptance.

It was a throbbing, unexplainable thing—that want, that need. No more moving. No more being alone. I wanted my own front yard, with my own child. I wanted what she had, and I wanted it with Joel.

Every part of my empty life came crashing down on me in that one second. It was empty because of me, because I was empty. I'd been in over twenty-three different towns in six years, but I'd never actually lived in any of them. I just went to school and then to whatever job would give me the most hours.

It wasn't until that day that I realized I, like Nathan, had been hiding from the world. For ten years, ever since my parents died, I'd walked through life zombie-like, feeling nothing, being nothing.

I didn't want to be like that anymore.

What had started with Joel's little flower, finished with a little boy.

In that moment I believed in miracles. It was a miracle I'd found Joel, a miracle I hadn't shut him out, like I did everything else.

I breathed in deeply. *Maybe there's still hope for me.*

rachel

chapter seventy-nine/ rushing waters

The fear of death follows from the fear of life. A man who lives fully is prepared to die at any time.
-Mark Twain

I started walking again, like I actually had a place I was heading towards. Weston's residential section isn't that big, only a three block area. At the end of it is the gate to Lambert, the other private school in Weston. It was open, so I walked through it.

The grounds were just what you'd expect from a school of horticulture. The lawns were perfectly manicured, all the hedges trimmed. The flower beds were bursting forth with new spring life. Daffodils, tulips, and crocuses neatly lined the edges of the arborvitaes that surrounded the clapboard buildings.

But I didn't stop at any of those. Instead, I walked past the buildings and continued towards the forest that was just beyond them. There were paths into the woods, but I didn't take them. I kept walking on my own path, straight forward.

It was a young forest, with many small saplings and thorns overtaking the ground. There was warmth on my face from the sun filtering through the pine trees mixed among the maples. It was a beautiful day.

I heard it before I saw it; the West River that trickled beneath the bridge in town roared furiously there. I followed the source of the sound as I made my way out of the woods that had turned into a clearing.

Immediately, I knew I'd found the place Joel had talked about; his hiding place. It matched his description exactly. There were mountains in the distance and a river that coursed around a bend and flowed out of sight.

There was a large boulder in the middle of the river. I walked towards it, and the closer I got, the more certain I became that there was actually someone sitting on it.

It was a man.

For some reason, it didn't seem strange to me that he should be there, past the woods, sitting on a large boulder. It felt like the most natural thing in the world. Until he spoke.

"Rachel."

I don't know if I fainted or if my legs gave out on me; all I know is that one minute I was walking towards the rock, and the next I was lying on the ground, face first in the dirt.

"Rachel, I need for you to do something for me."

My shaking hands involuntarily went up to cover my ears. But it didn't matter; the sound of him was everywhere, around me, inside me.

"I need you to take Joel to Newstead, and I need you to give something to Nathan."

And then the sound was gone. Even the river sounded quieter.

After a few minutes of hearing nothing, I forced one eye open, but from my vantage point on the ground, I couldn't see anything but the stubs of the grasses that filled the meadow. I closed my eye again and took in a deep breath.

Coward.

Damn straight, I answered myself. I'd seen and heard plenty of things during my time in Weston, but nothing—nothing—compared to what had been sitting on that rock.

Part of me knew he was gone, but I couldn't convince myself to get up. *What if I'm wrong? What if he's just waiting for me to turn around so he can blast me with his laser eyes or drown me with that voice? No, I'm just going to stay right here.* And I did, until I heard my bag with my dress in it start to blow away. That got me moving.

I sat up and tried to grab it, but it was too late for that; it was already halfway to the boulder, the empty boulder. He was gone. The river was gone, too. At least the rushing river was. Instead, it looked like it did in town, trickling along.

My bag came to rest by the boulder that was no longer in the middle of the river; instead, it was several feet away from it, or maybe it was just the river that had moved. I don't know, but the scene was definitely less than it had been just minutes before. I tried to forget the reason why that was.

On the flat surface of the boulder, there was a piece of paper that had been ripped in half, weighted down by a smaller rock. Its edges ruffled in the breeze.

It looked like regular lined notebook paper that had writing on it; the chicken scratch of a child. I leaned against the rock and read it. Then I read it again.

It was…it was beautiful. I didn't need anyone to tell me what I was reading; I already knew. I finally had my wish; in my hands was some of Joel's writing.

I folded the paper and placed it carefully in my pocket. I needed to see Nathan.

美人
rachel

chapter eighty/ nothing

There's a rebel lying deep in my soul.
   -Clint Eastwood

It was still early afternoon as I turned the last bend in the lane before my trailer came into view. It was quiet. It had been since Aunt Beth had suddenly reverted back to herself.

Actually, she was better than herself. She was whole.

She'd become almost catatonic a couple years after I'd come to live with them, usually spending most of her days and nights lying on the couch. Occasionally, she'd offer a nonsensical word, but conversations were unheard of.

The door swung open when I got to the top step, with my aunt smiling widely at me. I jumped when I saw her standing there. Some things were too hard to forget.

"Rachel, what are you doing home from school so early?" she asked.

I paused, not sure how to answer her. I wasn't used to having a parental figure, especially one who cared if I went to school or not.

Nathan came to my rescue by walking up behind her.

I stepped between them and turned so I was facing only

Nathan. "Can I talk to you for a minute?"

I'd mouthed the words. .

"What about?" he asked loudly. Sometimes Nathan was so dense.

"Outside."

"This better be good." He stomped out of the trailer and took two steps after leaving the stairs before turning to face me. "Okay, what's this all about?"

I walked past him deeper down the lane. He followed me, mumbling curse words under his breath. I could tell he'd reached the limit of his patience with me, so I turned around and just blurted it out, all of it.

His face froze in its place as soon as I began. "What did he say, exactly?"

"He told me he wanted me to take Joel to Newstead and that he wanted me to give you something. That was all."

"Did you see him or just hear him?"

"I saw him, but from far away. I could tell it was a man, but that was about it. But his voice sounded..." I paused, trying to think of a way to describe his voice. There were no words. "Very loud," I finally said to finish my inadequate description.

"What did he give you to give to me?"

I paused, unsure. I didn't see why Nathan should have Joel's journal entry–he didn't even like Joel.

"Give it to him." The words came from everywhere all at once.

Without thinking about it, my hand reached into my jacket and pulled out the precious paper. It dropped into Nathan's waiting hand.

"What's wrong, Rachel? What happened?" Nathan asked urgently. I'm guessing my face didn't look very good. I didn't feel very good, either.

"Nothing," I whispered, but Nathan didn't look like he believed me. Something in his face told me he knew from experience the terror I felt.

He scanned the paper and put it in a pocket of his own. I almost reached out and took it back, but I didn't. I didn't need to learn the same lesson twice. It wasn't mine. It was meant for Nathan.

I went inside the trailer and got ready to do the second part of what the man had asked. I had to tell Joel that I wanted him to take me to Newstead.

chapter eighty-one/ hallucinations

Let your plans be dark and impenetrable as night, and when you move, fall like a thunderbolt.
   -Sun Tzu, *the Art of War*

Monday finally came. At first I'd been dreading it, but somewhere along the line that dread had changed. Part of me was actually looking forward to it. It was the day I had to turn in my list of needed supplies. Only one question remained—would I be able to pull it off with the secrecy I needed?

The supply shed was on one end of the bunker. It was just a door on a smallish building, nothing spectacular, really. I pushed the button on the door and heard a loud buzzer echoing from somewhere inside.

I guess it's bigger than it looks from the outside. I took as step back and looked at it. *But then again, so is the bunker.*

A man I'd never seen before swung the door open and planted himself in the opening so I couldn't look past him. He crossed his arms across his chest as he looked down at me.

I took one step back and tried to decide what to do. If he was the supply officer, then he should've been expecting me. The man glaring down at me didn't look like he was expecting anyone.

Instead of guessing, I asked him.

He nodded once, but didn't move away from the open doorway.

"I'm Joel Cranston, the team leader of platoon Bravo. I was told to turn in my list to you."

Another nod was followed by a buzzing sound from somewhere far behind him. He turned and looked in that direction.

"Stay here. I'll be right back."

I reached out and stopped the door from closing. His back was just disappearing into the darkness. With him gone, I saw all kinds of things.

I pushed open the door the rest of the way and stepped inside.

The only empty spot was right by the door, past that was row after row filled from the floor to the ceiling.

It seemed like too much. There's no way they needed all that stuff just for FTX.

My eyes scanned along the rows closest to me. There were things on those shelves I never would've thought of. Hell, even my teammates hadn't thought of half of it.

I pulled out my pencil and started writing furiously. The three pages I'd had turned into ten by the time I heard footsteps approaching in the distance.

The supply officer appeared. He looked pissed that I was in there, but he didn't say anything. He only handed me the clipboard that was in his hand. "Fill out your requests on the lines and sign at the bottom of the page. As the team leader you are personally responsible for any loss or damage that may occur."

I nodded and thought back to the wasteland that the last two weekends had left. *Wonder if any of those team leaders had been held personally responsible.*

The supply officer didn't move from where he'd planted himself as I transcribed my list onto his form. After asking for more paper the second time, his arms re-crossed themselves over his chest. After I was done, I signed my name at the bottom of the last page. *Worst case scenario they can take over the lease on our apartment. I don't think we have anything else, maybe the Buick.*

I handed him back his clipboard and watched his face as he scanned each page.

"Eight coolers?" he asked incredulously.

"What can I say; we like to eat."

I smiled. He didn't.

Instead, he headed towards the rows to begin compiling the items on my massive list. I let myself out, still smiling. It was just what I needed: a long, in-depth list to hide the few oddities that needed to be hidden, like the extra blankets, food supplies, and tents. I hoped that instead of guessing my real plans, they'd just think I was being foolishly over-zealous.

I laughed to myself the entire walk to Rachel's.

chapter eighty-two/ the library

Life is divided between the horrible and the miserable.
  -Woody Allen

The surprised look on Joel's face when he came that afternoon was worth all the effort. His eyes skimmed over my body, a gesture I'd seen many times, but with Joel it lacked the sleaziness. He smiled warm and bright, his eyes dancing. I felt beautiful.

"How was your day?" I was wearing my new dress, and Joel seemed to like it as much as I did.

Joel's eyes shifted back up and his voice got excited. "Great. I spent most of my day in the supply room, ordering the things my team needs for this weekend."

I swallowed hard. I'd forgotten about his war in the woods. "What kind of supplies would you need besides tents and sleeping bags?" I asked quickly before my voice could betray what I was really feeling.

He smiled at my naiveté, about to respond. But suddenly, indecision clouded his face. He carefully looked around the trailer, his eyes briefly pausing on Aunt Beth's slouched form on the couch, taking her usual afternoon nap.

"That pretty much covers it," he answered.

He gestured to the door, suddenly ready to leave.

Once we were outside, the old Joel reappeared briefly. I watched him carefully to see if the day was going to be a wash. For some reason, *my* Joel was nowhere in sight. Thankfully, the calculating, precise look quickly retreated into the background, his broad smile in its place.

"You look beautiful," he said simply, genuinely. It was the first time anyone had ever said it to me when I believed them.

"Thank you," I answered. He pulled me into a light hug.

"Aren't you a little overdressed, though?" he asked, once again looking at me in my new dress.

"Overdressed for what?"

"I told you, remember? I'm taking you to my hiding place where you're going to force me to reveal my journals to you." He said it jokingly, but it was a little too close to what had actually happened that morning for me to laugh.

"Rachel, are you all right?"

My heart began to race. "I'm fine," I lied, and then I said the last words I wanted to say. "Actually, I was hoping we'd go someplace else instead."

"Really? But I thought you wanted to see my spot." He tried to hide his disappointment, but I could see through him. How could I tell him the truth; that I'd already been there?

"I want to go to Newstead." I forced the words out before I could change my mind.

"Newstead...are you sure?" He looked at me strangely, like he wasn't sure if it was me or not.

"Yes."

"...All right," he said as he took my hand and led me to the last place on earth I ever wanted to go.

chapter eighty-three/ desperate ground

On desperate ground, fight.
-Sun Tzu, *the Art of War*

The gates were still open.

Rachel stopped when she got to them. She hadn't said anything the entire walk through town, and she didn't say anything to me then, either. But she did reach out and grab my hand, clinging to it like it was the only thing that was keeping her standing upright.

I looked down at her pale face. She was looking straight forward. She swallowed once and then took a step, her first step onto Newstead property.

I followed slightly behind her, letting her decide how fast she wanted to go. She didn't go very fast. Her grip on my hand got tighter with each passing step.

When I looked up, I could see why.

It was a different Newstead than the one I'd left forty-five minutes earlier. This Newstead was utterly and completely still.

There was no one anywhere.

My eyes scanned the walk that went past the fountain, the outdoor rec area, even the buildings themselves. It looked like a ghost town.

But I knew better.

rachel

chapter eighty-four/ newstead

When you're fearful, you stumble.
   -Jenna Jameson

Newstead looked like Lambert, with brick buildings instead of clapboard. It lacked the hominess of Lambert, though. There it was spring; at Newstead, eternal winter.

As we got closer, I saw the brick wasn't the only difference. There was a fountain there, a freaky angel-lady holding a jar.

I shook my head. *What a sick joke.*

It seemed like that was all the founders of Newstead had added when they took over that part of the school.

My eyes stayed fixed on her. She was so beautiful, I wanted to touch her.

I stepped in her direction.

Her stone looks so smooth, so silky smooth and her eyes...

The hand that was holding mine jerked me to a stop. I glared up at Joel, but he wasn't looking at me. He was looking around the campus, so I looked, too.

"What is it?"

He didn't answer.

I gave all my attention to him.

Every muscle on his face, his body, was tensed up as his eyes roamed back and forth over the campus.

I looked too, to see if I could see what he was seeing, and surprisingly, I did.

There was no one there; no one.

There was only buildings and silence. There it was, an unseasonably warm spring day, a day where people should be outside, and no one was.

The silence was suddenly very loud.

That time it was me who pulled forward. I wanted to get whatever it was over with so I could get the hell out of there.

Joel turned to look at me then. He tried to hide his thoughts, but that was impossible; I know what it looks like when someone doesn't trust you.

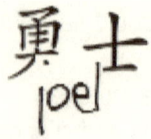

chapter eighty-five/ hell

He who exercises no forethought but makes light of his
opponents is sure to be captured by them.
    -Sun Tzu, *the Art of War*

Rachel kept walking even after we reached the center of it all:
the fountain. She turned to the left and walked past Chapman,
past the rest of the housing buildings. Finally, she stopped
when she stood outside the library.

She turned to face it.

I stepped past her and opened the door. The library, like
everything else there, was utterly still.

There was only one spot I could think to take her, so I
grabbed her hand again and led her to the back. It was the
place I used to go before it stopped being safe to be at
Newstead during daylight hours. It was the spot with the maps
and atlases where I'd found my copy of the Art of War.

She sat in the seat I pulled out for her. After an initial scan of
the premises, I took my seat beside her. There was no one in
there, either.

Slowly, I pulled Rachel's chair closer to mine, suddenly
needing to be near her. The temptation to talk about all that had
happened to me over the last month and a half became

overwhelming. Instead of giving into it, I bowed my head towards hers and told her the first thing to come to my mind; I told her why I'd taken her there.

The deep urgency left. I looked up to see where it'd gone. All too soon, I got my answer.

A version of Rachel's voice hit me then, sultry and smooth; hers, but not the same. I looked at her face. Instead of her usual softness there was only steel. Dean Erikson's words rang in my head as I watched her, listened to her.

We have ways of surveillance. Only then he'd been talking about Aunt Beth.

A low hiss left my mouth. They'd learned a lot about me over the past few months.

They knew the only way to get at me was through Rachel.

rachel

chapter eighty-six/ hell

Heaven has no rage like love to hatred turned, nor hell a fury like a woman scorned.
  -William Congreve

Joel led, his arm stretched out behind him, keeping me from getting lost. We made several abrupt turns, his hand locked on mine as I tried to keep up. He finally stopped when we got to a long wooden table in a remote corner of the library. It was surrounded by shelves of thick leather bound books. It felt private.

I sat in the chair he pulled out for me and waited for him to sit, too. He did, but for him it was more of a dropping, like he couldn't support his own weight anymore.

I closed my eyes so I wouldn't have to see that; Joel, looking broken.

As if to prove me wrong, his hands gripped on my chair and pulled it toward his, until they were touching.

I looked up then, but his head was bowed down. I lowered mine until it met his.

His breath hit my face in soft puffs until it held, and I knew it was coming, I knew the reason for us being there had come to fruition.

He exhaled. "This is where I go sometimes when I need to...research."

He looked outside my web of hair to the left, and then to the right, to see if anyone was listening, as if admitting you were researching in a library was a capital offense; treason.

"What were you researching?" The words forced themselves out, almost as if they weren't my own.

His head jerked up at the smooth sound of my voice. He looked deeply into my eyes, but it was a different kind of looking than he normally did when he looked at me. He didn't look like he liked what he saw there.

I was suddenly overcome with the need to know. A soft voice, not my own, whispered in my ear to ask again. The more I tried to ignore that voice, to hold onto some control of myself, the louder the soft voice became, drowning me out.

"What have you discovered?" the smooth voice asked from my mouth, smiling seductively. My frozen eyes were the only part of me that was still, at that moment, in my control.

Joel's hands dropped from my knees, slowly sliding his chair back so he could fully assess me.

My legs crossed and uncrossed as my body lounged back in the leather chair in a sensual way. The soft rustle of my cursed pantyhose was the only sound in the room as Joel attempted to regain control of himself. He was obviously affected by my sudden, forceful display.

My fingers began tracing along my arms, along my legs, pulling my knee length dress up, up, before silently resting my hands on his chair. Suddenly, I was gripping onto the arms of it, forcefully pulling the chair back towards mine with a strength I'd never known before.

"Tell me," I demanded, as my fingers began tracing along his arms, his legs.

I watched in silent horror, a spectator as someone else used my body, my voice, to seduce him.

He gently placed his hands over mine, stopping their inward progress.

"Well, you know about that FTX I'm doing this weekend?" His chair slid back to where it had been.

"Yes...," I said urgently, all attempt at seduction gone, as the impatient voice made its demands.

"Well I really want to win, you know, show all those guys that just because I'm new doesn't mean they're any better than me. So I found a map of the training field and found this really high spot. That's where I'm going to go set up. They won't even know what hit them." His face looked smug, but not his eyes, his eyes just looked sad.

The force inside me retreated somewhat, seeming to be satisfied with that answer, but I knew better. It didn't sound like Joel at all; it was almost like he'd just lied to me.

"Why do you want to win so badly?" It sneered. It wasn't releasing its hold on me just yet, not until it got all it wanted.

"I want to win because that'll show all them assholes who really should be their class chair for next year."

Joel smiled defiantly, that time the smile reached his eyes.

I had no idea what he was talking about.

"Good, very good," the voice answered, before retreating enough in the background for me to speak, to move.

I jumped up, determined to leave.

Instead of letting me, Joel gently eased me back down into the seat. With his hand still firmly on my shoulder he reached for one of the journals that lined the shelves, opening it to a page with a bunch of maps.

"This is the training field," he said, pointing to a big green blob on the page. "And this is that high spot I told you about. If Chad's team gets to it first, then we'll have to go here." He pointed to another spot on the map, just east of where he'd first pointed.

I'm sure my face looked as confused as I was. I had no idea why he was showing me all that.

"It's going to be so cool; there's no way Chad will be able to beat us."

He looked intently at me as I continued to sit frozen where he'd placed me. The whole conversation felt off. I nodded, because I could tell he wanted me to.

Joel put the journal back. "Was that all you wanted to see? I know you're worried about me being gone all weekend, but I'll be just fine; it's perfectly safe." His hand moved from my shoulder to my hand. He patted it and then left it there. It was a still a restraint, keeping me from obeying the voice inside my head that was telling me it was time to go. Right on cue he answered the voice, as if he'd heard it, too. "Are you ready to go now? I'm getting a little hungry, we can see if Fred's isn't too busy."

His free hand slid back my chair, giving me room to stand. I jumped to my feet.

He stood too, right in front of me. He slowly walked out of the library, forcing me to do the same.

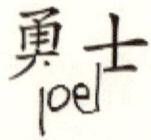

chapter eighty-seven/ silver lining

If his place of encampment is of easy access, he is tendering
a bait.
    -Sun Tzu, *the Art of War*

I recoiled, pulling my chair back away from the thing in
Rachel's body. It didn't seem to notice. Instead, it almost took it
as a challenge.

I always knew I could push myself further, I just never had. I
was already too much of a freak. But that day, at that moment,
watching Rachel's terrified eyes as she was being used like a
puppet to seduce me made me push. And I pushed hard.

I closed my eyes briefly and then opened them.

The world and everything in it was completely altered. I could
see everything and anything I turned my eyes to look at. It didn't
matter if it was in the room with me or not; I could see it, hear it,
smell it.

In the span on a single second, I located each and every one
of the hiding Newstead students and staff. Some of them were
even in that very library, in a secret room on the other side of
the bookshelves.

Erikson was in his office physically, but his real presence
actually rested right in front of me in Rachel herself, not trusting

the job to anyone else.

And I saw something else, too.

There was a tall form directly behind Rachel's back. His presence was obvious then, where during the previous second he'd been nonexistent: A tall blond man unlike any I'd ever seen before. His intense eyes turned to mine with the sudden realization that I'd seen him. A brief smile played across his mouth before he disappeared, vaporizing right before my eyes. Even with my new enhanced senses, I couldn't tell where he'd gone.

After he'd left, I turned my attention back to the matter at hand. Quickly, in my mind, I formulated a plan, which I speedily carried out.

My hands found Rachel's and put a stop to the useless seduction. Instead, I looked her in the eyes and pretended I believed it was really her I was speaking to.

I laid it on thick, using all I'd learned about my classmates and their behavior; what would've been expected of me if I'd been anything like them. The broad smile on Erikson's face in his office told me I was on the right track. He was just feeling me out. I guess he didn't wholly trust my quick change of heart, especially so close to the exercise when so much was at stake.

Even after he released his hold on Rachel, I could still sense him listening.

I took advantage of the opportunity to remove all doubt. Continuing with the charade, I pointed out with arrogance my obvious plans using maps and charts. After I finished with some lame explanation for having brought Rachel there in the first place, I closed my eyes to reassess the outcome of all of my statements. Erikson leaned back in his chair, satisfied.

"Go."

It was the same rushing water voice I'd been hearing for the last month, but with my augmented ears it sounded different, almost musical, like an orchestra on steroids.

I looked at Rachel. The voice was right; it was time to go. Her eyes were urgent, almost frantic.

I stood up and slowly led her out of the library, then Newstead itself. It would've undermined all my efforts if we'd broken out in a terrified run. If I was to be successful, Erikson and all the others had to believe the lie I'd just presented; everything depended on it.

I began to be grateful that Rachel had suggested bringing her there. I hadn't realized that I was still in danger. I'd been wrong.

Showing up that day with her seemed to be the missing piece I needed to convince everyone of my transformation. Seeing the smug look on Erikson's face was enough to tell me I'd done just that. Even before we left campus, life at Newstead went back to normal. Students piled out of the places they'd been sent to. Dean Erikson returned to his work, whistling softly to himself.

I closed my eyes again and pushed the voice in my head and all that my senses could do into the background. I opened them just in time to catch Rachel as she fell.

美人
rachel

chapter eighty-eight/ ferocious kitten

Failure is simply the opportunity to begin again, this time more intelligently.
   -Henry Ford

As soon as we'd passed the gate, my legs buckled beneath me, unable to support me anymore. Without stopping, Joel swung his arm under my useless legs and carried me, infant style.

I sobbed weakly against his chest as he strode towards town, past Fred's. He didn't stop until he was at the bend just before my trailer, where he placed me on my feet.

"What the hell happened back there?" I asked, finding my voice.

"Rachel, trust me, you're much better off not knowing."

I pushed off his chest. "But it was inside me! What was that inside of me?!"

Joel reached for me then, as my screaming turned into sobs again. His gentle hands were consoling, rubbing my hair, wiping the tears from my eyes. It was a wasted effort, since more just fell in their place.

"Honey, I'm sorry you had to go through that. It wasn't about you at all; it was just about me, okay?" He rubbed my back, trying to pacify me, as if somehow the thought that it was only about him made it all better. Didn't he understand I already knew that?

"Are you in danger?' I asked, not wanting to know.

"No." He turned from me then, trying to hide the lie.

So that's been it all along, he's *been the one in danger, but why? Isn't he one of them?*

No; I thought, answering my own question. *He's never been one of them.*

"What are you going to do?" I asked, clinging to him.

"Whatever I need to."

He stood even taller then, with his shoulders squared, his strong face intimidating. He hadn't reverted into intense Joel, but carried the same strength, as if the two had suddenly merged. But even with all of his attributes, and I knew better than almost anyone what those were, how could he have a prayer against so many of them? When they were so focused on destruction, on *his* destruction in particular?

"What do you want me to do?"

Joel chuckled at the sight of me; the ferocious kitten ready to attack the giant. Not realizing the overwhelming odds; possibly realizing, but still not caring. Despite all of that, I would've done anything Joel suggested, anything to ease the tension I saw in his eyes.

"Will you go back?"

He looked up then, towards them. "I have to."

I grabbed his face and pulled it back down to me. "No, you don't; come away with me right now; we can leave tonight."

I could tell I'd already lost by the look in his eyes. He would stay.

chapter eighty-nine/ visons and nightmares

When you can't make them see the light, make them feel the heat.

    -Ronald Reagan

I wrapped my arms around him, like I had a chance at restraining him. But he let himself be restrained, for a little while at least.

He bent his head down and lightly kissed me on my mouth, then again, still light. I reached up and pulled him closer, and that time, when his mouth came down, it was open and urgent. I didn't pull away. I didn't want to.

Our kisses stopped, but not the need. Joel drew back and traced his finger along the neckline of my dress, progressively going lower and lower, watching my face the whole time. I watched him, too.

I closed my eyes and my head tilted back as his hand slipped inside my dress.

The moment my eyes closed, a picture filled my mind. Not a dream, it was much more real than that; real enough to make me forget all about Joel and what he was doing.

The picture was of me. I was sitting inside Nathan's truck. I didn't like the look on my face. It was a dead look. Just as I was thinking that, the picture moved; the truck moved, and I moved with it. Once we were gone all that was left was Joel. He was standing where the trailer had just been. And he was alone.

I screamed his name, but he didn't hear me. He circled the spot where the trailer had been. In his eyes I saw the truth the same time he did; I was gone. I'd left him.

He fell to his knees.

I forced my eyes open to get that picture as far from me as I could, but it didn't work. Joel was looking down at me and his eyes looked the same as they had in my mind. They looked as empty as I felt.

His hands dropped to his side.

"Joel, I..."

He scanned my face. What he saw there made him pull back further, leaving a large empty space between us.

"I'm sorry." It was all I could think of to say. *How can I tell him the truth?*

"It's okay," Joel mumbled, looking away, trying to get control of himself.

I reached out to him, trying to erase the distance between us. "No, really, Joel, I'm sorry; I just..." I couldn't find the right words to say, but at least he turned and looked towards me instead of anywhere but.

"I get it. It's okay," he repeated, trying not to look dejected as he took my hands off him. I wasn't the only one interested in self-preservation.

"Joel...I..." The sorrowful look in his eyes made me continue, "I didn't stop because I don't want you. I stopped because I'm afraid if we do *that* and you or I leave, I'd never be able to get over it. I don't think either of us would."

It was as close to the truth as I could get.

His eyes softened. He understood.

I wrapped my arms around him, and that time he let me.

"It's okay," he repeated in a lighter tone, a completely different meaning tied to the same words.

I closed my eyes and buried my head in his chest. It helped with the emptiness. He seemed to understand, because he let me. By the time he pulled back, I'd forgotten about everything but him. Pretty much. .

"I have to go," he said.

I nodded, I knew he did. He kissed me lightly on the forehead before squaring his shoulders. He looked so alone.

So alone, just like in the picture.

I sat down on the steps and watched as he walked away. It felt like someone had dropped a ten pound piece of lead, right into my stomach. If that vision was true, then I would be leaving. Sitting there, staring at the empty lane that Joel had just walked down, I couldn't believe it. There was no way I'd leave him like that.

Then why was that vision so damn real?

I had no idea.

美人
rachel

chapter ninety/ the painting

What is a weed? A plant whose virtues have never been discovered.
    -Ralph Waldo Emerson

I dug under my bed until I found it, pressed right up against the wall. My fingers traced along the lid, hesitantly, reverently. I closed my eyes and pulled the box out.

It was a shoebox from a pair of light-up princess sneakers my mom and dad had gotten for me when I was five. But it wasn't the box that mattered.

Slowly, I brushed off the layer of dust that coated the lid and even more slowly I took the lid off and put it on the floor next to me.

Paints and brushes that used to be my best friends, friends that I hadn't seen in years, looked up at me. Everything looked exactly the same.

I picked up my favorite brush and brought it up close to my face and swooshed it along my cheek. My eyes closed again and I did the other side.

I'd come home.

I sat there for a while, looking down at the blank sheet of

paper. Usually I painted landscapes, occasionally animals, but I'd never painted a person before.

I dropped the brush and picked up a pencil instead, at least that way if I made a mistake, I could just erase it.

Very slowly I started; just some light strokes at first, followed by darker lines as my hands took over. It was like I'd never stopped. After I was done with the outline, I grabbed the brush again and started adding the pigments.

I was so focused on doing each part right: his hazel eyes that crinkled when he smiled, his hair that kept falling in his face, his flushed skin, that when I was done and took a moment to look at the summation of all the parts, I was awestruck. Not at my ability to paint, but at Joel.

My fingers traced over the picture just like I would've done to him if he was there. I shook my head in amazement. *After all these years my ability has never left me; even when I paint an angel.*

The picture took some of the sting out of the vision I'd had. Now he'd always be there, he'd always be mine; even if it was only in a painting.

I stayed up until after three in the morning telling the picture that I loved him and that I was sorry.

chapter ninety-one/ roles to fill

When the enemy has made a plan of attack against us, we must anticipate him by delivering our own attack first.
   -Ho Shih

Tuesday started where Monday left off, at least the part about everyone talking about FTX.

Steven and Marcus were both gone when I got up that morning. It felt strange without Steven there, he was *always* there; a permanent fixture in the background that you forget about until it's gone.

I walked into the mess hall and grabbed a bowl of cereal and milk. I waited a second to see if either voice would stop me, but there was only silence. *I guess it's safe to eat here again.*

I turned to go to the table I usually sat at during lunch. It wasn't empty. In fact, it was almost full with only one seat open, the one I usually sat at.

I paused then, too. Nothing. So I walked over, pulled out the chair and sat down.

I knew all of them; they were on my platoon. They were seven of the fourteen guys I'd decided were traitors. I sat back and waited for their schemes to begin. It didn't take long.

"Oh. Hi, Joel, I didn't see you sit down," one of them said. His name was Troy. He'd been the captain of the winning platoon for our class for the last two years. He was Bravo's version of Marcus.

"Troy," I answered and then went back to my breakfast.

"We're getting together later, you can come with us if you want."

I looked up at him. "Maybe, what time?" Both of us knew why I was asking.

"It would be before you have to go to work, probably right after Leadership."

A few of the other guys looked up. They weren't as good at covering up their real feelings as Troy was. I knew they didn't like me, but it wasn't until that minute that I realized it had a lot to do with my job in town, or maybe it was more my girlfriend in town.

Troy looked around at them when he noticed he wasn't commanding my attention anymore. Their eyes all dropped. "So, do you want me to count you in?"

I nodded. I'd been wondering when the sucking up would start.

And it didn't end with Troy, either.

Anthony, another one of the fourteen, sat down next to me in Biology. He started talking to me like it was something he did every day, instead of that being the first time ever.

"Joel. Good to see you, my man." He slid his chair next to mine and wrapped his arm around my shoulder. I looked first at him, then at his arm, but he didn't move either.

"There are some things we need to discuss, brother to brother."

"And what is that?" I asked as I slid my chair back. His arm dropped down, but he didn't seem to notice.

"FTX! What else?"

Anthony was Chad's best friend who, for some reason, hadn't been picked for his team.

"What about FTX?"

"Our plans, brother, our plans."

I relayed what I'd told Rachel in the library. He nodded, not looking very surprised.

"I'm talking about our *real* plans."

I flushed. "What do you mean by that?"

"Like where are you planning on putting the cylinder?"

At least Anthony got right to the point, not like Troy, who was planning on wasting my whole afternoon while he waffled around it.

I smiled at him. "I haven't decided yet. But I promise, when I do, you'll be one of the first to know."

His face went blank. I'm sure he'd never expected it to be that easy.

"Are you serious, or are you just messing with me?" He looked like he was going with option number two.

"Oh, I'm serious; I need a good man to keep an eye on it for me. I can tell that you're just the person I need."

His head started bobbing in his excitement. "That's right, and don't you forget it."

"I won't," I promised.

His head was still bobbing as he stood up and went to his usual seat.

chapter ninety-two/ auditions

He must be able to mystify his officers and men by false reports and appearances, and thus keep them in total ignorance.
-Sun Tzu, *the Art of War*

Leadership class was more preschool-level drills. I acted like I didn't notice. And really I didn't, I was too busy watching the interaction between Troy and Anthony.

Word must've gotten around to Troy about my offer to Anthony, because he looked really pissed. Not at me, I was just the mindless figurehead he was planning on using. He was mad at Anthony, who'd usurped him.

After class I followed Troy and a few other guys to the rec hall where he tried to fix the situation. He paused at first, like he didn't know quite how to bring it up. The bold honest truth wasn't his style, and true to that, he started on a completely unrelated topic.

I'd just popped the top off a soda when he sat down next to me. He looked briefly at the other guys who were waiting for his directions.

"So, Joel, it's been a while since you've been to Leadership class. Are you getting back in the swing of things? I mean if you need any help, you know I'm always there for you."

"I know." I took a swallow.

He blinked once and tried again, "I don't know if you knew this or not, but I've been the captain of two FTX platoons, two *winning* FTX platoons."

"I know." Another swallow.

Finally, he looked at one of the other guys for help.

After a brief pause, the guy he looked towards spoke up and his words sounded like they were being read to him. "Yeah, I was on his team. We creamed them, two years in a row."

I nodded and looked at all of them; then I looked up at the clock on the wall.

"It's getting late, I'd better get going. Thanks for inviting me." I stood up to leave and took one last long swallow out of my bottle before putting it next to Troy's. "Can you take care of that for me? Thanks."

I turned to go. Just as I reached the door to the rec hall, it swung open. It was Anthony. He looked past me to Troy, who at that point was standing, looking intently right back at him. Anthony led his group of six guys over to Troy's gathering or four. But it was soon equal as three other guys walked over to stand behind Troy; Troy who always kept some things in his back pocket.

I climbed the stairs and smiled to myself. They made my job too easy. I had two roles that needed to be filled and from the way auditions had gone that day I'd say Troy and Anthony would work out just fine.

Joel

chapter ninety-three/ reiterations

The general who thoroughly understands the advantages that accompany variation of tactics knows how to handle his troops.
-Sun Tzu, *the Art of War*

Rachel was sitting at the counter when I walked in. She was the only one, Fred's was completely empty. No dress that time, to my disappointment. I could've gotten used to that.

She didn't say anything as I walked past her to go into the back. The dishes were already done; the floor was swept too. By the time I came back into the dining room Rachel had her jacket on and was standing by the door.

She didn't suggest we do anything or go anywhere. Even when we got to the bend before her trailer she didn't stop like we usually did. She just kept on walking.

I paused, hoping maybe she just hadn't noticed where we were. She didn't. She just kept on walking.

I started again, picking up my pace so I could catch up with her before she reached her trailer.

She stopped then, but it was only for a second. She tilted her cheek up and I lightly kissed it. It was a kiss I would've given my mother, not Rachel.

She didn't say anything and she didn't look at me as she opened the door to her trailer and closed it immediately behind her, slightly harder than I was used to. Again I stood, that time at her doorstep, unsure of what to do next. There was no Rachel to speed up to that time, only a closed door.

At first I thought about going to the river where I usually went to be alone. But for some reason I didn't feel like it. Instead, I turned and went to the only place I could think of. I went back to Newstead.

The rec room went completely silent when I opened the door. Everyone froze. It'd been a long time since I'd made an evening appearance there.

I walked over and sat down in an empty chair and the activities slowly resumed. In my peripheral vision I could see Seth hesitating. I turned to look at him and smiled. He smiled back and walked towards me.

He was joined by John and Roy. They all sat down next to me. They were three of the six guys I considered my real team, although none of them knew that.

It was Seth who started talking, and of course it was about FTX, but his words didn't have the manipulative edge that Anthony's and Troy's had. He was just excited.

I leaned back in my chair and looked at team Bravo. They were scattered here and there throughout the rec room. I smiled to myself as I watched them. Yes, I was very happy with the selections I'd made.

chapter ninety-four/ choices

Concentrate your energy and hoard your strength.
-Sun Tzu, *the Art of War*

I almost didn't go to Fred's the next night, sort of an immature reaction to Rachel's behavior.

If it wasn't the last night before I'd get to see her again for a while I might've skipped it just to teach her a lesson. But I'm not that kind of person. So at seventeen hundred I headed out, walking towards Fred's for the last time.

Rachel seemed genuinely happy to see me, like she thought I wouldn't show.

The restaurant was moderately busy, at least compared to how it had been, with almost half the tables full. That's probably why Rachel was glad I was there, she needed my help.

I put on an apron and started clearing the stacked tables. *Apparently it's been busy for a while.* After that was done I went into the kitchen and let Rachel take care of waitressing without having to worry about being short order cook, too. The night went that way for some time. Both of us were too busy to take a breath, let alone talk.

My stomach growling made me glance at the clock. It was twenty hundred. *No wonder I'm hungry.* I looked for Rachel but she was back out in the dining room. I threw our pizza together and put it in the oven.

She came into the back just as I was cutting it. Without looking at me she grabbed a slice and headed back out into the dining room. I stood and watched the kitchen door as it swung back and forth until it finally stopped. I picked up one of my own slices and ate it, still watching that door.

They kept coming even after she flipped the closed sign. If it was me I'd have just told them to go away, but she let them in. It was twenty-two hundred when they were finally all gone and we could start on the closing work.

I kept looking at my watch as we washed the floor, as we rolled silverware. Finally I turned to her, "Listen Rachel, I have to go. If you want me to walk you home we have to leave right now or I'll never make it back on time."

At first she acted like she didn't hear me; she just kept on putting silverware in napkins. Finally, she looked up and nodded and put the half empty bin back under the counter. I grabbed her jacket from the back and handed it to her as I put on mine.

She was moving so slowly, indecisively. She looked flustered as she looked around Fred's; like it was the last time she was going to see the place. She paused at the door and looked one last time before flipping the lights off. She even hesitated at the rock as she put the key under it.

She was driving me crazy, and not in a good way. If I could pick her up and run with her to her trailer I would have. Actually I could, but something told me she would've minded that. Once we turned away from Fred's she picked up the pace, though. She almost looked like she was running.

Something's off. I turned to look at her.

Her eyes were straight forward, even though I knew she felt me watching her. Something about that alarmed me. She knew

I could read her eyes—is that why she wasn't letting me see them?

As if sensing my thoughts, she abruptly stopped and turned towards me. Her eyes were frighteningly blank. She mechanically put her hands on my arms and tilted her head back, eyes closed. It reminded me of another time when she'd done that, only that time it had been sweet. This time it felt forced.

I glanced around us. We were already at the bend by her trailer. She was just preforming her obligatory duties. She stayed that way, with her eyes closed, as I stood and watched her. Eventually her eyes opened, probably to see what my problem was. She scowled at me.

She wasn't taking no for an answer, not that night. Her hands became alive again and gripped my back pulling me closer to her. I let her. Her mouth forced itself on mine as her eyes slammed shut again. Mine stayed open. It felt too close to what'd happened in the library.

She was acting completely out of character. Her mouth and hands traced over my body, but not her eyes; they stayed closed the entire time.

I decided what the hell; I kissed her back just as forcefully as she was kissing me.

Her hands slid down from my hair to my shirt. She began fumbling with the buttons.

My breath held, waiting to see what she would do next.

Too soon I had my answer.

She jerked back, like I'd just hit her, and ran toward the trailer.

There was only cold air where her warm body had just been and that time my befuddled pause was long enough that I couldn't catch up with her. The slam of her trailer door was audible from where I stood, planted in the middle of the empty farmer's lane.

I looked at my watch; *fifteen minutes until lights out.* My indecision was palpable as I looked towards Rachel's trailer, and then towards the left, towards Newstead. The weight of uncertainty loomed in the air. And then I just did it. I made a choice and never looked back. I turned and ran to the left.

chapter ninety-five/ preparations

One who seeks to conquer by sheer strength, clever though he may be at winning pitched battles, is also liable on occasion to be vanquished; whereas he who can look into the future and discern conditions that are not yet manifest, will never make a blunder and therefore invariably win.
   -Chang Yu

Chad and I sat in the same office I'd seen both with my own eyes and with my augmented vision. It was as unchanging as Erikson himself, still an arrogant prick.

Making something of a ceremony of it, the man himself slowly opened the safe that was hidden behind some false book fronts. He looked at us with such pomp. I almost wanted to tell him the exact contents of the safe before he swung it open, one of the many things I'd been able to visualize during my time in the library. I'm sure that would've given him something to think about at night.

Thankfully I'm a self-preservationist, so instead of gloating, I looked appropriately awed as he withdrew the cylinders: Small, sleek silver capsules that would easily fit in the palm of your hand.

I quickly checked myself before I appeared over-anxious. That would've been just as lethal as indifference.

Erikson turned to us, leaving the safe wide open. My list would've been spot-on.

He immediately put one of the cylinders in Chad's outstretched hand. Then, turning to me, he paused briefly, something I'm sure he wasn't even aware of, before placing the icy object into my waiting hand. He turned back to the safe to get a third cylinder before swinging it closed.

He sat, we sat, and when we did he lifted the cylinder up until it was in front of his face. It was right at my eye level. It was all I could see. He pinched down simultaneously on both ends. Automatically a small keypad appeared on the face of the cylinder where only lustrous silver had been before. He typed in a series of numbers; an audible click was heard as the cylinder abruptly snapped open. It was empty.

I'm sure my face fell, I know Chad's did. Erikson looked at us with immense satisfaction before explaining, "Men, this is only an example of how the cylinders are to be opened. Rest assured. If you are fortunate enough to obtain the opposition's cylinder the rewards will be great indeed."

His eyes burned with an intensity I'd never seen in a living person before. My mind recognized it immediately. Erikson was enhanced, too.

Seeing him that way gave me an idea that had never occurred to me before. I could get what I wanted without all the trouble of FTX. I knew that when I was enhanced I could see through things. Why not avoid all the drama and just look into the cylinder right then?

So that's what I did.

I took a deep breath in and closed my eyes and pushed. When I opened my eyes again I looked intensely at the cylinder in my hand. The only thing I saw was Erikson's burning eyes in my peripheral vision. Whatever material they'd made the cylinders out of blocked me from seeing what was inside.

How could they have known? That's when it hit me; they knew all about me, all about what I could do, because they could do it too.

I glanced at Erikson and realized that meeting had more purposes than just handing out the cylinders for FTX. I was being tested and I'd failed. Or he'd won. Either way the end result was the same: It turned out I was one of them after all.

I'd gone for the easy win. In the few minutes I'd spent in Erikson's presence I'd become just like him. And the look on his face told me that was only the beginning. He planned on us spending lots of time together in the future. He wouldn't be finished until there was nothing left of me.

He smiled at me one last time to make sure I got his point. I nodded. I did.

Chad noticed nothing, said nothing. He was too absorbed in the moment. It was probably the single most anticipated experience of his life, being singled out by Erikson. His hand was still outstretched just as it had been when Erikson put the cylinder in it.

Into his other hand was placed a small piece of metal with numbers engraved on it. It was done with the same formality as receiving the cylinder itself. Erikson turned to me and handed me a similar piece of metal. It was the code for Chad's cylinder.

I slipped both the cylinder and the code into my front left pocket. Erikson looked surprised, surprised and disappointed. That time it was me who smiled. I might've failed the first test, but I was a quick learner.

I stood up to leave.

Erikson didn't stop me. He was too busy enjoying Chad who was frozen in place with his hands still outstretched. Erikson's eyes were burning again. He liked being worshiped.

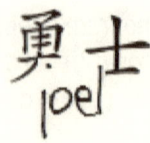

chapter ninety-six/ the heist

Humble words and increased preparations are signs that the enemy is about to advance.
    -Sun Tzu, *the Art of War*

I rushed to the store room to get there before Chad did so I could separate out my team's supplies from the rest of the façade. In five minutes there were three piles crammed in the small space: Alpha's, Bravo's, and mine.

I laid out a tarp and put all of my supplies in the center and then folded all the corners in. I knew I only had time for one trip, it needed to count. I lifted it off the floor; it was bulky, but do-able. I carried it to the edge of the playing field and placed it behind a large boulder. I got back just before Chad walked in.

We worked side by side, sorting through our piles. Mine outsized his by almost double. Occasionally he'd look over at my colossal mess and shake his head. *Amateur* his eyes said; victory was clearly within his grasp.

We finished shortly before nineteen hundred, working through dinner. Neither of us was willing to leave the other alone with their supplies. Both of us covered our neatened piles with a camo tarp before leaving together, locking the door behind us. Chad quickly walked toward the mess hall, probably hoping to guilt the staff into a snack, while I headed towards the front exit.

To the casual observer I was just doing what I did every other night, nothing unusual there. That was until instead of turning towards town, I slipped silently onto the path that had become well worn by my frequent passings. I quietly stole through the woods until I reached the boulder that hid the large pile of supplies for the seven of us who'd make up my *real* team.

I carried the load through the imposing forest going directly to my spot; the base of the Green Mountains. They were the invisible border of Newstead, the outer perimeter of the training field. It was there that I dropped the three tents, fourteen blankets, surveillance equipment, MREs, and water purification tablets. They were the supplies that'd been hidden in my grandiose list, unnoticed among all the fluff.

I walked over to the rocky edge of the mountain and found what I was looking for: a small groove in-between the jaunting rocks, a groove that the cylinder in my pocket fit perfectly into. My library experience had assisted me yet again. I knew all about it even before feeling it in my eager hands. I gently slid a flat rock in front of the cylinder completely concealing it. Quietly I turned to leave, eager for the sun to rise.

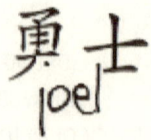

chapter ninety-seven/ before

In war let your great object be victory, not lengthy campaigns.
  -Sun Tzu, *the Art of War*

The weather was warm, which wasn't typical for that time of year. What little mud was left from the melting snow had dried up shortly after the thaw.

The locals at Fred's had been talking about it non-stop. They looked forward to spring all year to mock all those newbies who'd gotten their cars stuck. Instead, they were forced to keep themselves busy with the oddity of the weather. Who'd ever heard of an April with no rain?

I looked out the window. *It doesn't look like today's going to be any different.* I tried to close my eyes, to force myself to get more sleep, knowing I'd need it before the day was over, but I couldn't; too much was riding on this day.

In less than four hours it would all begin.

I waited until I heard other guys making noise before I got up and gathered my stuff to take my shower. Most of the things I needed were laid out on the foot of my bed; my camo fatigues, combat boots, face paint. But not everything. I went to my top dresser drawer and grabbed the silver eye glass cases and slid them in the creases of my folded clothes.

Steven and Marcus were still asleep when I came back in. They were the only ones, judging from the noise. Both were asleep for very different reasons. For Marcus victory was so certain anticipation wasn't necessary. Steven, on the other hand, didn't care either way.

None of us knew how close the shit was to hitting the fan.

chapter ninety-eight/ begun

On open ground do not try to block the enemy's way.
   -Sun Tzu, *the Art of War*

Everyone was supposed to meet outside the supply shed where our piles still sat, locked safely inside.

My team was all present and accounted for at zero eight–thirty. So was Chad's. They looked confident and eager, secret plans in their eyes. For a moment my previous certainty was shaken. *Have I misread them?*

It wasn't until the supply officer showed up and unlocked the door that I realized the reason. Instead of each team member gathering their own share of the supplies, all but two of Chad's platoon stood poised, ready for an all-out run; leaving the carrying of the gear to the unfortunate couple of guys who'd obviously drawn the short straws.

I gave myself a minute to be impressed with his simple plan. Sure, it followed the same outline I'd seen the other two weekends, but at least he'd come up with an original idea on how to get to the higher point first.

My own team, laden down with a ridiculous amount of stuff, looked even more dejected as they also figured out Chad's plan. They looked at me briefly, hoping I'd make a quick adjustment, give them a chance. Instead, I tried to look like I didn't even notice.

Dean Erikson arrived. Surveying the scene, he immediately read Chad's clear advantage. He smiled the brightest smile I've ever seen out of the guy.

But he didn't let himself get too excited, not yet, not when there were still the motions to go through. He turned towards us and gave a brief speech about sportsmanship and wished us all good luck. There was no need to go over the rules; the weekend had been the main topic in all our classes for weeks. We all knew what was expected of us. Instead, he took a moment to inspect each one, spending most of his time on team Alpha. All their eyes looked just like Chad's had: awed. Their god had spoken.

Only a brief glance at his watch made him stop. It was zero nine-hundred. He pulled a flare gun from his pocket. Immediately his arm shot up into the air, discharging the weapon. For better or worse, the games had begun.

chapter ninety-nine/ in-direct method

In all fighting, the direct method may be used for joining battle, but indirect methods will be needed in order to secure victory.
-Sun Tzu, *the Art of War*

We must've looked like a real life tortoise vs. the hare. Chad's unburdened team dashed immediately through the woods directly for the western elevation. My own team trudged slowly onward, heads down, not even bothering to follow. We all knew where we were actually headed. Consolation prizes all around; the eastern hill would be all ours and all of us knew what that meant. So much for my earlier speeches of victory; my temporary popularity was completely forgotten as each of my teammates silently cursed me.

Continuing to look like I saw nothing, noticed nothing, my face was a living stone. It showed nothing of what was going on inside me. I don't think I've ever been as excited about anything in my life as I was in that moment, before all of it began.

We got to the eastern elevation an hour after the flare gun was fired. As soon as the clearing came into view thuds could be heard all around as heavy packs were dropped. I didn't say anything then, and I didn't say anything when they started unloading and setting up without my orders. But I did stifle a smile as they noticed the heavy pie irons, one in each pack.

Troy and Anthony's feud had outlived the week. They set up their tents as far as they could from each other. I looked from one to the other to decide which one to activate first. I went with Troy; he seemed to be the most volatile.

I waited until I was done setting up the badminton set and then walked over to his tent. He was sitting on the ground just outside of it, not doing anything in particular.

I sat down next to him. He didn't even look at me, only kept staring straight ahead at Anthony's tent.

"Listen, Troy, I was thinking about what you were saying and you're right. I could use your help."

He turned to look at me and his face suddenly became animated. "Anything," he said. He looked like he meant it.

"I don't know. I guess I'm just disappointed Chad's team got to the other site first. I was really counting on getting that hill. But you said you were the team leader before, right? What would you do?"

His eyes shone with newfound excitement. I leaned back against the tree next to his tent as he rambled on for several minutes about all of his ideas. Finally he said the words I was waiting for:

"You know, it wouldn't be such a bad idea if we sent out a few guys to try and pick up anyone who gets too far from Alpha's home base. It'll bring up our numbers."

I nodded and attempted to look only marginally interested.

Troy's eyes gleamed as he continued, "You could be the one to lead them if you want, then I'll just stay back and make sure everything runs smoothly here."

I could see the plan unfolding in his mind. If *I* left, he'd be in charge, not just the runner up that he'd been willing to settle for. If I left and Bravo won, he'd just say I tucked tail and ran. Who'd be the wiser? Who would Dean Erikson believe? Hadn't Erikson already shown where his loyalties lay on that account?

He wasn't doing a very good job concealing how much he wanted it, but I was. I played along, hemmed and hawed before finally relenting. I didn't want to seem too willing.

"Alright. I guess you're right."

I pretended to look around like I was deciding who I'd take with me. Troy had suggestions about that too, but I just ignored him.

With Troy's grouping of tents set up on one side and Anthony's on the other, it didn't take me long to locate the ones I needed. Their tents were right in the middle; the rejects of the rejects.

I walked towards them.

Steven and Seth were done with their own tent and were helping Alex and Roy set up theirs. I stopped in the middle of their cluster of packs and supplies.

"Steven," I said. He looked up briefly but once he saw it was me he became very intense about setting up that tent.

"Actually, I need to see all of you." The group of them was standing in a loose circle around me, so I turned and looked at each one as I spoke. "We're going on a scouting mission in ten minutes. You can bring your personal affects, but that's it. I don't know how long we're going to be gone, so make sure you bring enough clothes for at least two days."

"Are you serious?" Seth asked.

"Very."

Steven looked up from the tent he was working on and looked at Seth, "Come on, you can help me take the tent down."

I met his eyes. "No, don't take it down."

"What? What exactly do you expect us to sleep in?" Steven asked.

"I'm bringing a tarp in case we're gone overnight."

His nostrils flared and his jaw clenched as he realized what I was saying. But he didn't tell me no. The rest of them looked at him, hoping he would say something, but he didn't.

"I'll be back in ten minutes, be ready to go." I looked at Steven for a full second before turning to walk away. Everyone there was completely silent.

I walked back towards Troy to tell him who I was planning on taking with me. It was all happening much better than I'd hoped. In the best case scenario I wanted to leave with my six men by morning. Instead, I found myself a whole day ahead of schedule, Troy leading the way.

Troy had a gathering around him: the six guys I saw in the rec room with him on Tuesday. They were talking intently and didn't seem to notice me until I was standing right next to them.

As soon as they did, their talking stopped mid-sentence. Troy turned to look at me with controlled calmness. "Joel. Have you gathered your team?"

I could tell that in his eyes, he was already in charge. I played along. "Yes, I will be taking Seth, John, Alex, Roy, Dale, Steven, and myself. We will be leaving in ten minutes."

He looked surprised. "Why so many?"

I'd expected him to ask that, so I repeated the answer I'd already come up with: "We need to have a mobile Prisoner of War camp for all the enemy we capture."

He looked at me. He knew I wouldn't be capturing anyone, no one would be leaving their home base, but he also knew that if he said that, I might change my mind about going. He wasn't willing to risk it.

"You're right. You need to have guards to make sure no one escapes." A couple snickers came from behind him. We both pretended we didn't hear them.

I nodded and turned to leave. I got five steps away from them when something gripped my boot. It wouldn't lift. I looked down and saw that I was stepping on my own shoelace. I swore silently as I bent down to tie it. As I did, a silver eyeglass case slid out of my pocket and landed on top of the boot I was tying.

My face engulfed in flames. As quickly as I could, I put it back in my pocket.

I looked around to see if anyone else had seen it. Troy was a few feet away from me, but he wasn't paying attention. Sweat began to trickle down my face as I scanned further out.

After a minute I stood. I was fairly certain that no one had seen; no one but me.

I walked back over to Troy's group. "Just a minute."

"What now?" Troy asked. He was losing patience with me.

"I forgot to hide our cylinder, isn't that part of the rules, that it has to be hidden in our home base?"

Troy looked at me like he thought I was a complete idiot. "Give it to me. I'll take care of it for you."

"No. Dean Erikson said it was up to me to hide it." He didn't, but Troy didn't know that.

He crossed his arms in front of his chest. "Fine, go hide it then."

He didn't move an inch from his position that was directly in front of me. So I walked around him. Two of the guys who were with his group were standing directly behind him. They didn't move either. I walked right between them, making my own space.

Troy was still watching me as I went to the spot I'd picked from one of my many previous trips to the training field. There was a large snake hole just past a cluster of boulders. I hoped its occupant still lived there and that Marcus would be the one who found it.

I carefully slid it in, covering it with a few loose twigs that were scattered on the ground.

I looked back and Troy's eyes locked with mine, which was a

problem. But thankfully it was a problem I'd foreseen. I knew Troy had been a team leader and would immediately recognize my dummy cylinder. I had to keep him away from my snake hole.

It was time to implement operation Anthony.

I walked over to his cluster of tents. His group had been watching my interaction with Troy with avid interest. Now it was time for the tables to be turned.

"Hey Anthony," I said.

"Joel." He was obviously pissed at me.

"Troy suggested that I take a scouting party and try to gather some wanderers from team Alpha. What do you think about that?"

Troy, who had moved within earshot, didn't appear to like that I was conferring with them. I ignored his loud coughs and throat clearings and waited for Anthony to answer me.

Anthony cleared his own throat in an effort to contain his excitement. "For once it seems like Troy had a good idea."

I thought he would. He looked at a few of the other guys who were standing with him. They seemed to think it was a good idea, too.

"When are you planning on leaving?" he asked eagerly.

"Right now. I just hid the cylinder, so there's nothing keeping me here."

"Oh yeah? And where did you hide it? Remember you promised you'd tell me." He tried to sound casual. He tried to sound like he really didn't care one way or the other, and if it wasn't for his hands clenching and unclenching, I might've believed him.

"Right over there, in a hole in the rocks." I pointed towards the snake hole. Even if Troy hadn't heard me, and I know he did, he wouldn't have missed where I was pointing at. He was well aware of where the cylinder was. And now so was Anthony.

I knew he'd keep Troy far away from that cylinder.

They didn't seem to notice me as I left their group to gather the six men I was leaving with.

Anthony's group quickly formed a perimeter around the location I'd indicated. Troy was joined by six men of his own. That's how we left them, poised, angry, in parallel lines. Seven vs. seven, with Anthony and Troy in the middle of their ranks glaring defiantly at each other.

My team, the true team Bravo, was standing by their tents waiting for me.

"Ready?" I asked as I walked up to them and then past them to the forest beyond. Slowly I heard their footsteps as they turned to follow me.

It was a bright day. The sun was streaming through the limbs on the trees as I started quietly whistling to myself.

chapter one hundred/ real team bravo

Carefully study the well-being of your men and do not overtax them.
    -Sun Tzu, *the Art of War*

We walked much longer than any of them probably thought we would. I purposefully circumvented the western elevation by several acres in case any of them decide to be chatty. That turned out to be unnecessary, since silence permeated the air.

Seth slammed into me as I stopped. We were at our true home base, the one I'd discovered after I tried to tear a chunk out of my face. It was there that we had our first real team meeting.

Everyone dropped their knapsacks just moments after I did. Somehow I still managed to have their respect as their leader. They watched in amazement as I lifted a rock colored blanket that camouflaged the supplies hidden beneath. Their surprise was more than I could've wished for.

"Now, gentleman, do you want to hear our real plans?'

It turned out they did. They stood in awed silence as I explained the details of our impending victory. Their blunted faces suddenly looked alive as they experienced true hope.

Even Steven smiled approvingly as I gave the game plan.

No one seemed to mind setting up tents for the second time in one day.

Initially, my intent was to go on surveillance alone, one of the few loose ends in my complex plan. Instead, I invited Steven to come with me. After watching him earlier in the forest I could see he was as surefooted as me and he wasn't prone to useless talking that'd give our position away. I handed him a pair of infrared binoculars, and left Seth in charge of defense until we got back.

I allowed myself a moment of satisfaction as we turned to leave. The camp was running smoothly, everyone settling into the routine. A rotating two hour watch had been set up. No one complained when I told them their shift was going to fall during the night. It was such a contrast to the other two weekends I'd witnessed.

It was good having Steven with me. It was good not to be in this alone anymore. I glanced towards him as we walked along, thinking I was sorry that I hadn't told him earlier and that I needed to thank him for all he'd done for me over the last few weeks.

I stopped to take a swig from my canteen but really it was because I'd decided it was time; time I told Steven everything. He stopped, too, and looked at me and I knew I didn't need to say anything. For some reason it seemed like he already got it. He smiled as he grabbed my canteen from me and took a big gulp.

Without another word we went on, together.

When we got closer to Chad's team we crouched low to the ground and went from cover to cover. We didn't make a sound. The practice runs were over; it was the real deal.

I led Steven to the marshes that I'd hidden in before. It was a good place to hide; far enough away that they wouldn't stumble upon us, but close enough for us to see what we'd come for.

They were all there, all twenty-one of them. There were campfires just like the last two weekends, only Chad's group looked especially euphoric. *Guess that's what knowing you're going to win will do for you.*

I handed my scope to Steven. I wanted to know if he saw the same thing I did.

After a couple minutes he handed it back to me. We both stood to leave. We had another platoon to spy on.

We walked deeper into the woods, not taking the easier path to get to the eastern hill. Any movement on our part would be sure to draw Alpha's attention. We saw that, too.

We saw them as they were perched on the edge of the ridge, watching team Bravo with a scope of their own. I don't think they were doing it to find out where our cylinder was, or anything else even remotely having to do with FTX. I think they were doing it to get their rocks off. And from the look of them, they were: rolling all over, laughing, pushing and shoving each other, each one of them trying to grab at the scope.

There were only three of them who looked even remotely serious. They were situated further back in the camp, away from the fires, away from the ridge. Just before I'd handed the scope to Steven those three were replaced by three others; the changing of the guard.

Chad was confident, but not stupid. He wanted his cylinder as far away from Bravo as possible.

chapter one hundred-one/ blood brothers

Keep your army continually on the move and devise
unfathomable plans.
-Sun Tzu, *the Art of War*

We came to the eastern hill from the backside. The tents had
been moved into two distinct groups with Anthony's closest to
the snake-hole. They'd even taken over the tents we'd left
behind. That was good. It gave the appearance of a much
larger group than what was actually there.

All was quiet, no fun or games like up on the ridge.

Defeat was clearly written across each face, at least the ones
who were still awake. Like Chad's team, they were taking
rotations guarding the cylinder: One of Anthony's team to guard
it, one from Troy's to guard him.

The opposing lines had been shortened somewhat; just two
guys, two otherwise hospitable classmates scowling at each
other. Neither one seemed to remember that the game
continued, that the real enemy was up on the ridge. Instead to
them the only enemy they saw was the one glaring at them
roughly three feet away.

How small people's worlds can become.

I was sorry to see it. My actions had brought out even more of their monstrosities. It had accomplished my goal though, another loose end tied up. The thought that Troy would see the eye glass case and know that something was up was a real threat to my greater plan. Anthony's mutiny would prevent that. Troy wouldn't get anywhere near that snake hole.

We spent much less time surveying our own team than we did team Alpha, partially because we didn't need as much information, and partially because watching them was depressing. They were a sad reminder of what we were capable of.

We slipped back into the forest and headed towards the mountain.

All was quiet at our camp. Too quiet.

I looked toward Steven, who was only glaring straight ahead.

Roy stepped out from behind a pine tree that had been directly in Steven's line of sight. He called out to us.

I looked toward Steven. "It's us," he answered. The fierceness in his eyes was gone; if it had ever been there in the first place.

"Good," Roy answered, walking out to meet us. "Seth just got done setting out the MRE's. Are you guys hungry?"

"Starving," we both answered at the same time.

We followed Roy deeper into our camp. With the pine trees you couldn't see it until you were standing right in the middle of the tents. The rest of them were sitting in a circle, like they were around a camp fire.

Seth handed each of us an opened MRE and we started eating. Mine was Chicken a 'la king. It wasn't half-bad.

After we were done, they all looked expectantly at me. I knew they wanted to know what we'd discovered. I glanced at Steven and nodded.

He began:

"Team Alpha has their cylinder by the tents facing us. At this point they don't realize we aren't at our home base. Our own team is too busy fighting with each other to worry about where we are. Thus far it looks like everything is going how we need it to."

I smiled at him. I really should have confided in him earlier. But then I remembered how he wasn't eating either, towards the end. Maybe for his sake it was a good thing that he'd been kept in the dark.

"I can't wait to see Marcus' face when he finds out we've one-upped him," Alex said excitedly. Then they all were saying it, laughing over it. I looked at Steven and he wasn't smiling, either. We both knew Marcus well enough to know how he'd feel about getting beaten.

I looked away as the glory stories got more and more grandiose. I hadn't really thought about the after. All I'd been concerned about was getting the cylinder. But once I did, what then? I swallowed hard and looked at Steven again. He was still looking at me and his face didn't make me feel any better.

I bet Dean Erikson didn't like getting beaten either.

chapter one hundred-two/ all of us

Surviving spies are those who bring back news from the enemy's camp.
-Sun Tzu, *the Art of War*

We finished eating, but none of us went anywhere. We just sat and talked, and after a little while, it was actually about something other than FTX.

"Hey, Joel—do you want to be our captain for the soccer tournament next week?" Roy asked.

"Thanks, but I won't be here. I'm going on vacation with my mom next week."

Roy's smile faded.

"What?" I asked. And then I looked at the rest of the guys who weren't talking anymore. They were all looking at me. *Did I miss something?*

"None of us have seen our mothers in a long time," Steven said quickly.

"Why not?" I looked around at them, but none of them answered me.

Steven spoke again for the group, acting as translator, "They just stopped writing, stopped coming. I guess they thought life was easier without us."

All five sets of eyes were fixed on Steven, but he was too busy looking at me to notice.

I almost said it, the one thing I shouldn't know but did because I asked my mom once about the strange scars I had on my arms and legs. I almost said I wasn't wanted, either. But I didn't. I couldn't. It was too real, too raw.

I took a deep breath and like the chicken shit I was, I said something else.

"Well that's how it's like with my father, he's never around, actually he never has been. I've never met the guy."

At first I looked at them, but then I couldn't. I looked down at my hands instead. It was like they could see right through me. I closed my eyes and sat and breathed in the silence.

It was Steven who finally broke it, "Joel, none of us know our fathers."

I looked up then and tried to focus on what he'd said. "How can that be possible?" I asked it to myself as much as anyone there. *I can't believe it. Even with the national statistics of single parent households, how is it possible that all seven of us come from one parent homes? Scratch that, fatherless homes?*

"Not just us," Steven said, gesturing to the small group gathered there. "All of us."

His eyes were intense on mine, trying to convey something vital, something I couldn't afford to miss. I closed my eyes and briefly pushed, letting the *other* come forward to analyze. I didn't trust my normal intellect with something that important.

All of us indicates all Newstead students, staff, and faculty past, present, and future, the voice informed me before obediently retreating to the back ground as I attempted to swallow that staggering bit of information.

"How could that be possible?" I repeated under my breath.

Steven's eyes closed briefly and when he opened them again

they were less intense than I'd ever seen them before. Whatever battle he'd been struggling with had apparently been resolved. He smiled a calm smile, a peaceful smile.

I guess he still doesn't notice the other guys glaring at him.

It was still quiet when I stood up, "Listen, I'm going to turn in. I'll be up in four hours for my shift of guard duty. Alex—could you wake me up when it's my time?"

"Sure," Alex said, but he wasn't looking at me. He was still too busy looking at Steven. They all were.

"Goodnight," I said as I turned to walk to my tent.

No one answered me.

chapter one hundred-three/ jackass

Let your methods be regulated by the infinite variety of circumstances.
-Sun Tzu, *the Art of War*

I wasn't tired. Even if I was, I doubted I could sleep; too many things were running through my head.

For the first time I thought about the after.

What am I going to do? It's not like I can just walk up and announce that I've found it. Game over. For five of the last six weeks I've been through every kind of hell as they did their best to destroy me and that was only when they thought I could get their cylinder. What will happen to me if I do?

Steven's eyes had warned me. It wouldn't be good.

And what about what he'd said about their fathers? What's up with that? What are the chances of having a school where all the students are huge, and strong, and fatherless? I knew there had to be a connection somewhere, something I was missing.

My eyes popped open as my tent shook around me. I glanced at my watch. *Zero four-thirty, time for my shift. Guess I'd fallen asleep after all.*

The zipper on the tent came down just enough for Alex to slip inside. He collapsed onto his blanket, not even bothering to climb under it. Instead of waking him, I just opened my own blanket and placed it on top of him.

After my two hour shift of guard duty, I asked Steven to go with me for surveillance again. Everyone at our old home base was just as we'd left them. Even team Alpha didn't look all that different. They were less jubilant. A sleepless night had left many of them groggy that morning.

The only glaring difference was the main reason for us going there. The previous night there had been three men guarding their cylinder, by that morning only one remained and he was half asleep. *Another loose end closed, almost tied shut now.*

The only large question mark remaining was timing. When would team Alpha decide to make their move? If they were anything like the other two weekends I'd witnessed it would be late Sunday night. But that was only an educated guess on my part. Timing would make or break us. If Chad's team made their attack without us noticing and found my dummy cylinder, all my plans would be for nothing. As soon as Chad saw the eyeglass case, he'd know all wasn't as it appeared.

So Steven and I made frequent rounds, checking out both teams, getting a feel for the tempo. Did they look like they were accelerating their plans? Sometimes overconfidence could make you restless.

At twenty-one hundred we went again. It was very dark that night, so I led. I felt Steven's hand on my shoulder as I walked to team Alpha.

The ridge was quiet. There were no campfires lighting the night. My heart began to race as I looked through my scope. *Did we miss them?*

"What's wrong?" Steven whispered behind me.

I shook my head as I took a step forward. And then I saw movement. It was Chad and Marcus standing by the ridge.

They hadn't left yet.

I let out a breath. "It's okay. I just thought they'd already left."

I handed the scope to Steven.

"No, they're still there, but not for long. Look at them, they're getting ready."

I nodded. He was right. For the first time that weekend Alpha was looking serious.

"Let's split up. I'll go to Bravo and make sure nothing is going on there. Can you go back to our home base and get our walkie-talkies and tell them to be ready for our signal?"

Steven hesitated and then nodded.

I turned and walked towards the eastern hill. No planning going on there. The game had been reduced to squatter's rights, with the outside world completely forgotten.

I didn't stay long.

I made it back to the marsh before Steven, even though I had more than twice the distance to cover.

I settled down in the cattails and watched Marcus through my scope. And still Steven didn't come. I was starting to get worried. It should've only taken him ten minutes tops to get there and back and that was me being generous. I could make it in five. But I knew the woods better than Steven. That's why he'd had to put his hand on my back.

I felt my face flushing as that thought sunk in good. *Shit.* No wonder he looked like he didn't want to go. It was pitch black out there, in a dense forest he wasn't familiar with. *What did I do? And I didn't even give him the scope either. What a jackass I am.*

I quickly stood to go find Steven. I looked once back at Alpha and swore again. It would serve me right if they left while I was out searching for him.

But Steven was right outside the marsh as I left it.

"Steven, I'm sorry. I shouldn't have—"

He smiled and handed me a walkie-talkie. "It's fine."

He walked past me into the cattails and I turned to follow him. We took turns watching the ridge. At twenty-three hundred, team Alpha formed a line; they were preparing to make their move. A series of beeps sounded just three hundred yards behind them, my own signal being given. The time had come.

rachel

chapter one hundred-four / moving on

Life's a bitch and then you die.
  -Nasir Jones

Tuesday was the day Aunt Beth announced that we were moving. Usually it was Nathan, and usually it was at night, just as he was about to pull out.

I was standing by the door, ready to leave for school, when Aunt Beth looked up from where she sat on the couch. For one minute I thought whatever gains she'd made had been lost. Her eyes were too bright. And what she said didn't do anything to convince me otherwise.

"We will be moving soon, Rachel." She watched to see my reaction.

My hand instinctively reached for the doorknob.

Nathan, where is Nathan?

He wasn't anywhere, at least not where I could see him. *Is it happening again?* I looked at Aunt Beth to see if I needed to make a run for it. She made no sudden moves. Instead, she sat still, waiting for my response. She never got it.

All the anti-moving arguments I'd planned weren't for her anyway. So I went outside to talk to the person I hoped to influence with my persuasive reasoning. But Nathan wasn't outside, either.

I don't know why I looked for him as I walked to school, but I did. It didn't matter anyhow, he wasn't there. He wasn't anywhere.

It'd been some time since I'd been freaked out. School had returned to normal and for the most part Aunt Beth had, too. Even Joel seemed to have found himself again.

Things were finally working out. It would figure now would be the time they'd decide to move. But did I have to go with them?

That was the big question.

It's not like I needed them. I could probably afford our standard of living on what I made. I tried to ignore the voice inside my head that said *they* needed *me*.

But ignoring it wouldn't make it go away. It even got louder, in fact it had pictures: One was of Nathan, the other of Aunt Beth, the week we'd gone without food. Neither of them had done anything to help themselves. They'd just sat in the trailer and waited for me to feed them. They were as helpless as baby birds.

I forced myself to acknowledge the truth of it. They'd starve if I left them.

So there it was. I had two choices. I could leave them and live the life I wanted with Joel, but I'd always know the outcome of that choice. Or I could stay with them and chew up worms to force down their throats.

But how does Joel fit in that choice? How do I?

I didn't. That was the point. That had been the point all along. I didn't fit anywhere with Nathan or Aunt Beth, but I was with them, anyhow. And now I couldn't leave them.

I went to work that night and sat down on the bench in the back. It was about an hour before I realized I'd never flipped the sign. I forced myself to stand up and do it. By then it was beginning to get dark out. No one came that night. I don't know if had anything to do with the sign reading closed until six or not. I guess I'll never know. I walked over to a swivel seat by the counter and sat down. That's where I was when Joel walked in.

I couldn't look at his face. I didn't even tell him what Aunt Beth had said. I don't know why, he deserved to know. But the idea was so exhausting I pushed it to the back of my mind. *Later, I'd tell him later.*

But there wasn't a later.

chapter one hundred-five/ left

The best way to keep one's word is not to give it.
-Napoleon Bonaparte

The quiet knock on my door just past two am on Friday morning didn't surprise me. It was like so many I'd heard before. The only difference was that it was Aunt Beth, not Nathan who stood at the entrance of my room. Aunt Beth who told me it was time to go.

To her surprise and mine I got up and walked to the truck; to sit in my usual spot, squeezed tightly against the passenger window with Aunt Beth in the middle and Nathan driving. The only time we ever used that old truck was to move. No wonder I hated it so much.

All was quiet as Nathan hitched up the trailer and slowly pulled out. Instinctively I turned to look back.

I didn't expect anything, honestly I didn't. That's what made the man standing there even more horrifying. I don't know how I knew he was the one from by the river, but I did.

That time he was less than ten feet away from me and I finally understood why Nathan had asked if I *really* saw him or not.

That night I really saw him.

He was tall, he was short. He was thin, he was fat. He was

nothing. He was everything.

He was a man and he was looking directly at me. I tried to look away, but I couldn't. I opened my mouth to speak, but the man slowly shook his head like he knew what I was going to say.

So I did it anyway. I screamed out Joel's name.

The man's face flashed with fire. And then the fire was just his eyes. His lips curled back over his teeth as I heard him, felt him all around me. There were no words, just the sound of rain drumming all around. And then the sound and the man were gone.

Nathan slammed on the brakes and turned to glare at me. But after looking at my face he didn't say anything, just started inching the truck forward again.

My face fell into my hands as we drove away. Away from Newstead, away from Joel, away from any shred of humanity I had left.

chapter one hundred-six/ the after

The good fighter will be terrible in his onset, and prompt in his decision.

-Sun Tzu, *the Art of War*

There was movement in the bramble just four yards behind us. My real team had arrived.

I looked through my scope one last time and then briefly raised my hand into the air. The movement got closer as my men made their way towards us.

Our group of two became seven. I didn't waste any time issuing my orders. I didn't know how much time we had.

"Seth, Alex, you will maintain our position here. Dale, Roy, you will guard our flank. John, you will position yourself in-between the two so that if either gives a signal, you can notify me. We are too close to enemy territory to use walkie-talkies. Any questions?"

"What about me?" Steven asked.

"You're coming with me. Alright men, this is what it's all about. Be as silent as the dead. We'll be back as soon as we have the cylinder."

And just like that we dispersed; each to his own spot. Steven followed me into their empty home base. Even the guy guarding the cylinder was gone. *Guess he doesn't want to miss out on the action. Good. It's much easier this way; no witnesses.*

I didn't waste time there, either. The last thing I needed was to have Marcus come back while I was still there. I could even see the silver end sticking up out of the ground, partially hidden in a pile of twigs and dried leaves.

Steven didn't follow as I walked over towards it, as I reached down and picked it up. I closed my eyes and slid it into my pocket. In its place I put a second eye glass case with a message in it, the first half of which was in a snake hole just waiting to be found.

I stood back up. It didn't feel like the victory that I thought it would. My insides were still about as tight as they could be, my heart was still racing. *Where's the release?*

There wasn't one. Maybe because I finally realized the truth of it; that the finding of the cylinder was the easy part. It was the after, the part I was totally unprepared for, that was the real challenge.

I swallowed at the lump that had suddenly formed in my throat and turned back to Steven. He wasn't looking at me. He was too busy looking deep into the forest.

chapter one hundred-seven/ the martyr

Rapidity is the essence of war: take advantage of the enemy's unreadiness, make your way by unexpected routes, and attack unguarded spots.
-Sun Tzu, *the Art of War*

We met up with John who signaled to the rest of them: We'd obtained what we'd come for. All of them were waiting by the marshes when we got there. I turned to walk back to our home base when Seth's voice stopped me.

"Aren't we going to watch? I mean I don't know about the rest of you, but I *have* to see their faces when they figure it out." He was eager, all of them were; all of them but Steven.

I should've said no. I should've known better. Get in and get out, that's what had kept me alive for the last six weeks. Twice that weekend I'd gotten distracted and made mistakes, but it was the third time that finally cost me something. It was the third time that cost me everything.

At my command we made our way through the woods towards team Bravo.

We arrived just moments before team Alpha did. At first I thought we'd already missed it, until I saw the familiar scene:

one of Anthony's men guarding the snake hole while Troy stood glaring at him. They were both completely unaware of the assault descending towards them, making their petty rivalry pointless.

Chad's team, like mine, had determined the location of our cylinder through means of scoping equipment. Not that it would've been that difficult to figure out. The rest of the camp was asleep in their tents. The only two awake were standing within feet of the fake cylinder.

Alpha platoon stole directly to the spot where Troy and Jackson stood.

Despite all the training we'd had on military tactics at Newstead, neither men flinched as twenty-one members of Alpha surrounded them. The first indication they were even remotely aware something was going on was when Troy unconsciously turned his head in the direction where Marcus crouched in the brush, greedily smirking at him.

It happened so quickly it was hard to tell who'd given the order to attack and who was the first to find the cylinder. My guess would be it was all Marcus, pulling off a last minute mutiny. He was unable to continue to follow, even if Chad was only a figure head, when victory was within his grasp.

It was Marcus who was holding the eyeglass case, trying to process what was happening. He looked confused. I smiled, knowing what he was thinking: He had seen cylinders before, having already been a team captain twice, and *that* wasn't it. Have they changed containers?

Unfortunately, he couldn't figure out the situation on his own; he had to reenlist the man he'd just over-thrown. Chad was dragged over and was quickly questioned about the cylinder. He refused to even look at him. Obviously, it hadn't been a peaceful coup. It wasn't until Marcus grabbed his face and shoved the eye glass case in front of his squeezed cheeks that

Chad began to respond with animation.

Troy was also brought to the enlarging group that was beginning to form around Marcus and Chad. I almost felt sorry for him. He looked completely taken by surprise, as if he really *had* forgotten about the game in his struggle with Anthony. He shrugged his shoulders at their intense questions and then pointed out into the woods, ironically pointing very close to the place where we crouched, binoculars in hand.

Realization hit Marcus long before the others. He gave a sharp order and began to sprint across the valley, back up the hill he'd descended just twenty minutes before. He was followed by each man; his team, as well as the rest of Bravo.

Some, knowing they'd been duped more quickly than the others, joined Marcus in his run. The rest followed, not sure why, but they knew *something* was happening. My own personal team followed me as I went back towards the marshes.

Marcus was crouched over the pile of sticks when I spotted him. He looked up and something about him made me flinch back. His face was wild; he didn't even look human. I almost ordered my men to put down their scopes as his murderous eyes scanned the forest for us, for me.

He turned in our direction, like he knew exactly where we were. His arm shot up in the air and I flinched again. But it wasn't what I thought it was; it was the eyeglass cases.

His lips were moving like he was saying something, like he was trying to communicate my tyranny to those who were crouched around me; like any of us would be able to hear him. Strangely enough, it appeared as if some of them did.

As if on cue, Seth's voice sounded from somewhere behind me, "Hey, why does Marcus have the two cylinders? I thought you told us that you hid ours somewhere at our home base..."

It didn't take long before I heard rustling as five men formed their ranks behind my back.

"Let me see that thing." Seth spoke again and there was authority in his voice.

The last thing I saw was Marcus's smile as I lowered the binoculars to turn and face my platoon. Steven lowered his just a moment after mine. His eyes sought my face and saw the sudden indecision there.

He quickly spoke for me, "Joel and I put a dummy one with team Bravo, Marcus must've picked it up. We needed to in order to convince them that they were the home base. Then I put one at Alpha's to trick them into thinking we hadn't gotten their cylinder." Steven's eyes spoke something urgently to me. "Give me the cylinder, Joel, so I can show them how much the dummy looks like the real thing."

I started breathing hard; to lose the cylinder so close to the end, it was unbearable.

Five men stood in front of me, suddenly untrusting. After all, I'd betrayed the rest of my team, what would stop me from lying to them too?

This was the after that I'd been dreading, the one I was completely unprepared for. I reached into the pocket that had the cylinder.

It sucked, but I had no other options.

Steven's hand grabbed mine and redirected it to my other pocket.

His actions had been so smooth, so instantaneous, no one but me noticed. His eyes were intent on mine. In my other pocket was the third eyeglass case, the one I'd planned on opening in front of the others. I'd known from my research that not one of them had been a team leader before. I knew they wouldn't know the difference.

I was going to keep the real prize all to myself. I knew that was the way it was supposed to be. I'd always known that in the end, it would just be me.

Steven held out his hand expectantly, looking impatient. Playing along, I reluctantly reached into my pocket and brought out the case.

"Keeping it all for yourself?" Steven asked. He reached for the case and slipped it into his pocket before anyone could see it.

"Of course not," I quietly answered.

"I'm in charge now, and I'll be the one to open the cylinder. Why don't you go run and cry to your girlfriend," he chuckled menacingly.

It was hard to tell if he was still acting or not. The rest of them didn't think so. They laughed along with him, snapping their jaws at me like a pack of ferocious wolves. Their line shifted as they re-aligned their positions, only that time they were behind him.

And that time I wasn't the one doing the pushing, it was me who was pushed aside as the augmented version of myself took over, knowing the very real danger I was in.

Steven stayed the same, a little brighter maybe, but nothing like the five guys behind him. They were more like the wolves they sounded like than the guys I'd grown to think of as my friends.

And there was a reason for that.

Erikson smiled at me from inside Seth; he was more visible than the rest, but that was more because of his abilities to show himself, than my ability to see. I'm sure the rest of them were just as occupied as Rachel or Beth had been; they just didn't have the same reasons Erikson had.

He wanted me to know it was him.

I took a step back. *Why did I think they'd let me get away with it? Of course they're watching; they always are.*

"Just get out of here," Steven said, refocusing me. His face was intense.

I nodded once and walked past Steven and then past the rest of them. They weren't looking at me; they were too focused on the one who had the cylinder. I tried to do the same with them.

I almost made it, too. My shoulder just skimmed Roy's and I automatically looked that way and found myself staring face to face with Mike. He smiled; that same hateful smile he'd had in St. Louis.

His smile got bigger when he saw that my hands had become fists. I closed my eyes and willed myself to keep walking.

It was the hardest thing I've ever done.

Steven had only given me a few short minutes, and I wasn't going to waste any of them on a frickin' liar like him.

I whispered a silent thank you before breaking into an all-out run down the familiar path.

chapter one hundred-eight/ the cylinder

If you know neither the enemy or yourself, you will succumb in every battle.
   -Sun Tzu, *the Art of War*

Where to go? I wondered as I headed straight for Rachel's, as if I had any other choice. The town was dark as I sped by, unnoticed.

But I didn't notice them either. I was too busy planning all the speeches I was going to give Rachel and her family about why I was there so late and why we had to leave, *now*. I turned the last bend and stopped.

It was just woods and pastures and a staircase going up to nowhere. Rachel and her trailer were already gone. They'd left without me.

They left without me.

I fell to my knees. I couldn't breathe as the words went through my mind over and over again. *They left without me.*

I closed my eyes and tried to focus, but I was out of ideas. For weeks I'd done nothing but come up with ideas and only then, when it was too late, did I realize I'd been too worried about the wrong things. The after was here and I was completely unprepared for it. Sure, I had the cylinder, but what good was that going to do for me when I was dead?

The cylinder.

I reached into my pocket and pulled it out. It was mesmerizing just like I'd remembered; smooth and cold, looking like one solid piece of perfectly polished metal. How could I have thought a simple eyeglass case would fool them? Marcus had certainly recognized the difference. Anyone would.

Without pausing, I recreated the motions I'd seen Erikson perform just four days before. And just as it'd done in his office, a slight audible click was heard as a small touch pad smoothly rose out of the middle of the cylinder. There were two seams where none had existed before.

I typed in the numbers I'd memorized and the cylinder responded with a gentle hiss as the pressure lock released, causing the smooth side to spring open. Two pieces of paper dropped to the ground.

Part of me was surprised. I hadn't fully trusted Erikson to give me the real numbers.

Two pieces of paper, that was all. I don't know what I expected, but paper certainly wasn't it. Not worth risking my life for, Steven's life for.

I raised myself off my knees and slowly headed to the concrete steps to read what had cost so many so much.

The first page was a chart made up of five vertical columns. At the top was a heading for each column: Name, Date of Donation, Donator/Son of God, Rank of Donation, and Current Location of the Donation.

The first column contained a long list of names neatly typed in a font unknown to man, it was so small. I scanned the information to look for some kind of pattern or clue. After not seeing anything, I permitted my "other" to come forward again. I needed all the help I could get.

As if seeing the information for the first time, a trend instantaneously appeared. The names were all male, listed in descending dates of donation. My eyes were quickly drawn to a slight deviation in the pattern; small handwritten script right in the middle of the page.

The words 'Joel Cranston' had been squeezed in-between two other familiar names, classmates of mine. Next to my name, in the date column, was penciled in a year: 1992. I'd been born in 1993, not 1992, so that eliminated date of birth from the equation.

Under the Donator/Son of God and Rank column there were just question marks. The Location column listed the word Newstead, like the other names close by mine. A quick scan revealed mine was the only one like that. My mind quickly counted; out of 667 names, mine was the only one hand-written.

There was something there, I felt it, but I just couldn't figure out what it was. I put that sheet aside and grabbed the other one. But it was no help. It was written in a language I'd never seen before.

I pressed my hands to my temples trying to will the answer to pop into my head. For almost a full minute there was nothing. And then I heard a familiar voice.

We don't have fathers, none of us do, the voice in my head said, repeating Steven's words.

I thought back to the other night when he'd told me that. His eyes had said more than his words and the betrayed looks on my teammate's faces said it as well. He was telling me one of their most highly guarded secrets; something they all knew. All of them but me.

And the voice didn't stop there. It took advantage of the momentum of my working mind and flashed a picture into my head.

I could see it clearly: My exhausted mother, stopping home briefly to tuck me into bed before leaving for her second job; I was looking up at her, asking yet again about my father. Instead of the usual way she talked to me, she turned on me with scorching words I'll never forget.

"Joel, you were nothing but a donation to him," she'd said. Her eyes were immediately remorseful, seeing the effect it'd had on me. In those few short words she'd killed what little hope I'd had left. At least she got one of her wishes that night. I never asked about my father again.

Nothing but a donation. *Could the dates possibly be the dates of conception, the dates of sperm donation?* It would be true in my case, at least.

It is true. For all of you, the voice in my head stated, agreeing with me.

So that was it. That's why the list was so important. From the looks on my teammates faces the other night I knew any one of them would kill to have what I was holding. To see, to know. To have their father's names listed in black in white. No more wondering, no more making up stories. To really know.

But I still didn't know. My name only had a question mark next to it. So then why was it so important that *I* find the cylinder? It didn't mean anything to me. And why was Erikson so worried about me getting it? What was so vital that he'd rather have me die than see it?

I closed my eyes and pushed again, trying to draw something, anything out of me. I knew my time was very short.

Why are the donators called Sons of God? my voice continued, prodding.

I shrugged. I didn't know. But I sensed that question was at the heart of it all.

It was then that I heard a faint rustle of pages fluttering in the sudden breeze. I looked down. There was a book lying on the concrete by my right foot, completely unnoticed until then. It was a Bible. I reached down and picked it up.

There was a paper jammed inside, at the beginning. Quickly, I flipped to the marked page and read the highlighted words. Genesis 6:4; *The Nephilim were on the earth in those days— and also afterward—when the sons of God went to the daughters of men and had children by them. They were the heroes of old, men of renown.*

There were no big lights going off, just a quiet understanding. Newstead and all the people there were Nephilim. I was a Nephilim.

But what the hell is a Nephilim?

I had no idea.

I snapped the book shut. *It figures.* I was more confused than ever, and my voice was done giving me clues. I reached my hand back over my head to chuck the Bible into the woods when the piece of paper that had been stuck in it caught my eye. It wasn't blank.

There was handwriting on it, my handwriting. It was a page from one of my journals, and from the yellowed look of it, it was one of my early ones. I'd probably written it years ago while I was still living in St. Louis. I had no idea how it got there.

I skimmed the page.

I can't believe it.

I'd written in a journal almost every day since I was about eight, so there were a lot of them out there. Most of the stuff I wrote I never remembered or thought about again. But I remembered the page I had in my hand and the day I'd written it.

It was just shortly after I'd joined the JV football team and I didn't know I was a freak yet. I just thought I was lucky. And I wrote about it; how it'd be when my dad showed up at one of my games. How proud he'd be when he saw how well his son was doing. But he never came.

I ended it with a poem which was probably the reason why it stood out for me. It was the first and last poem I'd ever attempted. That poem was what had been jammed in the Bible.

I read it again, my foolish words that suddenly weren't so foolish.

Nature's abominations from
Earth's own daughters,
Purposed for her destruction:
Heroes of old.
Infested with the seed of
Legions of fallen angels,
Inflicted upon men, creating their sons:
Men of renown.

My mind saw the acronym; what I'd always known, even when I was just a kid writing down what I'd thought were random words. I guess the augmented side of myself made appearances even back then.

A Nephilim was nothing more than a fallen angel's son. And Newstead was nothing more than a place to gather and train them. All the pieces clicked together in my mind.

Rachel discovered the truth and fled, probably terrified at the thought of me. Who else would've left me that message? I didn't even want to think about how she might've gotten her hands on my journals.

Okay. So now I know, but knowing doesn't help anything.
They're still going to come after me, no matter how much I
know. Or maybe they're going to come after me because of
how much I know. Either way, they're coming.

I sat still and listened to the forest that had suddenly gone quiet.

I could run. I knew I could outrun them. I'd done just that for months. *But where will I go?*

Anywhere but here, my voice answered.

I nodded as I stood up. It was time to leave.

I closed my eyes and pushed my hearing further. I needed to know where they were coming from. That'd be my only guide from then on, going in the opposite direction from them.

There were fourteen of them, just past the sheep pasture that was behind me. I sensed a trap. *Why wouldn't they go through the town, take the lane?* And I knew they had way more than fourteen waiting in the wings. I had the list to prove it.

Before I could turn and head in that direction, another sound hit me square in the chest. It was a car, and it was coming down the very lane I was about to make a run for. And it was coming fast. There was no way I could outrun a car.

I stood frozen by the stairs, listening. It was a terrible thing, hearing both of them coming, knowing they were coming for me. From the sound of it, the car was going to make it to me first. And it did.

A black Jaguar came around the last bend and slid to a stop just a few feet from where I was standing. The door opened and a tall blonde man got out. My eyes followed him as he walked past me to the passenger door and yanked it open.

It wasn't at all what I'd expected. I'd expected it to be one of them, but it wasn't. It was *him. What is he doing here?*

"Get in, Joel."

I flinched when I heard him. I knew that voice, too. It was the rushing water voice that'd told me about the cylinder in the first place; the voice that told me to trust him.

At that moment I made a choice, although looking back now I know I had no other options, not really. It was either go with him or stay, and let the Nephilim find me. And that time, after what I'd done, they wouldn't bother with their pretenses.

It was simply a choice of the known versus the unknown. I already knew what *they* were capable of, but the gleaming man standing next to the Jag? He'd at least never steered me wrong. Tucking the pieces of paper into the worn Bible, I tossed the cylinder where Rachel's trailer had once been.

What the hell; I'm too young to die.

a bridge/ gerrard

I obediently slid onto the smooth leather seat, past the door that'd been opened for me, the door which slammed shut the minute I was in. And then he was back, too focused on pulling away to say anything.

We took the farmers lane at about eighty. When he got to the end of it he didn't stop, just did another sliding maneuver like the one he'd done at Rachel's place. *Or what used to be Rachel's place.*

I knew we'd be driving by Fred's soon, so I tried to turn my head to look at it. That was the first time I realized I couldn't. My eyes were glued to his face.

I pushed at that moment harder than I've ever pushed before and with all the strength I had I forced my eyes away. He smiled, still looking straight forward.

We were already past Fred's by the time I could look out my window.

I didn't realize that it wasn't just my eyes that were frozen as whatever that man was immobilized me; it was my mind, too. Because as soon as I looked away all sorts of thoughts came flooding back in. Mainly they were thoughts about Steven; that he was still out there.

I carefully looked straight forward and for the first time I talked to the man who'd spent the better part of two months talking to me.

"We need to go back and get Steven. I think he might be in trouble."

"Steven has been given his options and he has made his choice," he answered quietly, but it still felt loud.

"What the hell does that mean, made his choice? Do you know what they're going to do to him?" I turned to look at him, but I shouldn't have. My train of thought was completely gone.

"I know."

I forced my eyes away again. It wasn't as hard that time. "And you're not going to do anything about it?"

"He is not my responsibility."

"And I am?"

"Yes."

That wasn't the answer I'd expected. *Who is this guy?*

"How did you know my name and where to find me?" I looked at him from the reflection in the window, it was easier that way. He almost looked bored.

"I know many things about you, Joel, which made locating you not difficult." His gaze was still forward, his affect still unchanged.

"Who are you?"

"My name is Gerrard," he answered, like I was only asking his name.

"Never heard of you."

He frowned, like my answer disturbed him. "No, I don't suppose that you have." His face looked momentarily troubled before smoothing back to the blankness that'd been there before.

Should I have heard of him? My mind quickly scanned my memories. Besides that fleeting moment in the library, I'd never laid eyes on him before.

I looked out my window again, at the road speeding by.

"Where are we going?"

His face remained forward. His eyebrows furrowed momentarily before settling into that irritating smoothness again. "Away."

"What's that supposed to mean?"

"Joel, from what I know of you, you usually don't ask so many questions. Now why don't you go back to being *that* Joel and just let me drive." His eyes were suddenly dancing and there was a half-smile on his face.

I sat up straight. "Know me? How do you know me?"

His smile vanished. It was his turn to look away.

I caught a glimpse of his reflection in the window. The last thing he looked was bored. He looked tortured.

"Joel..."

He glanced at me. He'd never looked more human.

And then I knew. I gripped the handle. "Pull over." *I should have stayed at Rachel's. If I'd known who he was, I would have.*

"Joel. Be reasonable."

"Be reasonable? Who the hell do you think you are?"

His frown deepened as he said the last words I wanted him to say:

"Your father."

The story continues with
The Bashan Agenda
November 1, 2013

Acknowledgements/

Elohim; first, last. Always.

My husband David, my harshest critique and my best friend. God was very good to me the day he shared you with me.

My daughter Mikaela, who very kindly helped me take care of this; my fourth child.

Hannah and Jacob, for giving me two precious hours a day to work on this project.

My mother, for everything.

My dad, for teaching me about everything outdoors.

Matt, for editing, listening, and helping Joel's voice be authentic.

Alex for your amazing advice and line editing skills.

Emily, my copy editor, thank you.

Thank you to all of my blog followers who so patiently read my posts and respond encouragingly.

Tenth Avenue North- you have no idea how often I listened to your music as I pushed my soul to feel and love deeper. Joel and Rachel would not exist without you.

melanie schulz/ a note

I live in upstate New York with my husband and three children, where I've pretty much been planted my entire life. Which is fine, because it's beautiful here. My only complaint is that most people assume that New York means NYC, which it doesn't. There, I've done my part in exposing the truth.

Truth. The truth is I'm not a writer, storyteller maybe, but not a writer. It wasn't something I spent years dreaming of, or even what I went to school for. I'm a nurse. I love being a nurse. So why write? I don't know. I do know when it started, though: September 3, 2010. I know this because I nature journal and on that day Joel made it into my notes. I guess that's fitting. Someone like him needed to be birthed out in the woods.

If you were to meet me, and I hope someday you do, you would not connect me with this story. I'm a wife, a mother, a nurse. The person who wrote this should've been a guy, first off; secondly he should be some militaristic strategist; that's who you'd expect to see if you were to come to a book signing, not me. But I'm there, in every line. So if I don't have the pleasure of meeting you in person, I hope to see you in the Newstead Saga.

www.melanieschulz.com
black and white publishing co.

www.ingramcontent.com/pod-product-compliance
Lightning Source LLC
Chambersburg PA
CBHW022242020726
47496CB00004B/1029